MADONNA RED

JAMES
CARROLL
MADONNA RED

Rediscovery Books
HILL & COMPANY, PUBLISHERS · BOSTON

Library of Congress Cataloging-in-Publication Data

Carroll, James, 1943–
  Madonna red.

  (Rediscovery books)
  I. Title. II. Series.
PS3553.A764M3 1987   813'.54   86-33537
ISBN 0-940595-02-8

Designed by Milton Glaser, Inc.
Printed in the United States of America

In memory of Jim Young

I

TUESDAY, APRIL 22, 1975

The trouble started Tuesday morning when Cardinal O'Brien heard the knocking on his door. He had been leaning against the left edge of the Victorian bay window that divided the broadest wall of his office in half, looking at the tiny new leaves of the huge oak that stood like a guard in front of the cathedral rectory. What could go wrong with the world, he wondered, when the city was waking to one of its perfect spring days? Washington did nothing so well as April.

He walked the ten paces from the window to the large Jacobean desk that occupied the dead center of the office. With each step his body tilted slightly, almost imperceptibly, as he favored his left leg.

It was the cardinal's habit, before grunting his "Come," to consult the appointment sheet that Mrs. Keegan prepared each morning and slid under the glass top on his desk. But this time, even before reading it, he knew: Tuesday, April 22, 1975, 8:30, Sister Dolores Sheehan CSC. He opened the center drawer of his desk, took out a single manila folder, and placed it on the otherwise vacant surface, squaring it with the near edge of mahogany. He adjusted the broad red cincture of his cassock, brushed his right fingers over his bishop's skullcap, and only then grunted, "Come!"

The door opened slowly in front of a fifty-year-old woman. It was Dora Keegan, his secretary. As she entered she said, "Sister Dolores, Your Eminence," and gestured toward a second woman, who was coming in behind her. Mrs. Keegan stood with the knob of the door in the small of her back as Sister Dolores Sheehan walked by her into the office. The secretary's gaze bounced over the nun, a hint of disapproval.

The nun's eye quickly took in the details of the room: the mammoth oriental rug that seemed afloat on a sea of polished dark parquet; the bright bay window; the eighteenth-century desk; the paneled walls; an alcove to her left, reminiscent of the sleeping corners in the chambers of French palaces, its long Catalonian refectory table with a dozen medieval chairs in attendance. Her eye went to the three portraits on the broad wall to the right: Pope Paul VI, looking slightly frightened, John XXIII, benign and harmless, and a bishop whom she did not recognize looking vigilant, impatient. It was probably, she thought, John Carroll, first archbishop of the United States, first ordinary of Washington. Justin Cardinal O'Brien quoted Archbishop Carroll the way presidents quoted Lincoln.

"Good morning, Sister."

The cardinal watched her intently. He considered, not altogether accurately, that his sixty-eight years had given him, in addition to an arthritic leg, an uncanny knack for reading people, sizing them up, taking the measure of their spirits.

"Good morning, Cardinal," she said from where she stood just inside the door.

He took note of the fact that she did not say "Your Eminence." He took note of the fact that she was dressed in a green wool suit, the skirt of which came to her knees. She wore a white frilly blouse and a green silk scarf at her throat. He noted that her hair, uniformly brown, was long to her shoulders. Certainly not much like a nun so far, he thought. The clothes — that's how it always starts.

The cardinal looked at his secretary. She held her steno pad against her breast. She was waiting to be told to take her place at the refectory table, from which she discreetly took notes on the cardinal's official conversations. But Cardinal O'Brien hesitated. Perhaps, for what he had in mind, it would be better if he were alone with the nun. He looked at her. Yes, below the composure was subservience. He would surface it. It would be better to be alone. He would forgo the notes. He would risk not having a witness.

"Thank you, Dora," he said, nodding at his secretary pleasantly.

She hesitated, then glanced at the nun, who was awkwardly looking around the office. It was obvious that Mrs. Keegan expected and wanted to remain.

"That will be all," the cardinal said more firmly.

"Yes, Your Eminence."

Mrs. Keegan slipped out of the office, closing the door behind her. Sister Sheehan stood where she was on the edge of the oriental, not half a dozen paces inside the room. She was trying to decide whether to move forward when the cardinal began moving around his desk to greet her.

He was aware of the pain in his left knee, but gave no indication of it. He was nearly used to it. He held his right hand out to her. She walked toward him. They met in the open space halfway between the desk and the door.

The cardinal knew that visitors were often intimidated by the room, its size, its antique furnishings that achieved a kind of monkish elegance. He liked his office for its formal dignity, but he always found himself trying to put people at their ease, usually by greeting them away from his desk, by offering the simple gesture of welcome. He did so now with the nun.

She took the hand he offered to her. It was the hand that carried the large green jewel of his bishop's ring. Though he gave her the hand cupped, facing directly downward, she turned it slightly in her own and held it momentarily as if that was what she was expected to do. She did not bow to kiss his ring. He took note of that.

"Do sit down, please." He gestured to the braced-back Windsor chair that faced his desk, at a slight angle. He returned to his side of the desk and, looking up, saw that she was standing next to the chair.

"Please, Sister, be comfortable."

"No thank you, Cardinal. I prefer to stand. Really."

"Oh." The cardinal shrugged slightly. He would not press it, but he noted it. "As you please, Sister. If you don't mind, I'll sit." He gathered the folds of his cassock, eased into the high-backed leather swivel chair, pulled up to the desk, deftly adjusted his red skullcap, then rested his hands on the manila folder.

"Well, perhaps, Sister, if we both recall that our shared concern, our first concern, is for the good of the Church, the whole Church, what we have to do this morning may be less unpleasant."

"Unpleasant, Cardinal?" She tilted her head at him, then continued. "It needn't be unpleasant. In fact, I'm glad to have the chance to explain what actually happened."

He was surprised. The woman's composure seemed to increase. She was showing little or no nervousness. She was looking directly at him. As she went on, she put her purse on the chair, opened it, and withdrew a plastic cigarette case.

"The media have misrepresented what took place in the chapel that day, and some remarks attributed to me were done so falsely or taken out of context."

"Is that so, Sister?" The cardinal's right hand left the manila folder and went to the gold cross at his breast; he fondled it.

"Yes. Quite so. I don't blame you for being upset in light of what was reported." She lit a cigarette, then looked about for a place to put the match. The cardinal did not move. Their eyes met.

"Do you have an ashtray?" she asked.

"I don't smoke."

"Oh." She paused. She glanced about again, then said evenly, "Well, do you mind if I do?"

"You may smoke, Sister."

"Thank you."

As she removed the pack of Kents from the case there was a slight tremble in her hands, and Cardinal O'Brien noted it. She juggled the cigarette pack, the case, the burning cigarette, and the match. Finally she succeeded in putting the match in the case.

The cardinal allowed himself to smile. "You balance all that pretty well. You couldn't have been smoking that long. It wasn't permitted before, was it?"

"Before? Oh, before the renewal. Well, no, of course not. Nothing was permitted." She said it with a hint of laughter, her response to his smile.

"Now everything is permitted," Cardinal O'Brien said. "You are even allowed to give yourself cancer."

The woman looked at him. Was he rebuking her? But his glance was benign, pleasant even. She decided he was not. She took a long pull on her cigarette and began speaking even as she exhaled.

"Actually, Cardinal O'Brien, I know that not everything is permitted. After twenty years as a grade school teacher I'm something of an expert on the need for limits. That is why I am happy to have the chance to explain to you that I did not, as I have been accused of doing, celebrate the mass at the student chapel of American University last Tuesday."

"Excuse me, Sister," the cardinal corrected, fingering the left edge of the manila folder in front of him. "You are not accused of celebrating mass. Obviously, since you are not ordained, you can only be accused of *attempting* to celebrate. You are not accused of *celebrating* the mass. That is out of the question. You couldn't do that even if you wanted to. You are not a priest and . . ."

"I understand, Cardinal," the nun interrupted. "All right. But that's not relevant since I didn't *attempt* to celebrate mass either."

"You didn't?" Cardinal O'Brien leaned forward. He sought out her eyes with his, found them, stared into them, trying to see behind them.

"No." She did not blink. He leaned back in his chair, stretched his left leg in the desk's cave, rubbing his knee with his left hand. He never took his eyes from her.

"Well," he said slowly, "perhaps I need some help in understanding the source of all this uproar. Why has my phone been ringing all week? Why is the *Washington Post* running a series by Roberta Winston on the oppression of women in the Church with your photograph on the front page? Why is the National Organization of Women threatening to picket this very building? Why do I have fifteen telegrams from brother bishops around the country? Why is the apostolic delegate forwarding questions from Rome about what goes on in my archdiocese with people who are in my employ? You mean it has all been a misunderstanding?"

"Yes, I do, Cardinal. A horrible misunderstanding. It troubles me as much as it does you."

"Perhaps so, Sister. Please help me to understand." The cardinal brightened, not, as she thought, with relief, but with anticipation. She was giving him the opening he sought.

"You see, Father Baron was out of town Tuesday. The priest who was supposed to take the noon mass didn't show up. Well, there we were, a dozen of us in the chapel, waiting. Since I am Father Baron's associate in the ministry, and since clearly we owed those people some opportunity to worship that day, even if the Eucharist wasn't possible, I conducted a short, informal service with Scripture readings and meditation and the Lord's Prayer and that sort of thing."

"But not the mass?" The cardinal's left hand went from his knee to the manila folder. He squared it with the edge of the desk again.

"No, Cardinal. Not the mass. I'm not ordained."

"I know that, Sister."

"I believe in Holy Orders, Cardinal. I would like to see women ordained someday. But in the meantime I believe with you that the order of the Church must be maintained."

"Sister, I can see we're going to get along better than I

expected. But let me be so clear on this. You believe in the sacrament of Holy Orders?"

"Yes. Let me tell you something about myself, Cardinal. The most honored member of my family was my uncle, a priest of this archdiocese . . ."

"Who?"

"Monsignor Peter Keller."

"I knew him. A fine man."

"Indeed. He was. I loved him dearly. Perhaps, having known him, you can understand when I tell you that I was raised with an intense reverence for the priesthood. I continue in it, Cardinal, and not as a mere act of childish devotion, but in considered appreciation for the fact that the priesthood is the central structure of the Church. I've argued this very point with some of my closest friends, women who have left the religious life and who now hold the Church in some . . . contempt. I do not agree with them, Cardinal. I agree with you. I would never celebrate the Eucharist myself, or *attempt* to."

The cardinal took note of the conviction with which the woman spoke, the sincerity, the obvious feeling. He was delighted to hear her denial. He hoped he could make the most of it. When he spoke now there was a confidentiality, almost an intimacy, in his voice.

"Sister, I am glad to hear your side of this. I had been quite concerned."

"I can imagine, Cardinal."

"Since you didn't attempt to celebrate the mass, perhaps you can help me straighten out a couple of items on which there seems to have been particular misunderstanding."

"Certainly."

"First, the matter of reported remarks. Roberta Winston has you saying in this morning's paper, if I remember correctly, 'I said mass. Let them burn me at their male chauvinist stake if they dare.' "

"I did not say that, Cardinal." She made the denial with

such force that he lowered his eyes. She continued, "That statement was made by a young woman, an undergraduate, who is one of several members of the Women's Collective, as they call themselves, who have consistently tried to use me as a rallying point for other women on campus. I am being manipulated by political forces over which I have no control, Cardinal. And the press just uses anything that's sensational whether it's true or not."

"I understand that, Sister. I myself have been misquoted a time or two. I know how frustrating that can be. You must be very upset about all this."

"Yes, I am. I profoundly regret the trouble it's caused the diocese."

"The *arch*diocese, Sister. I'm sure you do."

The nun visibly relaxed. She had been standing straight and rigid. Now, breathing more easily, handling her cigarette more casually, she shifted her weight to her left leg. She was beginning to feel relieved.

"For the record, Sister, there are certain questions I must ask you directly."

"Of course, Cardinal."

"It's not that I don't believe you, just that the record requires definite information on certain points of fact."

"I understand." She took a long drag on her cigarette, exhaled, was ready.

"Did you wear the vestments of a priest?"

"No. I did not." Her denial rang.

"Did you say the words of consecration over a paten containing twelve hosts?"

"No."

"Did you say the words of consecration over a chalice of wine?"

"No."

"Did you distribute communion in any way?"

"No."

"Did you conclude the service with the priestly blessing?"

"No."

The cardinal stopped. He glared at her. Suddenly his manner seemed different. As he spoke now, slowly, officially, he drummed the jewel of his ring rhythmically on his desk, on the manila folder.

"Sister Dolores, because of the publicity associated with this event, which publicity has made it a celebrated cause and a source of serious confusion for the people, the Church has no choice but to respond to this event in a clear, unambiguous fashion. The order of the Church must be maintained. We are not Episcopalians. Consequently, you must either acknowledge that you attempted to say the mass and thereby, in the very deed, have submitted to me your resignation from the Archdiocesan Campus Ministry and from the Sisters of the Holy Cross. Or, if you continue to deny having done so, you must submit to the formal ecclesiastical procedure as set forth in *Liber Quintus* of *Codex Juris Canonici*. If, in that procedure, you are found to be guilty as charged, you will be formally excommunicated from the Roman Catholic Church."

The woman seemed at first not to have understood. Her face reddened. Her mouth opened, then closed, then opened again as she said, "But Cardinal O'Brien, I'm telling you the truth. I have been a Sister for twenty-four years. Whose word are you going to take? Mine? Or Roberta Winston's?"

That is when he did it. He replied to her question with silence. He sat forward, put the fingers of both hands on the edges of the manila folder. His eyes fell to it. He slid it slowly, deliberately, across the desk.

She looked at the folder where the cardinal pushed it, then looked at him, trying to find his eyes. But he would not show them. He was looking at the jewel of his ring. He said nothing. She looked at the folder. She crushed the cigarette out in the plastic case and put it down on the desk. The folder was plain, unmarked, bearing no indication of its contents. Suddenly the first wave of real panic rolled through the woman's stomach. She looked at the man again. If only he would lift his eyes. But he would not. He would not take his eyes from his ring.

The nun opened the folder. She began to read. Then stopped.

Her vision blurred. She closed her eyes, opened them. She read further. She stopped breathing. Her teeth bit her lip. She turned the page. The next one was identical to the first. She read it. She turned it. The third was the same. She read it. She turned it. A fourth. She turned it. A fifth. All the same. A sixth. Only the signatures in the lower right-hand corners of the pages were different.

"Eight, Sister," the cardinal said at last. "Sworn affidavits stating in detail what you wore, what you said, what you did."

Now it was she who wouldn't look at him.

"Eight," he said, "of the eleven who were there." And then, in the voice he used at funerals, "I have no choice, Sister." She had given him the opening, and he had shut it on her.

"Oh . . . Your Eminence . . ." She said it in barely a whisper. But he heard it. He noted it.

She doubled over, slowly, as if reeled by a blow to the abdomen. He thought she was falling, but she sat in the chair behind her, curled her face down into her lap, and shook with sobs.

He watched her. She seemed small, helpless, completely at the mercy of the shame that poured out of her in stifled groans. He wanted to touch her, to say "Daughter, daughter."

He did not move.

After several minutes she sat up in the chair, drew her hands slowly down from her face. It was wet with tears. There were dark streaks in the hollows below her eyes, the wreckage of mascara. Makeup, he thought, noting it; it all began with makeup.

But now it was the woman who was trying to see into the man. Her eyes met his, burned into them with their question. What human being would so entrap another? Would so coolly await such humiliation? Would plan it?

"A well-laid trap, Cardinal," she said. There was iron in her voice.

He looked away from her. He hadn't expected resistance from her now. She had been beaten, hadn't she? Caught? It had been almost inconceivable that she was lying.

"Sister, you lied."

"Cardinal, we both lied. You told me you believed me. You didn't. We both lied, but I knew it. You lied to yourself."

"I did not." He squirmed. She was not asking for his pity. He would have given it.

"Your concern is for the Church?" she snapped. "What has that to do with your calculated plot to humiliate me? You led me on. You had your evidence. Why didn't you say so?"

"Led you on? I simply gave you a chance to state your case, and you lied."

"As you hoped I would. You thought to destroy me, to obliterate whatever self-respect I had left so that you could sweep me into the gutter without so much as a whimper of protest."

She stood again. He made ready to defend himself. Suddenly his heart was beating in his ears.

"Not so much hoped, Sister, as expected. I know your kind, full of bravado at your demonstrations and press conferences. But in private, when called to account for your deeds, you crumble."

The nun's face was as red as his garment. She was supporting herself against the desk with the tips of her fingers. Her lower lip began to tremble again, but she forced it to stop. She knew he was waiting for more of her tears, but he had had the last of them.

"Cardinal, I will not crumble. You have helped me to see what I must do. My regret now is that I chose such an undignified way of responding to my own fears. I did lie. Yes. I was terrified of you. Of what I had done. I do understand exactly what's at stake in this. It is not child's play. But you have done your worst to me, and it isn't enough. Instead of crushing me it has opened my eyes. I was wrong to deny what I did, because what I did was right. The Church — "

"Sister, the Church — "

"The Church is wrong!" Now she was nearly screaming, not with panic, but with anger. It poured out of her forcefully, cleanly. "Let's join the issue then! You snared me, now get rid of me if you can. I will not deny what I did. I will not repent of it. I will not apologize. Neither will I resign from the Archdiocesan Campus Ministry nor from the Sisters of the Holy Cross. I will have a trial. I will have a public airing of what I did and why. I have no desire to hurt the Church, but it is clear to me now, Cardinal, that, exactly because I love the Church, I must defend what I did. The Church must end its contemptuous treatment of women — "

"Sister — "

"Such as you have displayed for me just now."

"Sister Sheehan — "

"And which every woman experiences every time she approaches the altar of God which is presided over exclusively by men. Cardinal, we will not be treated like your laundresses any longer."

The cardinal stood then. His face was pale, white against the red of his cassock. He reached across the desk, closed the manila folder, and pulled it back to himself. He squared it with the mahogany edge. He raised his head.

Their eyes were joined. The issue was joined. They were locked together in the ancient energy. All right, the silence between them said. All right.

He leaned toward her. His voice was rigid, controlled, as he said, "You may leave now . . ." He paused, leaned closer: "*Miss!*" He said it like a curse. It was his first blow in what he knew would be a difficult battle. He had misjudged her. He was, perhaps, growing less astute with age. She was more than he expected. She would be, he knew now, a worthy adversary. He would not be gentle.

The nun turned, strode across the carpet to the door, opened it, closed it behind her, was gone.

The cardinal dropped his left hand to his knee and rubbed it. He stood straight again, stepped away from his chair, turned and walked the ten paces to the window. In a matter of seconds the nun walked out into the street from the main entrance of the rectory directly below. He looked at her closely. She was walking quickly. Her face was turned from him. He couldn't be sure, but she seemed not to be crying at all. He noted that.

He watched her walk down Rhode Island Avenue. When she turned up Connecticut, his eyes fell to the new leaves of the mammoth oak. He could almost touch them. Soon they would block his view entirely.

A sigh came out of the man then with such sadness it surprised him. What, he remembered thinking, could go wrong with the world? What indeed, he thought to himself, shaking his head. What indeed?

He moved out of the window's bright bay and, favoring his left leg, walked across his office past the portraits of the popes and Bishop Carroll to the shadowed corner in which, disguised in the dark wood panels, was his private door. He went through it. It opened onto the arched passageway that led from the offices to the cathedral proper. He walked the forty-five feet to the large doors that were carved with scenes from the life of Christ. He pushed through them into the church and stopped while his eyes adjusted to the dim light. He heard the familiar drone coming from the main altar in the distance.

He eased himself into the nearest pew and slowly lowered his body onto his right knee, keeping his left as straight as possible. He covered his face and tried for a moment to pray to the dark place his hands gave him. But his head was still loud with the sound of his heart; he felt the vein in his temple throbbing. He looked up. Banks of blue vigil lights flickered at Mary's feet in the far left corner. A dozen worshipers, old women mainly, were scattered in the pews. His eyes were drawn to the pair of tiny but brilliant red lights over the confessional booths halfway up the far left side of the apse. The two lights flashed on to indicate that a penitent was behind the curtain seeking forgiveness from the priest. The weight of the penitent's knee on the step inside the confessional triggered the light that was the Catholic code for *occupied*. One light went off, and an old woman emerged from behind the curtain, which she then held in the usual courtesy for the next old woman. The curtain fell behind her, and the light went on. And the cardinal, taking note, was consoled by such simple signals of belief.

In the sanctuary the tall white candles were lit, the six of them. A tall young priest was saying mass. It was John Tierney. Cardinal O'Brien watched him hold the wafer high, pause and genuflect. There was no bell. There were no altar boys at the morning mass on weekdays. Tierney took the chalice, bent over it, whispered, held it high, and knelt. The cardinal watched him carefully; the priest moved with such grace, such reverence, such strength. Tierney believed. Tierney carried on what had been given, the treasure, the trust. It was so fragile, carried in vessels of clay; it could be broken so easily. It could be lost. Vessels of clay, he thought, like himself.

Cardinal O'Brien's eyes bathed in the sight of the priest moving through the ritual carefully, exactly. There *was* a way to do it. A way to touch God. God Himself. To *touch* Him. To *eat* Him. Oh, how to keep it alive at a time when even what is sacred is disputed, challenged, denied. At a time when even nuns disregard their vows, dress like actresses, and hold the tradition of two thousand years in contempt.

Join the issue with me? he thought. The woman has no idea what the issue is. The issue is God and how to touch Him. The issue is passing that touch, that loving touch, from one generation to the next. It was a gift born in fire and in blood. The touch of God was the most precious experience human beings had ever become conscious of. It was so subtle it could be forgotten. The woman doesn't know, he thought, doesn't know the damage she could do.

But was it her fault? Hadn't she been failed by her leaders, her shepherds, who were themselves confused, who hadn't spoken clearly? He could not be angry at her. She was lost in a crowd of the confused and the frightened.

The cardinal knew he was appointed, not for the healthy, but for the sick. He felt the weight of his burden, the weight of disillusion that lay on his people like a shadow of death.

Well, he would carry the weight. He would speak clearly. He would protect the fragile vessel even if it meant pain to the woman and others. Pain to himself. The order of the Church must be maintained. He would be a shepherd to the flock and lead it faithfully through these perplexing, dangerous days.

Justin Cardinal O'Brien put his hands over his face again. He spoke into them. "Forgive her. She knows not. And give me strength, Almighty Father, to defend the faith. Defend us in battle, Saint Michael the Archangel. And hail holy queen, Mother of Mercy, our life, our sweetness and our hope."

John Tierney prayed out loud, "Lord, I am not worthy that you should come under my roof." He prayed according to the rubrics, holding the bread high. The people were supposed to say the prayer with him. They never did. He didn't mind.

He bent over the consecrated wafer and ate it in one bite. He paused, straightened, brushed his fingers across the sacred cloth to their places on the edge of the altar. He nodded his head slightly, froze for an instant, then slowly fell until one knee touched the floor. He froze again, but only for the count of two. He rose slowly to his full height, six feet three inches, and drew his feet together until the heels of his shoes touched. He picked up the chalice, swirled the two ounces of mediocre burgundy in one circle, clockwise, and raised it to his lips with his left hand. With his right he brought the linen purificator to his chin beneath the rim of the chalice. He drank the wine, the blood of Christ, in one swallow.

The people were coming to communion. Tierney went to the tabernacle that sat, enthroned, on the high altar behind him. He genuflected and took the large ciborium full of consecrated wafers. He walked to the low, gleaming rail where the dozen women and a couple of old men were kneeling.

Almost no one goes to mass on a Tuesday morning anymore. Not even at Saint Matthew's Cathedral. Tierney was used to it. In his five years as a priest he had served in three Washington churches. It had been the same in each place: fewer and fewer worshipers, fewer and fewer children in the school, no altar boys on weekdays, less and less money in the collection. Signs of difficult days for the Church, for the people of God.

"The Body of Christ," he said, placing a wafer on each of their outstretched tongues. They were supposed to say "Amen." They never did. He said it for them, but not out loud.

It was while looking for others who might be coming to communion that Tierney saw the cardinal in a pew near the back of the church. Light flashed off the jewel of his ring. His hands were covering his face. The priest turned back toward the altar. What would the cardinal be doing at his mass? he wondered. Checking up on him? No. The cardinal had been known to do that with the newer priests, but not with him. Tierney knew he had the cardinal's confidence. Then what? Maybe something was wrong. Illness. Maybe Edna, the cardinal's sister, was sick. Maybe the cardinal himself was.

Maybe he just wants to pray, Tierney thought as he returned to the lectern for the final prayer. He chided himself for ferreting out a problem, a pain. Priest's syndrome: smelling out the secret chaos of every heart. Even the cardinal's. Maybe he just wants to pray.

Tierney turned the pages of the heavy book, extended his arms, and said, "Let us pray." The people stood. "Oh God, you have fed us . . ." He read the words slowly, deliberately, meaning them. "We give you thanks . . ." And he did.

He always felt genuinely grateful at this point in the mass. He was a fortunate man. He knew it. He had been fed. He was not hungry. He believed. He was of use to some people. Sometimes he thought he even loved them. He looked out at the dark and nearly empty church. Whoever was there had been fed, too, their hunger abated, if only for a time. The mass done rightly had this power to ease loads and sustain nerve and keep lives going. It was so with him. And with those few who knew enough to leave their cozy rooms when the last of night was still on the city. Now he would send them out into the day. A warm, lively April day. A day in the season of rebirth.

John Tierney raised his right hand. "May Almighty God bless you . . ." He made the large sign of the cross with his hand, God's signature on the air. ". . . the Father and the Son and the Holy Spirit."

The people were supposed to say "Amen." They never did. As he picked up the chalice from the altar, perfectly covered by its square of white, paschal silk, Tierney said "Amen" for them. And then he said, "Go in peace to love and serve the Lord."

They did not say, "Thanks be to God."

Neither did he.

He turned to the high altar, genuflected, and walked across the slick marble slowly, gracefully, with perfect posture.

Janus had the feeling she was being followed. Even as she walked hurriedly down the long terminal concourse she turned her head and let her eye drift expertly back along the floor-to-ceiling window. Other travelers moved swiftly toward their gates, a maintenance man pushed his broom lazily, a pair of Pan Am stewardesses walked in stride, chatting. No. If she were being followed she wouldn't see them. Her eye was drawn to the image in the glass of the attractive woman who walked beside her, keeping up with her.

Bridgit Connor hurried toward gate number 17C. She was nervous. If she missed her flight her aunt wouldn't know when to expect her and then she would be in trouble. How would she get in touch with her? And her mother, who'd written specially to Aunt Nell, would be furious, would say it was just like her to lose her way. The huge London terminal had confused Bridgit. She'd been lost twice already. It was nothing like the simple counters and gates at the small Derry airport she'd flown from that morning. Bridgit looked at her watch. It had stopped.

Janus noted the time. The digital clock hung from the ceiling read 13:56. Four minutes before her plane would go. Heathrow was mammoth, but she knew it well. Gate 17C, where the BOAC 707 to Dulles waited, was nearly half a mile away. She was relaxed even as she clicked briskly across the polished terrazzo. As she angled into the long C concourse she dropped her small bag on the conveyor belt and approached the arch of the metal detector. No problem. She was not armed.

When Bridgit Connor walked through the arch, the buzzer sounded. The policewoman took her aside and began whisking the phone-sized metal detector up and down her slim body. Bridgit couldn't imagine what was wrong. The policewoman sensed her nervousness and reassured her, saying, "Terribly sorry, ma'am." And then, with her voice lowered, "Probably your brassiere, dearie."

"My . . . my . . . brassiere?" Bridgit could feel her face going red. She glanced to see if anyone had heard. In the reflection of the window her eyes met those of the woman she'd been walking by. She seemed to be listening.

"Well," the policewoman said. "the underwires. Sometimes the tiniest bit of metal . . ."

"Oh," Bridgit said, blushing still, mystified. She hadn't worn a brassiere in years, not since moving out of her mother's house on Landown Street to get married. Her breasts, as Peter had teased her, wouldn't fill a champagne glass. The brassiere had been the unnecessary formality that only embarrassed her more with its uselessness. And now she felt as though the policewoman, running the humming instrument all over her body, would know. But then Bridgit looked down at herself; the woman couldn't know, not through her raincoat and her wool suit. It was a metal detector, she reminded herself, not a bust measurer.

"Thank you, ma'am." The policewoman had been thorough, polite, chaste. She stepped aside and smiled at Bridgit. "Have a pleasant journey." Bridgit nodded, smiled, tugged at the bright, blue scarf she wore at her throat, and hurried into the flow of people. She checked her watch. She had forgotten that it had stopped.

Janus noted the time on a second digital clock; three minutes. She began to move quickly, cutting left, then right, in front of one person, by another. She moved faster and faster.

Her timing had been perfect up to now. She was at her most alert. This was the mission for which she had honed her every nerve. Let them try to stop her. Let the best of them try. She bumped an elderly woman who pulled her purse to her breast, turning on her fiercely. But she moved by her. She looked ahead for gate 17. In the distance she saw 11, 13, and 15, but not 17. By her calculation one minute remained; just right. She began to run.

Next to her, reflected in the window, another woman was running. It was the Irish good-looker who'd become flustered at the simple English security check. Janus eyed her discreetly in the glass. She had to admit that the woman was beautiful. Very slender, tall. Her hair was short, brown, and unexceptional, but her face was stunning, all angles, high cheekbones. Blue silk drew attention to her long Nefertiti throat. She looked the perfect candidate for fashion pictures. Janus imagined her face on the cover of a Yank magazine. Yes, perhaps so. An unspoiled Irish beauty. Ideal for selling signed Waterfords.

But then, as she ran with her, Janus saw the woman the way the English guards had no doubt seen her, flustered, close to panic. God, Janus thought, the ineptitude of Irish tourists. In from the farm or just out of the schoolroom, innocent even of her own good looks, off to visit relations in the States. And on the verge of tears, for the love of Christ! No wonder the bleeding English think us all buffoons. Brassiere, dearie, indeed!

Bridgit saw the number 17 hanging from the ceiling fifty feet ahead. Now thirty. Now ten.

"Hello. Hello," Bridgit said. The young woman she greeted was just sliding the narrow board that read WASHINGTON D.C. out of its slot on the wall behind her counter. The waiting lounge was empty; the plastic benches yawned. Bridgit saw the door in the left corner close as another late passenger went into the entry tube. It was a woman.

"Am I tardy?" she asked, breathlessly, fearfully. She would not cry, but what would she do? How would she contact Aunt Nell?

"Yes, ma'am. It seems you are. I'm sorry."

"Oh," she said, shoving her ticket at the woman. "But the plane's still there, isn't it? Oh, please, miss."

"Well, ma'am, I'm sorry. I just boarded one late passenger. And the captain has already . . ." The clerk looked through the window. The 707 was not moving. She looked at the harried woman in front of her. Irish. Frightened. Lovely face. Could do with a coif.

The clerk opened the top left drawer of her counter and picked up a pale blue telephone. It was the color of her dress. She fingered the dial in the spine of the phone three times, put the phone in the bend of her neck, and took Bridgit's ticket. Bridgit's face broke into a broad smile. She was trying not to breathe so hard.

"Hello. Yes. Penelope again." The clerk was very brisk. English. "One more. No, the very last, I promise. Can you hold? Right." The clerk dropped the phone to its cradle and slammed the drawer, whether in haste or pique the Irishwoman couldn't tell. She snapped the ticket in two, giving the bottom half to Bridgit. The clerk led her to the door in the corner of the lounge, opened it, and said, "Have a pleasant visit, Miss Connor."

"Thank you so much." Bridgit understood how the clerk could know her last name from the ticket, but she wondered why the clerk called her "Miss." As she walked down the tube to the plane, she also wondered how the clerk knew that she was off on a mere visit.

Nine minutes later the big plane left the runway. Behind her closed eyes, Janus was seeing the 707 spec sheets she had memorized the year before at the Black September training camp. She waited for the first change in engine pitch that signaled the end of the critical takeoff phase, the period of seven seconds during which forty percent of all 707 equipment failures occur. It came. Janus knew the aircraft. She could take it if she chose to.

She pushed her head back against the seat and turned slightly to look out the window. She saw the small houses, each with its square of mud, its stunted street, its chimney and ribbon of smoke. As the plane banked to her side of the fuselage she saw the graceful highways carving into the sprawling terminal complex. The dark spots of automobiles slid along them like bugs in a stream.

Then suddenly she sat up and put her face to the glass as she saw the lights, blue flashing crowns, on the tops of two cars. No, three. She watched them race by the other vehicles toward the terminal. What were *they* after? As the plane continued its steep reach for the ocean she lost them. She sat back in the seat, considering what could have gone wrong. What did they know? Only three members of the Action Council knew of her mission; they were absolutely trustworthy. The English therefore could know nothing of it, she decided. And of herself, even less. They didn't even know at last report that Janus was alive. And they had never known that Janus was a woman.

Bridgit Connor considered meanwhile that if she lived through this she could live through anything. But the sound she took to mean the plane was coming apart meant, in fact, that the landing gear had been retracted and secured.

Here rested the remains of President Kennedy at the Requiem Mass, November 25, 1963, before their removal to Arlington, where they lie in expectation of a heavenly resurrection.

John Tierney was standing on the edge of the white Carrara marble crest that marked the place where the cathedral's central aisle intersected the sanctuary. He remembered listening to the broadcast of the President's funeral on Armed Forces radio, and as he looked around the cathedral now, he realized again that the familiar old church had over its eighty-five years been the scene of countless stately, even historic, occasions. Tomorrow's ceremony would be momentous for him; for Saint Matthew's it would be just one more in a line of assemblages of the mighty.

As his eye drifted around the vast open place, it seemed to Tierney that the cathedral had the air of a veteran butler. It would not deign to share his excitement, his anticipation. It had seen everything: the funeral of a President and, before him, of a Supreme Court Chief Justice; the christening of a prince; the wedding of a famous general. Every day it saw God come down to its altar in the form of bread. What would the conferring of the papal Order of Gregory the Great on an ambassador, even the British ambassador, be to Saint Matthew's?

It would be something to Tierney. For one thing, he was the master of ceremonies. It was his show. For another, Sir Alisdair and his wife were, well, almost friends — a relationship that had grown easily over the previous months while he prepared their daughter Melissa for her first communion. The investiture must come off without a hitch, he thought.

He began to walk slowly across the width of the cathedral. Though he was looking at the sanctuary, the priest was careful not to step on the circle of marble that marked where Kennedy's coffin had rested. His eyes moved from the high altar to the Caen marble statue of Mary to the Venetian candlesticks on the smaller forward altar to the linen cloth that poured perfectly over the edge of the altar. He was looking for any disorder, for signs of dust, for a fallen petal, for an imperfection. The floor, polished Botticino marble with inlaid floral patterns, was spotless and shining. As he walked along the altar rail, Tierney ran his finger inside its bronzework designs, over the edges of the crosses, the peacocks, the wheat stalks and grape clusters: nothing. It was clean. The sacristan, Jimmy Wilson, and his crew of women had been doing their work. Tierney resolved to commend them.

The exterior of Saint Matthew's, with its gaudy red brick and the harsh green patina of its copper dome, had always left Tierney cold. But the interior of the cathedral was like an emperor's icon. Laid out on the lines of a Latin cross, it combined an Italian perfection of scale with a Byzantine subtlety of color. The nave and transepts were exactly fifty-four feet wide and their walls were fifty-four feet high. An open view, unusual in a space of such great size, had been achieved by running the support arches for the two-hundred-foot dome from the walls and not from obstructing pillars. There was no part of the church from which the rest could not be seen.

Tierney was looking at the thirty-five foot mosaic of Saint Matthew in the niche behind the high altar. An angel, benign and affectionate, enfolded the evangelist with his huge protecting wings. Above that was a second, larger mosaic, which pictured a lamb about to be slain. Eight angels bore the instruments of passion and death: one a spear, others a hammer and nails, a crown of thorns. One angel bore a wooden cross. In the lower right-hand corner of the mosaic was a small coat of arms. Tierney smiled, remembering that it was the crest, surreptitiously installed, of Robert E. Lee. One of Lee's nephews, Monsignor Richard Lee, had built the cathedral in 1890. Though he had converted to Catholicism, he had apparently maintained his Virginia loyalties. Tierney loved the man for his small act of stubborn resistance.

He stepped inside the altar rail and turned to face the main body of the church. He wanted to trace the route of the next day's formal procession with his eye. After the cardinal greeted the dignitaries on their arrival at the main entrance, he, together with the ambassador, the apostolic delegate, and other clergy, would wind his way from the sacristy behind the sanctuary down the right aisle to the center of the cathedral, across and then back up the center aisle.

Tierney stopped. His eye was caught by the sight of the hunched figure in one of the rearmost pews. The priest knew immediately, even through the darkness, that it was Cardinal O'Brien. He was still there, though the mass had ended ten minutes before. Except for him and the usual lingering women with their shopping bags, the cathedral was empty. Tierney wondered again if something were bothering the old man. Involuntarily the priest's hand went to his throat; the collar of his long-sleeved black shirt was open. The cuffs of the shirt were rolled back. As was his habit, Tierney had resorted to such comfortable informality immediately after the mass. The cardinal, who preferred that his priests wear the traditional cassock when they were in the cathedral, would be annoyed. "Shirtsleeves!" Tierney could hear him. "And collar open, and before the Blessed Sacrament! Really, Father!" Tierney turned back toward the altar, chiding himself for thinking about clothing. The cardinal made him nervous.

Tierney saw the mural on the far transept wall, *The Martyrdom of Saint Matthew*. A Roman officer who had just given the command to behead the evangelist stood neatly, waiting for his order to be carried out. The executioner was unsheathing his sword to strike the blow. Above the bent Saint Matthew, angels appeared carrying a palm branch and the martyr's crown. Altogether gruesome, Tierney thought, turning his attention to the floor again. But there was no dust anywhere. He moved to the elevated pulpit on the left side of the sanctuary, turned, and took in the entire scene again, envisioning the various movements of the ritual.

When he was interrupted, Tierney was compiling a mental list of the paraphernalia that would be needed for the service. He wasn't sure what such an investiture required. In checking the cathedral *Acts*, he had discovered that no one had ever received the Order of Saint Gregory the Great at Saint Matthew's before. In fact, that honor was usually conferred at the Vatican itself.

"Father." Though the voice was hushed he knew it at once as the cardinal's. Tierney turned. The old man was standing at the altar rail. He had made his way down the red-carpeted center aisle without a sound.

"Good morning, Your Eminence."

The cardinal was in his usual full regalia — red cassock, pectoral cross, gold chain, skullcap. Tierney was pleased that the cardinal had come up to him, but was anxious to know why. It was not like the cardinal to casually approach his priests, and he never did so inside the cathedral itself.

"Come to my office." The cardinal's whisper was softer than the priest's, but it was hard with authority. When the older man turned abruptly and strode up the aisle, Tierney wondered if he'd spoken too loudly or too casually.

"Yes, Your Eminence." He said it inaudibly, aware of a certain unarticulated resentment. It wasn't the cardinal himself Tierney resented, so much as the ease with which he was intimidated by the man. They walked the length of the aisle, neither of them making a sound on the carpet. All that Tierney could hear was the soft grunting noise the cardinal made in rhythm with his slight limp.

At the rear of the cathedral they left the carpet for the side door to the rectory. Their feet clattered across the stone floor then, and the noise seemed to Tierney to fill the dark reaches of the church. At the private entrance to the cardinal's office a near-collision occurred when O'Brien stepped back to let Tierney go first. Tierney hadn't expected the courtesy and bumped the older man slightly. Each recoiled from the other instantly.

"Sorry, Your Eminence."

The cardinal did not answer, but only walked into the office ahead. It seemed to Tierney that he was angry, and the priest could feel the quickening of his usual nervousness. While he followed the cardinal across the oriental to the desk in the center of the room, Tierney's hand was at his throat again: no collar. When O'Brien looked up at him from the chair he had taken behind his desk, he seemed to note it. Tierney dropped his hand. The cardinal said nothing. He was trying to catch his breath and only stared impassively at the priest for nearly a minute. He had an annoyed, agitated expression on his face, one Tierney had seen only a few times before. The lively blue eyes were stilled in their dark hollows, as if gathering energy for a new effort. Tierney had the impression that the pupils of Cardinal O'Brien's eyes were about to leap out at him. At the edges of his mouth and in the recesses at the sides of his nose there seemed a new weariness.

Tierney wondered at the trouble that had made the cardinal seek him out. There was nothing on his desk to indicate what it was. Perhaps it was the special liturgy for the ambassador's investiture. O'Brien was a stickler for ceremony; he would want it right. Especially this one, with the apostolic delegate and the Catholic Diplomatic Corps and senior State Department people in attendance.

But the way O'Brien was staring at him with that annoyed gaze made Tierney sure it was something else.

"Father, tell me," the cardinal said at last.

"Yes, Your Eminence?"

"Did you read the paper?"

"No. Not yet." What could be in the paper?

"Well, you have been following the story." The voice was edgy and raw.

"I'm sorry, Cardinal. What story?"

"The nun."

The nun? What did a nun have to do with anything? Unless . . .

"You mean the nun who said mass?"

"*Attempted* to say mass, Father. Yes." The cardinal glared at him. Tierney saw with sharp surprise that O'Brien's hands were shaking, even as the cardinal, aware of the priest's gaze, clasped them firmly in front of him. Suddenly a knot formed in Tierney's stomach, and the old instinct that warns of serious trouble began to unfold itself like a message until just as suddenly it faded and the knot dissolved.

"Right," Tierney said.

Which also seemed wrong. The cardinal leaned back in his chair, his annoyance giving way to a vast weariness. Tierney resolved to say nothing until asked. O'Brien pointed distractedly to the Windsor chair opposite his desk. Tierney sat.

"In my forty years as a priest I've never known such contempt." The voice was mournful and humiliated. O'Brien's eyes sank. Tierney felt a tug of sympathy for the man, but could never have expressed it without seeming false or silly.

"That's just the *Post*, Cardinal," Tierney said, thinking the newspaper must have criticized him. "They've gotten carried away since they brought down Nixon."

"I'm talking about that nun, Father. She's a pathetic, misguided woman. I would like to feel sorry for her, but I can't because she's dangerous."

Dangerous! What was he talking about? It was startling to discover beneath the inexplicable anger and the hint of self-pity a core of fear.

"Dangerous?"

"Yes, man, dangerous! Think a moment, will you? What will happen when any disgruntled layman or religious takes it upon himself — or *herself* — to say the mass?"

"I understand that, Your Eminence . . . ."

The cardinal shook his head. "No, I don't think you do."

Now the old man was getting angry at him, and Tierney could feel the blast coming. It would be indecent and wrong of the cardinal to empty his spleen on me, Tierney thought. How to protect one's self-respect and one's innocence without giving O'Brien real cause for anger? And what had happened this morning to provoke him so? Tierney decided not to wait impassively for the old man's bitterness to spill over him.

"I don't understand what you're angry about, Cardinal," the priest said firmly, with the barest note of defiance.

O'Brien paused, the acid in his manner visibly ebbing. He ran the tips of his fingers over the lower edge of his chin. When he spoke then his voice was worried, thoughtful.

"Father, sometimes I think that the Church is held together by Scotch tape and thin wire — it's that fragile."

For that single moment the cardinal was transparent to Tierney; the old man was feeling fragile himself. Tierney was moved as he listened to his sorrowful rambling, but not so as to forget that however vulnerable he might appear for the moment, the cardinal was streetfighter tough.

"The Church is battered and beleaguered. People don't know what to believe at a time when belief is more needed than ever. Even her priests, some of them, and sisters, these new-breed sisters that look like actresses or worse, sow seeds of doubt and confusion in the minds of the faithful."

He paused, smiled thinly, then went on, his voice rising. "Well, Father, the more fragile the battered Church, the more certain and steadfast those of us who lead it must be!"

No hint of self-pity in that. No fear. The unwanted and

useless emotions had been dispelled. He would maintain a level of anger because it would be efficient for him to do so. The priest could see the cardinal's resolution defining itself, and he tried to ease his own anxiety and relax the tension he could feel in the air by assuming a studied, casual manner. He pushed his weight back, lifting the chair on its two hind legs. He slid his hands into the pockets of his black twill trousers.

"Maybe once you talk to her . . ."

"I talked to her this morning . . . already."

That was it! That was what brought him to mass. That was what stirred him to anger. Abruptly, O'Brien leaned toward the priest, transparent again. "Do you know what she said to me? You could never imagine. How long are you ordained?"

"Five years."

The cardinal leaned back in the chair, thoughtful, a bit surprised. "You look older."

"I am older. I'm thirty-seven. I started late."

"That's right. You were in the army, weren't you?"

"Yes." What was the old man getting at?

"Well, you couldn't appreciate then what an abysmal, heart-breaking moment we've come to. You have no idea what it was like before."

"Before . . . ?"

"Before it was thrown in the gutter!"

Tierney felt a certain revulsion at the ugly vehemence with which the cardinal spoke. The man wasn't being guarded with him at all.

"I'm sorry, Your Eminence, but what . . . ?"

"The tradition. I'm talking about respect, obedience. I'm talking, Father, about the pride priests used to take in themselves."

Tierney returned the chair to its four legs, cursing himself for his open neck, for his slouching manner. But then he felt a wave of his own anger back at O'Brien. What did he want of him? Why should the cardinal badger him with the condition of the modern world? What was the calculated, inexorable will behind the cardinal's bitter fussing? An anxious mood caught Tierney again, threw his breathing off, magnified his uneasiness. The cardinal was practically ranting.

"Nobody laughed at priests, at the priesthood. No newspaper, not even the high and mighty *Washington Post*, would dare mock an archbishop by giving such space, such support to such contempt. No nun would ever think to disobey . . ."

He stopped, looked at Tierney, seemed to collect himself, to return from a distant place. He went on, more thoughtfully. "Do you know what Pope Paul said to me once? He said, 'The sisters in America are the treasure of the Church.' "

Tierney slapped his thigh with a counterfeit enthusiasm. "That's still true, Your Eminence. You're only talking about one . . ."

"Does the 'treasure of the Church' lecture the cardinal archbishop of Washington about discrimination in his archdiocese?"

"Is that what she did?"

" 'Laundresses,' she said! Like laundresses we treat them!"

Tierney resisted the impulse to smile at the irony of the cardinal's last outburst, for in the basement of that very building some nameless nun was bending over the day's third load of dirty clothing, washing it, laundering it — a laundress exactly. Nuns cooked the priests' meals in the cardinal's house and did all their laundry. When Tierney had first been assigned to the cathedral it bothered him. He remembered washing his own underwear at the sink in his room. But at some point, he forgot when, he stopped caring. He sent his dirty clothes down the chute like everyone else.

"Maybe she has personal problems," Tierney said, pushing all sarcasm out of his voice.

"Indeed she has. And now she has a new one. She asked for a fight and she'll have it." He delivered the line like the Barry Fitzgerald pastor in a dozen movies: he's a swell fellow, that cardinal, but don't cross him.

"You expect that conflict will be necessary?" Tierney asked

respectfully, not wanting the question to sound like a challenge.

"Inevitable, I'm afraid. A major conflict. She refuses to resign."

"Well . . . " The priest shrugged in his chair. He didn't like the sound of the words even as they came out of his mouth. "Perhaps you should fire her. It would blow over. If people can't play by the rules, they ought to get out. She should have known that."

"That's the point, Father. This is one we don't *want* to blow over. It's time to take a stand, especially on this woman thing. Now that the Episcopalians have given in to their lunatics, the Catholic people are more confused than ever. Now's the time to demonstrate that the order of the Church holds. They can depend on the Rock of Peter; however fragile the Church appears to be, it is built on a solid foundation. There is a Catholic way to do things, established by the Lord Himself. Violations of that way must be swiftly and clearly punished."

"Punished, Your Eminence?"

Tierney's voice, unfortunately, was crisp with surprise. He fell silent, wondering if the cardinal sensed his shock at his sudden, ruthless tone. He watched the cardinal's face, which was lively and alert, nothing remote about it. His eyes were luminous. Tierney understood finally that the old man prized the energy and excitement that the woman had stirred in him. She represented a danger that heightens exquisitely one's consciousness of being alive. Though he saw her as a threat primarily to the Church and only indirectly to himself, the cardinal was still too much a man, too much aware, to be unmoved by her. His response was visceral, total, almost sensual. Tierney didn't know when he had seen the cardinal so agitated.

"Here, look at this . . ." O'Brien reached into the top left drawer of his desk, grunting slightly as he did so. He brought out a thick maroon volume entitled *Codex Juris Canonici* and slapped it down on the desk. He opened it to a page in the middle, withdrew a marker, and slid it across the desk. Tierney took the book, but did so slowly, already imagining what it said.

"Numbers 802, 803, and 804," the cardinal said, then leaned back in his chair, swiveling it slightly, watching. If you had the right page in the right book you could rule the world.

Tierney read, "*Caput I. De sacrosancto Missae sacrificio. Art. I. De sacerdote Missae sacrificium celebrante. Canonicus* 802. *Potestatem offerendi Missae sacrificium habent soli sacerdotes.*"

He translated his way through the canons as quickly as he could. He had never fully mastered Latin. A thin line of perspiration formed above his brow. Finally he looked up and said, "Well, that's pretty clear, isn't it?"

"Yes, it is. And she's in violation of all three. The penalty is clear enough too."

"And she wouldn't resign?"

"No. She wants her fight. Well, she'll have it."

"You know, Eminence, uh . . ." Tierney paused. The knot in his stomach was back. ". . . the publicity on this could be enormous. It plays right into the vogue for women's liberation. The networks and papers made the Episcopalians look like fools with the Foresman trial. A trial of a nun would be worse. It could be a real circus."

"That's why I asked you to stop in here, Father." O'Brien leaned back in his chair and suddenly beamed at Tierney with a genial, intimate air — an air that, either for its contrivance or its sincerity, made Tierney uncomfortable.

"Me?"

"Yes. I want you to be the canonical advocate."

"I'm sorry, the what?" Tierney barely remembered the phrase from his seminary courses in canon law.

"You prepare the Church's case. You present it. *And* you represent the Church's position in the public forum."

"Your Eminence, I'm hardly qualified. Don't you need a canon lawyer?"

"No. I don't." O'Brien leaned forward. He began to wave his right hand, gesturing as if it held a cigar. "You will have canon lawyers for assistants, a dozen of them if you want. But, frankly, what I need is an attractive, articulate man who can win our case not only behind the closed doors of the metropolitan tribunal, but — and this is more important because the ecclesiastical case is already settled — who can win it on television *and* in the *Washington Post*. I want this whole city to understand that this woman is not the victim of a capricious, vicious, female-hating fossil of an archbishop, but is merely being faced with the consequences of her own deed, that the very existence of the Catholic Church is at stake when unordained persons claim the right to preside over its central act. You see, it is more than my hurt feelings or outraged pride that is at stake here. I have no personal issue with this poor woman at all."

"I know that, Cardinal."

"Well, you must make the argument then."

"I don't know if — "

"Father Tierney, do you understand the weight of this question?"

"Yes, Your Eminence. I assure you, I do." It was, in fact, as if he were standing under it. Tierney grasped that the issue was fate-laden, and not abstractly so, not merely for the Church at large. He could feel the weight pressing down on his own frame. As if to resist it, he stood up and paced the width of the cardinal's desk. He did understand, and he agreed that the integrity of Holy Orders, of the sacrament, had to be protected. He shared in both the broad assumptions and the details of O'Brien's argument. But something gnawed at him. "Isn't it possible to avoid a major, public confrontation?" he asked.

"Well, it might have been if she'd resigned, confessed her offense, and disavowed the controversy that others — the press, women's-libbers, rabble-rousers — are stirring up in the wake of what she did. But the nun won't resign. We have no choice. She's already made it a circus." The cardinal's eyes glinted, sharp, focused.

"I see what you mean."

There hadn't been a canonical excommunication in the United States since Leander Perez had been condemned for public and extreme racism in New Orleans in the early sixties. The thought of embarking on such a rare and loaded procedure now, particularly in the face of the immense social and political clout the women's movement had engendered, sent a spasm up the priest's spine. The thought of presiding over such a procedure turned him cold. He made as if to hug himself and sat down in the chair again.

"Really, Cardinal, I'm not sure I'm your man."

"But you agree with me."

"Yes."

"You *are* the man, Father."

Was it settled then? That simply? Tierney knew: one does what one must do.

"Well, perhaps if someone else talked to her. Perhaps she was just reacting to you as an authority figure."

"You talk to her if you like. When she lets her venom go on you as she did on me your uneasiness about this affair may not evaporate, but you will see there is no other way. Yes. You talk to her. Then, Father . . ." O'Brien paused, staring hard at Tierney, who knew a command when he heard one, "you teach her."

"I'll talk to her."

"Good."

Tierney stood. The cardinal wasn't looking at him. In fact, the old man's eyes seemed to have focused on a point inside himself. Tierney sensed for the second time how humiliating it must all be for him, how rarely in his life the man's will had been thwarted.

"Cardinal, there was something else."

"Yes? What?"

"The ambassador's investiture."

"What about it?" O'Brien's tone was dull, indifferent. Tierney was surprised. The business with the woman was serious, but it couldn't cast a pall over everything. The ambassador's reception of the Order of Gregory the Great at the explicit direction of the pope himself was the most important event of the cathedral's year. Yet the cardinal was still looking vacantly, wearily, up at Tierney.

"I wanted to confirm with you, Your Eminence, that the ceremony is tomorrow at five-thirty."

"Right. I'm planning on it."

"And the apostolic delegate?"

"Whatever you do" — the cardinal sat up, abruptly alert — "don't mention it to him."

"What?"

"The business with the nun."

"Of course not, Your Eminence." Tierney was startled at the cardinal's distraction.

"When I spoke to him yesterday, he didn't bring it up."

"But he will be coming?"

"Oh, yes. In fact, he has the papal medal, the ribbon, and the ceremonial sash. And His Holiness sent a gift for Ambassador Ferris-Cogan by the same courier."

"Oh?"

"Yes. A fragment of parchment from a letter written by Pope Paul the Third to Saint Thomas More. It was never delivered because More was in the Tower."

"A perfect gift! You know the Cogan side of the ambassador's family lost their title and most of their land when they remained Catholic at the time Henry the Eighth broke with Rome. Sir Alisdair will treasure a relic of More's."

"Actually," O'Brien said too sharply, "it's a relic of Paul the Third's."

"Of course." Tierney was surprised at the edge in his own voice.

"Ferris-Cogan was one of Cardinal Heenan's advisers in London, you know." O'Brien said it pleasantly, as if he too were aware of the mood in the room and was trying to break it.

"So I understand." Tierney wasn't giving away anything now.

"And a chairman of the World Laity Council. An exemplary Catholic."

"I'd guess there's been some political maneuvering involved." The priest had turned his attention to the edge of the cardinal's desk, was tracing it with his finger. Something was wrong. He had no idea what.

"What do you mean?" the cardinal asked.

"Has to do with Ireland, I'd imagine."

"The pope doesn't hand out such honors for mere political achievement." The cardinal was speaking in his official capacity: papal spokesman.

"Well, if Ferris-Cogan does go from D. C. to home secretary, as I've heard at the embassy he might, it wouldn't hurt Wilson's chances to pull that nut out of the fire if England's man for Ulster after all these centuries was finally a Catholic, *and* a favorite of the pope, *and* a descendant of the Thomas More wing of fiercely loyal Catholics."

"Well, there's a touch of politics in everything." The cardinal withdrew into distraction again. Obviously he hadn't left his thoughts of the nun behind. Tierney said nothing. The silence that settled between them seemed after some moments to lend a warmth to the air. The two men were on separate edges of the same hole. When the cardinal looked up at Tierney finally, his eyes had a kind of gratitude in them.

"So," he said, as if the silence hadn't interrupted him at all, "if His Holiness can help bring a little peace and order to that heartbroken island from which so many of us spring, well, he would do so gladly. If the ambassador is England's showcase Catholic, it's our privilege to shine him up a bit tomorrow."

"Before he goes on display." Tierney said it easily, with a sweeping gesture, matching O'Brien's reconciling humor. "I'm seeing him today. I have my weekly instruction with his daughter."

"How's she coming?"

"She's an exceptional child and very charming." Tierney felt a calm infuse his manner. The thought of Melissa eased his keyed nerves. "I like her. And her father's very good with her. Her mother, you know, isn't a Catholic. He taught her all the prayers himself, and he's quite interested in my lessons with her. Though, actually, theologically speaking, he's a bit conservative."

"Well," O'Brien smiled, "when he asked me to appoint a chaplain he told me not to send over any liberal new-breeder."

"So you sent him one of your good, reliable stuffed shirts, eh?"

"Right." The cardinal chuckled. Tierney felt an immense relief. Perhaps he had just been making it all worse than it was. His relief showed in his voice.

"In any case, I'll go over the ceremony with him today. By the way, is the pope's gift a surprise?"

"Yes. Don't mention it. I want to give it to him myself."

"Right." The priest was respectful and easy. "And when can I go over the ceremony with you then, Your Eminence?"

"You needn't worry about me, Father. You're the master of ceremonies. You just tell me what to do when we're on the altar." Cardinal O'Brien's gaze was full and direct; it had Tierney as if by the shoulders. "You just tell me what to do. I can follow orders."

He spoke as if what he said were a joke. But it wasn't.

In the warm quickening of April, Rock Creek Park coursed through Washington like an artery, the deep wild source of its life. From Military Road in the north to the Tidal Basin in the south, the windows and balconies of senators, generals, diplomats, one Vice-President, several Cabinet members, the Shoreham, the Sheraton Park, Walter Reed, the townhouses of Georgetown and Foggy Bottom all opened onto the slash of tidy reborn forest that could fool a man into thinking the world was still a simple place in which to live.

In the spring the high waters of its stream rushed down from the Maryland hills past the cages of animals in the District Zoo, under the high, arched Roman bridges of great avenues, by the colonial burial place at Dumbarton Oaks, over the forgotten locks of the Chesapeake and Ohio Canal and through a floodgate, the Watergate, into the Potomac River, where, under the gaze of Thomas Jefferson, they swirled toward a point on the Arlington shore between the great cemetery and the Pentagon.

By nine o'clock the grass in the meadow below the P Street Bridge was just about dry. The dew had been baked off by the sun. The steep ravine of Rock Creek Park flattened out at that point into a broad field that was several hundred yards nearly square. There were boundaries of trees to the north and south. On the west the field sloped down across a bridle path to the creek. On the east a sharp hill, nearly a cliff, rose a hundred feet toward Twenty-second Street and the Dupont Circle section of the city.

The chill of the night was gone. The birds had taken over the meadow from the swamp crickets and the other creatures that owned it in the dark. They were busy collecting the new seed that the spring winds had discarded between the blades of grass all over the meadow, and so they disregarded the muffled sounds of hooves.

A large black horse burst into the field from the woods to the south. Its feet slammed into the earth, shaking it. Yet from the distance it barely seemed to touch the ground as it streaked along the bridle path by the creek. Pebbles jumped and dust rose in small clouds until the horse angled off the path and dashed headlong into the meadow. The feeding birds continued to ignore the horse, except those that were directly in its path.

The man on the horse's back sat squarely in the straight line of its motion. He controlled the motion, but without effort, without excessive dominance. His legs rode the flanks of the animal the way muscle rides on bone.

They took the meadow in a series of sharp, quick turns. The rider raised his left arm, swung it in circles above his head, and then slashed it down as if stroking a polo mallet, as if knocking the small sphere of willow, of *pulu*, as the wood is known in the language of the Tibetan inventors of the game.

39

The rider drove his horse into a wrenching turn and swung his arm down again, gave chase to what he saw, and swung again. A great hearty yell came from him as he gave himself up to the shot on goal that he and his horse made in the imagination their movement showed they had in common.

"Shot, Ambassador!"

The rider drew his mount abruptly to a halt. He looked up at the bridge over P Street where the man who had hollered was standing. About forty feet separated them.

"Good day, Parsley."

"Yes, sir." The man on the bridge was calm and sober, dressed in a dark business suit and tie. It was difficult to imagine that he would have jovially shouted "Shot!" after Ferris-Cogan's simulated goal. But the ambassador knew that the man's cheer had been simply a calculated notification that he was there, watching.

Alisdair Ferris-Cogan hated to be surprised, and in particular he disliked being observed in the act of indulging his passion for the ride and the game. Ordinarily, especially with staff, he was an aloof and formal man. He drew his horse closer to the bridge, having resumed his casual dignity. He squinted up at Parsley.

"So this is as far as I go, eh?"

"If you please, sir. We've no men posted farther up the path."

"You're the only man on my staff that tells me what to do, Parsley. Did you know that?"

But the man hardly reacted. "I didn't know, sir."

"I'd have thought my security chief would know that. Seems a choice bit of intelligence. You and my wife, Parsley. And Melissa, of course. You're the authorities in my life."

"Yes, sir." Parsley smiled pleasantly down at Ferris-Cogan, but still refrained from the banter. He was all business. Ferris-Cogan held his reins loosely in one hand. The horse was still, obedient. With his free hand he rubbed the broad neck of the animal, a slow sensual stroking.

"Why don't you ride with me, Parsley?" Ferris-Cogan felt a

mild resentment toward the man. "Frankly, I'd prefer your company to your detached observation."

"Procedure, sir. In any case, I don't ride. Nor do any of my men."

"You inquired?"

"Yes, sir."

"Which means I submit to the limitations of your office."

"Sir?"

"I thought you security people were all crack athletes, National Service with the Gurkhas and all that."

"No, sir, I was RAF."

"How are you going to protect me on the ground?"

"I'm qualified in pistol, sir." He said it matter-of-factly, not indicating the bulge of the weapon over his heart, not using the truer word: expert.

"We're wandering a little far afield, so to speak." Ferris-Cogan leaned back on the haunches of his animal, enjoying himself. He was beginning to understand that Parsley's dryly given responses had their own self-mocking edge. "I suppose what remains is for me to turn back and seek the safety of the compound as swiftly as possible."

"Not at all, sir." Parsley spoke without the slightest hint of irritation. The man's patience itself was beginning to seem a parody to Ferris-Cogan. "As long as you stay south of this point, sir, and north of the canal, you will be in sight of my people at all times. As long as that is the case, I have no requirement for you to return to the embassy."

"Thank you," Ferris-Cogan said, his sarcasm stifled.

Parsley did not reply. He understood perfectly when no reply would suffice. Indeed, Reginald Parsley understood when no reply was the best reply of all.

From his place below the bridge, leaning back on his horse, Ferris-Cogan gave Parsley a frankly admiring smile. The man struck just the right note of impersonal competence. Which was why he could be so irritating and why, finally, the ambassador was willing to entrust him with his life and those of his wife and daughter.

Ferris-Cogan shrugged. "Right, Reg." He clucked his horse, drew in his reins, turned, and moved off, riding south. "See you," he hollered over his shoulder.

"Sir," Parsley said inaudibly, watching the figure of the ambassador shrink until it presented too small a target for anything but a sighted rifle.

"Sister Dolores Sheehan? I was told she would be at this number. Oh. Well, it's important that I speak to her. This is Father John Tierney. Saint Matthew's. Yes. It's about that. Yes. Thanks."

"Sister Dolores."

"Hello, Sister. This is John Tierney."

"Who?"

"Father John Tierney."

"Do I know you?"

"No. We've never met, but I'm a friend of Hank Baron's, and I've heard about your work at A.U."

"I'll bet you have."

"Right. Can the small talk, huh?"

"Right."

"Okay. Look, I just talked to the cardinal . . ."

"That's a switch."

"Sorry?"

"I thought he did the talking."

"I know what you mean. That's why I'm calling."

"Why?"

"Well, maybe things were pushed too fast and far this morning . . . between you two, I mean. It occurred to me that everyone might be served better by a reasonable discussion. Do you know what I mean? Sister? Sister? Sister, are we cut off?"

"Are we connected?"

"Well, look, I'd like to head off the escalation. He's ready, reluctant but ready, to bring out the bombers."

"Are you the point man?"

"What?"

"You tell them where to dump?"

"Look, I'm not interested in fencing with you. I'd really like to help."

"I know you won't believe this, Father, but I don't need your help. I'm not one of the helpless and harmless little nuns you call the 'good sisters.' You're not going to sweet-talk me into what the cardinal couldn't threaten me into."

"Sister, you're entitled to full ecclesiastical due process, and you'll get it if that's what you want."

"If that's what I want?"

"Yes. Actually the entire mess could be avoided."

"How?"

"Well, I was hoping we might get together to talk about it."

"Talk now, Father."

"Wouldn't you rather . . . ?"

"No. Why don't you just say what you have to say?"

"All right. It's occurred to me that everybody's best interest — yours, the cardinal's, the Church's — would be best served if you resigned — "

"Come on, Father! Do you expect me to give up my way of life to appease an old man who hates women?"

"Wait a minute. Wait a minute. His age has nothing to do with it. He does not hate women. And I'm not talking about your way of life. I'm talking about your job at A.U."

"He wants my resignation from the Order as well."

"I'm willing to recommend that he waive that demand if you resign from the campus ministry and accept an assignment with your Order in another diocese."

"I refuse to apologize for what I did."

"You could just say you accept the Church's dogma that only the ordained can celebrate mass."

"Only men, you mean."

"That's not the point, Sister."

"That's exactly the point, Father."

"You're being unreasonable."

"Am I?"

"Quite."

"I'm only doing what Jesus would do were he a woman in this Church."

"That's an almost laughable statement, Sister. I don't know, frankly, that Jesus would do what I'm doing were he in my position, but I do know that there are other ways to accomplish the kind of change you advocate. I happen to agree with you that women should be ordained — "

"Aren't you the perfect liberal?"

" — but I do not agree that unordained persons serve the Church or Jesus Christ by celebrating the mass."

"*Attempting* to celebrate, Father."

"What?"

"Forget it."

"Look, if you want a fight, Sister, you'll have it."

"Don't *you* threaten me, Father."

"It's not my intention to threaten you, Sister. If you want to play it this way you'll be left with nothing. Believe me, I'm trying to help you."

"Perhaps so, Father, but no thanks."

"Look, I was afraid this would happen. Can't we get together?"

"To what purpose?"

"I'm the canonical advocate in this thing, as it's called."

"The prosecutor."

"Exactly."

"And you want me to get you off the hook you're squirming on now."

"I just want to talk to you. I want to meet you."

"Shake hands before coming out, huh?"

"I refuse to play Bobby Riggs to your Billie Jean King."

"Afraid you might lose?"

"Look, Sister Dolores, if you're that sure I'm a male chauvinist pig, why don't you just hang up on me? . . . Sister? . . . Sister? Oh, God. Great. Bitch! What was that number? Here. Five, four, seven, two, two, nine. Now, answer. Answer. Come on, answer it."

"Sister Sheehan."

"Sister, I just called back to commend you."

"On what?"

"On the nunlike docility with which you hung up the phone at my suggestion."

"Look, Father, that's exactly what I . . . Father?"

In his room on the third floor of the rectory, Tierney sat looking at his telephone. His heart was beating so that he could feel it.

"Oh, you bitch," he said aloud. He reached past the phone for his pack of Pall Malls. He banged one out into his hand, put it in his mouth, slapped his shirt pocket for a match, but he had none. He opened the center drawer of his desk and groped under papers and bent envelopes until he came up with the Key to His Future. He read the inside of the matchbook, decided not to send off for the free application, ripped a match loose, closed the book, and struck it. He inhaled deeply, stood, and fell back onto his bed. He lay there, feeling caught between Cardinal O'Brien — the weight of tradition — and Sister Sheehan — the dash for freedom.

Great, he thought, I *am* the point man. I'll be the jerk in this one. I'm the damn laundress to both of them. What next? What next?

Next his phone rang. It was the last thing he expected. He leapt from the bed and reached for the phone. He forced himself to wait for the third ring. When he put the receiver to his face he forced himself to be calm.

"Hello. Father Tierney."

"Hi, dearie."

He sat back on his bed. The most familiar voice in his life. The Irish lilt.

"Oh. Mom. Hi."

"You don't have to sound disappointed."

"I'm not disappointed."

"Don't get cross."

"I'm not cross, Mother."

He was cross. What did she want anyway? He'd been over Sunday. She couldn't complain about not seeing him. But, dutiful as he'd been lately, the old guilt began crawling out of its cave in his stomach.

"You sound cross."

"No, really, Mom. You just caught me in the middle of something."

"Oh. Well, I'll let you go."

"No, I'm through. What's up?" He turned cheerful. Cheerful affection was the tamer's chair with which he forced the monster guilt back into its cave where it had lived since the moment in his boyhood when he admitted that, in addition to loving his mother, he hated her.

"Well, I got a letter today from your Aunt Moira."

"Oh, yeah? What'd she have to say?" He lay back on his bed, smoking.

"Guess who's coming to the States?"

"Aunt Moira?"

"No."

"Uncle Mike?"

"No."

"I give."

"Guess."

"Aunt Tess?"

"No."

"Who?"

"Guess."

"No, who, Mom?"

"Your cousin, Bea."

"Bridgit?"

"You guessed it."

"No, I didn't."

"Well, you almost did."

"That's great! What for?"

"A visit, Moira says. I'm so excited."

"She's coming here?"

"Of course. To see us. She'll stay here, with me."

"Great. When's she coming?"

"Today."

"Today!"

"Yes. Moira said she'd call from the airport."

"What flight?"

"She didn't say. When she calls, could you get free to pick her up?"

"No, I can't, Mom. I'm tied up. I'm surprised it's such short notice. It's kind of a big deal for Bridgit to travel like that, isn't it? She's never left Ireland before, has she?"

"No. But Moira says she was so excited about my letter she decided to come on the spur of the moment. I'll just have her take a cab, then."

"Your letter?"

"Well, she wants to go to the ceremony tomorrow."

"What ceremony?"

"With the ambassador, you know. The pope's award. Moira was bursting with pride and envy. They're all so proud of you, son. And you know how fond Bridgit is of you from your visits."

"How'd they know about the ambassador?"

"They read about it. It's in all the papers at home."

"But how'd they know I had anything to do with it?"

"I told you."

"You did?"

"My letter. I wrote them you'd be presenting His Honor to His Holiness."

"His Excellency to His Eminence."

"Whatever."

"I'm just the master of ceremonies, Mother."

"You're the ambassador's private chaplain."

"Yes. Private."

"What do you mean?"

"It's not for you to be telling that around."

"What's the difference? You'll be a monsignor next, Johnny. They're training you for it."

"Mom . . ."

"It'll be no trouble. I'll bring Bea with me."

"Okay. I'll get you good seats."

"I knew you would."

"It's the least I can do, if she's coming all this way."

"Well, it's such an honor."

"Yes, but not to me, Mom."

"Well, it is to me, darling."

"Okay, Mom. Look, I'll get out to the apartment for dinner."

"Fine."

"What are we having?"

"What do you want?"

"Anything."

"Prime rib? Something special for Bea?"

"Good. Yeah, let's give her a real nice visit. She's shy, you know."

"But she's nice, and so pretty."

"I know she is. I really like her. In fact, I wish she weren't my cousin."

"Johnny! You're a priest!"

"I know, Mom. See you later."

" 'Bye, darling."

Tierney put the receiver back in its cradle and sat looking at it. How about that, he thought, banging out his cigarette in the ashtray. All this way for the ceremony. All this way — could it be — for me?

Brigadier Frank Cameron, military attaché to the British Embassy in Washington, sat stiffly upright at his desk in his office on the second floor of the modern chancery wing. A moustached man in his early forties with graying hair, closely cropped, he wore a stern tweed suit with matching vest, a light brown tie perfectly knotted at his throat. He would have preferred, of course, to be in uniform, but British policy followed the American custom; Washington military officers of field rank or above dressed in civilian clothing except on occasions of ceremony or official function. Cameron thought it a degrading policy, as if soldiers should be ashamed of themselves. But Americans did not know the difference betwen discretion and disgrace.

He wore half-lens reading glasses, and was frowning at the paper he held in his hand. He studied it. He stared at it. He memorized the ribbon lines that were pasted on it.

It was the message he'd been waiting fifteen months to receive.

He took off his glasses, dropped them on his desk. He reached over to the intercom beside his phone and smashed its button down.

"Stone! When did this dispatch come in?"

The intercom murmured back at him: "About seven minutes ago, Brigadier."

"*Exactly* when?"

"One moment, sir. Sir, the cryptogram was received at 1042 hours, processed 1045 hours."

"Why wasn't it brought to me immediately?"

"Sir?"

"Immediately, Stone!"

"Yes, sir!"

Cameron snapped off the intercom and sat back in his chair. On the wall behind him were several photographs, each showing the brigadier himself standing in the midst of a small number of soldiers. In one photograph all of the men were dressed in mottled green parkas and baggy trousers bloused into boots. All of the men wore dark berets with the crown insignia. Underneath that photograph was the word ULSTER.

Second and third photos showed similar groupings of soldiers around a Cameron who looked younger. In all the pictures his moustache was the prominent feature of his stern face, flowing as it did down the creases of his chin. Thick hair grew on the bridge of his nose, making his eyebrows one continuous dark line, a kind of symmetrical repetition of the line his moustache drew across the bottom third of his face. Below the other two group photographs were the words ADEN and MALAYSIA. The men in these pictures were dressed in khakis, their sleeves rolled up, their necks open. But all wore the dark berets with the crown insignia.

The fourth photograph showed Cameron walking on a city street between two young boys. He towered over them, an exceptionally tall man. He was dressed in the camouflage green of the ULSTER photo. He was carrying a large automatic rifle, the long fat barrel of which protruded from beneath his right armpit. The two cocky lads beside him both walked with their hands in their pockets. One wore short pants; the sock of his left leg fell to his shoe. Both boys looked directly at the camera, laughing, but the brigadier's eyes were turned toward something to the right of the lens. He was staring intently, alert, as if something was about to happen. As if he knew, and the boys at his side didn't.

Two yards to each side of these photographs were two flags that fell in thin furls down their mahogany staffs. One was the Union Jack. The other was the gold and violet banner of Her Majesty's Special Guard. In the left corner of the medium-sized office was a small table holding four copies of the same thin book, *Urban Operations — Cameron*. In the right corner was a narrow floor-to-ceiling window that opened onto the courtyard of the embassy. It was ajar. The breeze lifted the white curtain, which rose and fell lightly in the sunlight.

Cameron swung around in his chair and looked absently out the window. He was intent upon his thoughts and hardly noticed the tall young woman in a gray skirt and paint-splattered black smock crossing from one wing of the building to the other. She wore her blond hair up off her neck and carried half a dozen artist's brushes in her hand. When the door slammed behind her in the far corner of the yard, it seemed to jolt Cameron out of his grave reverie. He turned back to his desk and slammed the button down on the intercom. "Stone!"

"Sir!"

"Get Mitchell in here!"

"Sir!"

A moment later, Captain Ronald Mitchell came into Cameron's office, brushing by the wood plate on its door lettered BRIGADIER FRANCIS A. CAMERON, H.M.S., MILITARY ATTACHÉ. Mitchell was Cameron's executive officer.

"Yes, sir!"

"We've got it, Mitch."

Cameron held out the dispatch. "Read that. Just in from M.I., Whitehall."

Mitchell read silently: Highest priority. Confirmed source reports Provisional Officer "Janus" arrives D.I.A. 22/4/75 at 1336 hrs. on BOAC 924 from Hthr. Expect high intensity operation, unspecified. Prevent.

Mitchell lowered the paper and looked at Cameron. He smiled and said, "Janus!"

Cameron nodded. "We haven't heard from him since the Parliament bombing."

"Nearly two years. I'd heard he was dead."

"Intelligence reported last August that he was one of the prisoners in the Maze. They did their usual timid interrogation and, of course, turned up nothing. In my time we'd have nailed him."

"They say even the other Provos don't know who he is, though."

"That's because he's their gun against their own. He's their executioner, their enforcer. He killed Roring and probably MacCauliff. The Officials wanted him more than we did in my time."

"Was he on the subscription list?"

"Yes. The last four months we had the sales program. We'd have sold him too, but . . ." Cameron stopped; his glance drifted away from Mitchell momentarily as his mind ran on with the bitter memory, rehearsed and familiar. The fucking Labourites just then started crying "torture," and when the government changed and Wilson sent over his citizens' commission to wipe the noses and kiss the arses of the bloody internees, Whitehall panicked, canned the in-depth interrogation, obliterated the Military Reaction Force, denied it ever existed, transferred Cameron to this cream-puff post lest he be uncovered for the ogre that he was, and, in the process and among other things, assured that "Janus," the only skillful assassin the IRA has produced, would be alive and free to join him in this fair city today!

Cameron slammed his fist down on his desk and turned to the captain.

"Mitch, I want this bugger! They have given us *carte blanche*. He's ours."

"All we have to do is find him."

"And stop him."

"What's your guess about the operation?"

"High intensity? More of their bloody shit on each other no doubt."

"The IRA kill each other, you know, because they've no other worthy opponents."

"Very funny. It's because they'll kill anything that breathes. They're the most vicious bastards I've ever seen. And I've seen viciousness."

"Sorry, sir."

"You were in Ulster as long as I was. You've seen what they do."

"Yes, I have. And, frankly, sir, faced with such inhumanity, all one can do is make light of it."

"No. One can defeat it."

"What's procedure, sir?"

"First, we keep it military for now. I'll not have the locals in at all if I can help it. And I'll tell Parsley myself when it's appropriate. Second, put the blade to our stateside sources immediately. Get on to Seton in Boston. Review the transcripts on the Shannon tap here in D.C. and see what clicks. Tell McQuaid to surface everything at his end — rumors of arms deals, talk of turncoats, big money flow from the Northern Aid Committee, whatever dung the Irish are throwing at each other on this side of it. Third, I want the whole staff in here now. Among the nine of us we might trip the bastard at Dulles. It may be our best shot at him. He won't be armed coming off the plane, for one thing. We have to move fast though. He comes down in not three hours."

"We have no idea what he looks like?"

"Not Michael Collins, for certain. The goddamned thing is we know nothing personal about the bastard at all. Even the fucking informers are useless. Nobody ever *sees* him, not even the Provos. He knows better than to trust those fools. Which is why he's still at it, why we've not nailed him."

"I was hoping he'd be wearing a bush hat at least, like the old IRA."

"Right, and a gold lanyard to his pistol. No, this one is the real thing, Captain. Get the men."

Mitchell turned smartly on his heel and left Cameron's office. The brigadier fingered the dispatch again, read it, grunted at it, and crushed it into a ball.

He withdrew a single key from the pocket of his vest, leaned down to the third drawer of his desk, inserted the key in its lock, and opened it. He dropped the balled message into the drawer.

He lifted out a holstered pistol. It was not his service revolver as he'd have preferred. That would be too bulky. It was a .357 Magnum Model 19 with a two-and-a-half-inch barrel. It would do. He stood, withdrew the belt of his trousers from half its loops, fed it into the holster, and slid the weapon around it to the small of his back. He fastened his belt again and drew the edges of his tweed coat together, but did not button it. With his left hand he slapped the place on his lower back where the gun nestled now.

It was the moment he'd been awaiting for fifteen months.

The heavy wood door leading from the courtyard to the rear wing of the embassy slammed behind Nancy Ferris-Cogan. She walked quickly across the wide enclosed portico, through a pair of smaller doors, and into the solarium that a previous ambassador had added to the building to house his collection of exotic plants. It made an ideal painter's studio.

Instantly the warmth of the place hit Nancy. The fresh morning sunlight poured through the glass panels that formed the east wall and the outer half of the curved ceiling. The room was about the size of a squash court; an easel stood in its center, angled with its large canvas to avoid the sun. A clutter — canvas scraps, bits of wood, half-started paintings, folded tripods — was pushed to one side in disorder. Records were piled in a corner by a turntable, which sat on one floor-sized speaker. The other speaker stood next to the easel and held two coffee cups, an ashtray littered with used cigarettes, and a broken pencil. On the other side of the easel was a high table, half the size of a door, covered with spread-out newspapers that held a dozen tubes of paint, variously squeezed, a palette, rags, and three cans with brushes set in murky fluid. Away from the easel facing the glass wall a chaise longue stretched out under a Scottish wool blanket, Black Watch, which was stained here and there with splotches of paint. The wall opened on the broad lawn that ran level from the building a hundred yards before falling off into the ravine of the park at Dumbarton Oaks.

No one was on the lawn. No other windows of the embassy faced the solarium. To have such privacy in the sunlight at the foot of an open field under the perfect blue sky, and to have the warmth of her own cluttered space spared the chill of the April morning — it was a luxury she cherished.

Nancy dropped the brushes she carried onto the worktable, moved to the chaise, and lay down. She unbuttoned her paint-stained black smock and opened her breasts to the sun, closed her eyes, and lay motionless.

She became freshly aware of her body as the sun caressed its warmth down on it and lulled her into the familiar pleasure she took in her own beauty. She was thirty-three years old, but her bright skin, ripe eyes, and slim shape made her seem younger. She knew it and enjoyed the polite but unmistakable regard her appearance always drew from men.

She tightened the muscles in her thighs, thought of stripping off her gray skirt to lie fully nude in the sun, but decided against it. She put her fingers to her tongue, then rubbed saliva on her forehead, under her dark blue eyes, over the high thin arches of her cheekbones, over her nose. She lay motionless again, feeling the moisture give itself to the sun. Motionless in pleasure.

She remained so for nearly ten minutes. But then she thought of the painting, of the work, of what remained to be done. She hoped to finish it today, to have it for him in time. She tried to conjure up the painting in her mind. It would not come. Her mind was blank. That was the trouble. She had so far over six weeks managed to come up with a canvas that still eluded her.

It was the first time she'd ever tried to do a portrait of her husband. After all these years, finally sensing she was ready to do it, she had hoped to capture several things: the romance he stirred in her at the beginning and, still, the pride he wore like the family arms, his love of the danger in the sport, the madness in him for wanting such danger between his legs. Between his legs, she thought. Yes, the madness and the power. She roused herself, rubbed her face vigorously with her hands, and got up.

At the easel she grimaced. Yes. Between his legs, a horse, her husband on a horse, on Gandalon, his great horse. The horse he rode for two seasons, the two best seasons, '64 and '65. The first time Nancy saw her husband was at the National Polo Finals at Hurlingham, the club outside London where polo had been introduced to England by officers back from India in 1856. Alisdair had been riding with Prince Philip himself, and she had been enraptured by the dash of it all, the romance, the pride, the danger, the skilled madness.

But when she looked at the canvas she knew that what she had painted was not alive with the primal spirit she sought, not her husband's, not hers.

There was motion; she had him lunging off Gandalon's left flank, out of the canvas as it were, poised to strike his mallet in the very next instant. It was an unusual composition. She liked the idea of it — to freeze the moment in which the timing of several relationships climaxed: between horse and rider, between stick and ball, between ball and goal.

But standing now with her eye heavy on what she had done, Nancy decided she had frozen not only the moment but the man as well. That was the problem; the horse was alive with its terrified eyes, steaming nostrils, straining muscles, but her husband's image lay flat and lifeless on the canvas.

She looked more closely at his figure, trying to see the key, trying to track down the hole in her vision through which all the juices of the man were seeping. His upraised arm, tense with readiness, about to slam the circling mallet down, was the center of focus in the left mid-quarter of the painting. It was done superbly, slightly distorted, forearm exploding with power, all shades of mauve, green, rust. Her eye ran down the arm to the shoulder, to the shirt which was dark along the twisted ribs with perspiration, reds, grays, the startling white of the shirt's trunk, the blue band cutting it in the center, slashing across his chest, across the painting, breaking the vertical and thereby making it all the more dominant. Above the shirt, the neck with its wedge of shadow pointing down his chest to bring his head all the more forward, his head, helmet, whites, blues, strap to the chin, perspiration, flaring mouth, a yell of triumph, attack, closing to strike.

There was a feverish tension in the face, a power, a soaring delight in the bodily stress of the moment. That much was real and alive and his. But there was something else — what was it? She wanted to put her hand inside the eyes she had painted to feel, to touch what was behind them. The eyes, yes. Something in the glint. Something like a barb, an edge, an unevenness. Something unmeant.

She took a further step back from the canvas. Yes, the eyes. She glared at what she had done. The eyes she had fashioned of blue dabs, white, ocher, black, were not the eyes . . .

The house phone rang. She went to it.

"Yes."

"Mrs. Ferris-Cogan?" It was Radford, the ambassador's secretary.

"Yes."

"The priest is here."

"Oh."

Her hand went involuntarily to her breast. Her smock was still unbuttoned. She fumbled with it, wedged the phone in her neck, and started to slip the buttons into their slots.

"Well, is Melissa ready?"

"Not quite, madam. Miss Wells says a moment more."

"Have Father Tierney come back here then. Have Miss Wells send Melissa back when she's ready."

"Certainly, madam."

"Thank you, Mr. Radford."

Nancy looked around the solarium. It was a mess. The servants were instructed not to touch it. She smoothed the plaid cover on the chaise, kicked random papers into the corner with the canvas bits, the naked frames. She turned to the glass wall, trying to find an image of herself in its reflection. She opened one of the French doors so that it angled away from the direct rays of the sun and gave her the mirror she needed. She pulled the smock straight, caught a long wisp of her blond hair, and fixed it in the comb at the nape of her neck.

She returned to the canvas, where her eyes fell again on those of her husband; they wouldn't do at all. She took up the number 9 brush that soaked in the clearest can of turpentine, squeezed the excess fluid out of its soft bristles, and then stopped. She did not know what to do. She stood staring at the painting for some moments until there was a faint knock at the door.

"Enter please," she said, loudly, cheerfully.

The door opened and Father John Tierney entered, dressed as usual in black suit and Roman collar.

Nancy was glad to see him and said so with the enthusiasm of her greeting. "Hello, hello, Father. Come in. Come in." She put the brush and the rag on the worktable, wiped her hands on her smock, and stepped around the canvas toward him.

"Hello, Nancy. How are you?" He took her hand, pressed it firmly, bent toward her so that she could kiss his cheek lightly. As he lowered his gaze it unconsciously slid along the frank lines of her body until he checked it, raised it to meet hers. Her wide-set eyes, gray and unclouded, fixed upon him. He felt himself blushing.

"Isn't it a lovely day?" she said.

"Certainly is, beautiful." Tierney deliberately began looking around the solarium and out at the lawn. "And what a marvelous room in which to enjoy it."

"Oh, this is where I work. I have my delicious isolation here. The world leaves me utterly alone . . ."

"Oh, I'm sorry. I'm interrupting."

"Not at all, Father. Not you. I've been wanting you to see it actually. It's only the last month or so with the warmer weather that I've been out here."

"You showed me your studio upstairs a couple of months ago." He remembered a small, close room with eaves. Its musty, intimate smell filled his nostrils for an instant.

"Well, I work here now." She gestured toward her easel. "Care to look?"

"Certainly."

Together they moved to the easel, came around it, and faced the canvas in silence. Nancy watched his face. She was anxious for his reaction because he was the first person to see the work and because she instinctively trusted his responses.

He stepped back, saying, "I'm speechless. It's magnificent."

She was delighted. Perhaps the rag and spit of her work had not missed its mark after all. "I'm still at work on the face, actually."

"God, it's powerful. I ache for the horse."

"For the horse?"

"Yes. It seems about to explode with suffering and ecstasy both."

"What about the man?"

"It's your husband."

"Yes. A gift for him, in fact, for tomorrow."

"Oh, he'll love it, Nancy. I'm sure of it."

"I have to redo the eyes. They've . . . eluded me."

"It can't fail to — "

"I *must* get the eyes right, otherwise I'm afraid the horse dominates. It's the man I want to celebrate *with* the horse."

"Yes, I see. Well, he'll love it."

"Thanks. I'm glad you think so. I wanted to do something very special."

"You've done it."

"Guess what else?"

He turned from the painting to face her. The top of her head came level with his eyes. She was taller than most women.

"What?" he asked, finding her eyes.

"I just received word that I'm to have a one-man show in London in October."

"You're kidding? That's wonderful! Congratulations!"

"I'm delighted, of course. It's my first."

Tierney met her broad smile with his own, took her hand into both of his, and shook it heartily, playfully. He was thinking her eyes held all the pride he ever wanted to feel. "A one-man show!" he burst out. "Wow!"

"One-*person* show I should have said." She was pretending to be repentant.

"One-*person!*" Tierney dropped her hand and covered his face in mock horror. "Don't tell me you're a feminist too!" He leaned back against one of the frames of the door that opened onto the broad lawn.

"Watch your suit. This place is tacky." Nancy reached over to draw him away from the door, touching his sleeve. But he put her off with a wave.

"It's all right."

"That black you've on will show it all. Be careful of the paint." Her solicitous tone became quick and assertive then. "*Of course* I'm a feminist. Wouldn't you be?"

He turned slightly to peer *at* the windowpane, not through it. He could see her image in the glass. She was sparkling in the sunlight.

"God, no," he said. "What's the kick in hating men?"

"Hating men? God, Father — pardon the pun — what a Sicilian notion of feminism."

"Sicilian?"

"Stream of consciousness, followed on 'godfather.' "

"You've lost me."

They laughed, gloating together upon their silliness, until Nancy decided to answer him seriously. "What women want will not be sliced out of a man like a pound of flesh . . ."

". . . or like a rib."

". . . or like a genital organ," she rejoined, "which is the real issue, isn't it?"

Tierney didn't reply immediately. There was an abruptly sensual character to the silence between them. When Tierney spoke, it was with an abstract air that dispelled it.

"Well, it's the real fear, I suppose."

"*Mythic* fear, not real. Freud aside, we are all capable of other envies, other conflicts than the merely Oedipal." She was drumming absently on an edge of the easel with sharp almond fingernails.

"Don't be so hard on myth."

"Don't be so easy on it."

"Oh," he shrugged. "*That* discussion."

"Yes. What a bore." There was in Nancy a store of chic ennui. "You'll not convert this pagan, Father."

"If you were a pagan, I wouldn't try. Pagans are more religious than any of us.'

"What am I, then?"

"You're an artist," he said simply, as if it were explanation enough.

"At least no 'Prince of the Church' appears to tell me I can't paint."

There was a second of sharp silence. Tierney lifted his bony spine away from the doorframe.

"You read about it."

"That's what's bothering you, isn't it?"

Tierney's even breathing broke pace. Was it so evident?

"Yes," he said slowly, "it's my bad fortune to be involved in the thing."

"I'd say it's the sister's bad fortune to be involved."

"She started the millstone turning."

"I think she's right," Nancy said, lifting her chin slightly, showing him the creamy white hollow of her throat.

"Of course she's right," Tierney said a bit quickly. "Everyone's right! There's no such thing as wrong anymore, is there?"

"Wait a minute, Father. We're not talking about the breakdown of western morality."

"You think not?" he replied evenly. "Perhaps we are. Perhaps *exactly* that."

"The woman said *mass*. That hardly rates on a scale with, say, what's going on in Vietnam this week."

Their answers were increasingly flinty, but were still well within the good-natured mood of mock argument.

"All I'm saying is that if every woman starts celebrating mass, then the mass is gone. The priesthood is gone. The Church is gone. And if the Catholic Church falls, what can stand?"

"That's how my father used to talk about the British Empire." Nancy bent, brushed her fingertips across her left thigh, as at an insect, then picked up her cigarettes from the floor speaker by the easel. She took one, then offered the pack to Tierney. They were, he noticed, English, Rothschild Filters. He took one and fumbled in his pocket for a match. Nancy lit her own cigarette with a chrome lighter and then held the flame for the priest. He bent to it, touched her hand with his, and inhaled. Neither mentioned their use of the new protocol, but both noted it and smiled.

As the smoke came out of his mouth, he laughed and spoke. "Do you appreciate the irony of this? Here I am defending the ancient tradition to you, a titled woman, a 'Lady' no less."

"Well, you're titled yourself, *Father*."

"But I'm not nobility."

"Neither are we, much to my husband's regret."

"What do you mean?"

"Alisdair was made a life peer for exceptional services to Her Majesty's Government, et cetera. By virtue of his knighthood, he is 'Sir' and I am 'Lady.' But the titles die when we do. He is not nobility as he would have been, as earl of Surrey, were it not for another moment when Christians started to break the rules."

"The Reformation."

"So called, yes. Frankly, the tradition of the family line is much more important to my husband than to me. He would like nothing better than, even as a prominent Catholic layman, to be restored to the earldom. *Especially* as a Catholic layman, actually."

"Ah, so the ancient tradition can continue."

"Yes, but the Cogan history is instructive. There are times when one's reverence for one's tradition means that something of the tradition must be forfeited. For the Cogans once, either their Catholicism or their place in the king's court. Alisdair's ancestor — you've seen his portrait in the family dining room — had to choose, much in the way it seems to me that your nun-friend had to choose. Sometimes one can't have it both ways."

"He had to choose between his conscience and obedience to the king."

"I don't agree. He had to choose between the obediences owed to the *two* kings in his life, the pope and Henry. Conscience is simply the place in which we make choices like that."

"So the nun is choosing between obedience owed, say, the pope, and obedience owed . . ."

"Her integrity as a woman."

"Perhaps I don't understand the urgency of that."

"Not many men do."

"Does your husband?"

"Better than most. I've my own life, my own career. He lives with it." As she said this, her lips parted in a whimsical but wonderfully endearing smile.

"You make it sound . . ."

"It is. Like most men he'd like a nice submissive serving girl who could double in the evening as a pin for his lapel. Like most women I'd like a daddy to tell me how good I am." She stopped, met Tierney's eyes, and held them as she went on. "But we chose each other and we've helped each other to grow up."

She said this with such obvious affection for her husband that Tierney had nothing to say. He was moved by it. He envied it. They looked at each other in silence for a moment. Tierney had the unaccustomed thought that a man could get lost in a woman's eyes.

Finally, Nancy leaned toward him to toss her cigarette out the door. As she did so she said lightheartedly, "It works for us, Father, because *he's* the one who's religious and *he's* the one who likes to cook."

"A little role reversal always helps."

"And we both raise our daughter. Look."

He followed her gaze to a point in the middle of the broad sunny lawn. He saw a man on a large black horse cantering in a slow graceful arch toward the house. He was holding a little girl between his own body and the horse's neck. Tierney could hear the child squealing with delight. He could see the man's face beaming with pleasure, laughing.

"That's a beautiful sight, Nancy," the priest said.

"Yes." She uttered the word so simply, yet so fully, that Tierney looked at her. He saw the easy glint of an eye that loves what it sees.

"Daddy! It's Father John!" The little girl was pointing at Tierney. Her father was waving.

"Greetings, Father," the ambassador said, easing the large horse to a stop just outside the door to the solarium.

"Hello, Sir Alisdair." Tierney dropped his spent cigarette in one of the coffee cans Nancy used as an ashtray. He stepped outside and went to the horse with his arms reaching for the girl. He was saying in a singsong imitation of Cary Grant, "Melissa, Melissa, Melissa." She gave him her weight, grabbing his neck, squeezing, laughing, "Hello, hello, hello."

Ferris-Cogan leaned down to wave at his wife, who waved back. Their smile to each other was all that passed between them, but the woman held her husband's eyes, as if studying them.

Then the ambassador turned to the priest. "Sorry she's late. Miss Wells told me you'd be waiting, but we took a detour around Dodge City, that is to say, the garage."

"I was just about to send the posse out after you," Tierney said, matching the ambassador's tone, then rubbing the crown of his head into Melissa's chest in one last burst of affection before putting her down. He loved her warm weight against his chest.

"You're staying for lunch, Father?"

"Yes, Sir Alisdair. Thank you."

"Fine."

"In fact, I hoped to have a moment with you to talk about the investiture."

"Good. I've been wondering about it. Why don't you come by my office when you and Annie Oakley have finished up?"

"Okay," the priest said, and then to the girl, "Do you hear that, young lady? You're not to wear me out."

"Father John," she said, swinging his hand, "I want you to ask me the Apostle's Creed today."

"You do, do you? You couldn't possibly know the whole thing already."

"I'll bet I do."

"I'll bet you don't."

"Come on." The girl tugged at him. They started to move back into the solarium.

"I'll see you later," Tierney said, looking first at Alisdair and then at Nancy. He rolled his eyes at both of them as he allowed himself to be dragged through the cluttered studio and out into the corridor.

Alisdair shifted slightly in his saddle to look at Nancy. In the flood of sunlight he saw that freckles, small as pinheads, had come to her nose already. She leaned against the door, crossed her arms, and gave him an easy smile. She seemed to him to be growing more beautiful all the time.

"How's the job?" he asked, leaning to rub the withers of his horse.

"Coming."

"May I look?"

"Not yet. Someday."

"I'll be old and blind."

"You already are," she teased, straightening herself, swinging her hair in the sun.

She walked back to her easel, picking up a rag from the floor as she did. She looked through the glass at him again and waved. He returned her wave and, making sounds at the horse from deep in his throat, backed away from the door, turned, and rode off. Nancy watched him until he turned the corner and disappeared.

She faced the canvas. She picked up the number 9 again, touched it to the turpentine, and immediately began to remove the oils from her husband's eyes. She worked efficiently, unhesitatingly. She knew what she wanted to do.

Janus pushed the bolt home, locking the door. The fluorescent light blinked on. She turned in the cramped corner toward the mirror. Neat plastic signs purred their series of polite commands at her: TOWEL DISPOSAL, PLEASE DO NOT FLUSH FOREIGN OBJECTS. USE THE TOWEL TO WIPE THE SINK. PLEASE CONSIDER YOUR FELLOW PASSENGERS.

Janus considered her face. At a new mirror she always looked for the scar below her left ear. She never saw it. The surgery had been perfect. Roring's stiletto had been sharp, clean. It would have done more damage had he not been dead by the time his hand reached her face.

Bridgit Connor took a copy of the *Ladies' Home Journal* from the wall rack at the rear of the cabin. She walked unsteadily to her seat. The flight was smooth, but Bridgit found walking difficult. She was feeling a big dizzy.

When she sat down she opened the magazine in her lap. She read that Danskins are not just for dancing. She didn't understand. Two little boys were holding a kite. Maybe they were girls; they wore their hair in bangs. One of them had on striped red shorts, the other, blue ones, solid. Danskins must have been the name of the clothes manufacturer. "This crew flies Danskins for comfort, style, endurance." She put her hand to her head and closed her eyes. Endure, she thought. She didn't want to be sick. Maybe this was airsickness.

She forced herself to pay attention to the magazine. There was an article about alimony. She turned the page. "My brand is Fruit of the Loom," she read, "now more than ever." A beautiful woman in a pink nightgown was leaning on her pillow holding a mug that had the Fruit of the Loom seal on it. As if Fruit of the Loom were coffee. The woman's hair was long and smooth, off her left shoulder. Bridgit touched her own hair. It was short. She decided again to let it grow out.

She turned the page. There was an article about Robert Redford. A photograph showed him sitting on the edge of an old-fashioned airplane. He was wearing a leather helmet, with goggles hanging to one side of his face. He was smiling. She thought he had a very good-looking smile. She turned the page and another photograph showed him hanging from a long rope ladder off the airplane, which was flying. A wave of nausea rose in her stomach. She closed the magazine.

"Hello, miss?" Bridgit raised her hand at the stewardess who was passing in the aisle.

"Yes?"

"I hate to trouble you."

"It's no trouble. Can I help you?"

"Yes." The stewardess seemed very nice. Bridgit tried to smile at her, but even her face felt sour.

"Do you have something for a queasy stomach?"

"Certainly. You're not feeling well?"

"Just a touch of . . . perhaps airsickness."

"Do you feel inclined to . . . ?"

"No," Bridgit said. She could feel herself blushing. She would be mortified if she vomited. "Just dizziness. My stomach is uneasy, but I won't . . ."

"I'll get you something." The stewardess moved down the aisle then, swiftly, briskly, but, as Bridgit noted, not urgently. It wasn't urgent, she told herself. Just a minor queasiness, she said, just minor.

The first thing the reporter noted was that the cardinal shook her hand rather timidly, almost as if he wasn't sure how to do it.

"I'm sorry," he said apologetically, "to have kept you waiting, Miss . . . uh . . ."

"Roberta Winston, Your Eminence. And you certainly didn't keep me waiting. I'm grateful to see you on such short notice."

She sat in the chair to which he showed her, an authentic Windsor, she noted, facing the handsome desk in the center of his office.

He was shorter than she had expected him to be. Otherwise, she thought, right from central casting. The proper red garments, the splashy jeweled ring, the old man's girth and slouch, the fusty manners, an affected courtesy that had nothing to do with reality; he had not kept her waiting at all.

"Would you like some coffee?" the cardinal asked. She had not expected that. It seemed a much too ordinary offer from such a man in such a room.

"Why, thank you, yes."

As the cardinal took his own chair behind the desk, he pressed a button on the phone. She could hear it buzz beyond the large door through which she'd just entered. The door opened and the gray-haired woman who'd showed her in appeared on the threshold.

"Yes, Your Eminence?"

"Dora, would you bring Miss Winston a cup of coffee? How do you take it, Miss Winston?"

"Oh, Your Eminence," the reporter said, "aren't you having some?"

"No." He smiled. "I've had my quota."

"In that case I'll just skip it."

"It's no trouble."

"No, thanks, but no."

"As you wish," he said. He looked at the gray-haired woman, who shrugged. "Thanks, Dora," he said. She closed the door behind her.

There was a longish pause. Finally, Winston said, "Your Eminence, may I ask a few questions about Sister Sheehan?" She sat with a pencil ready on a small notebook.

"Yes, indeed."

"Is it true that she has been or is about to be dismissed?"

"Not at all. As you know, she has been involved in what may be a serious breach of Church law. The regular canonical procedure which will determine the facts and their consequences has been initiated. No other actions have been taken as of now."

The reporter was writing in her notebook. She was aware that the cardinal's voice was even, almost easy. She was thinking that the knife he wielded was sheathed in manners.

"Would you describe that procedure to me?"

"I'd rather not go into the details of it . . ."

"Why?" Her head shot up from the notebook. "Is it secret?"

"Oh, not at all. It's outlined in the code of canon law, a thoroughly public document. I'd have thought you'd be familiar with it."

"You would have? Why?"

"Well, you've been writing with a certain air of expertise about church matters recently."

"Thank you." She smiled at him, deliberately turning the little blade of his sarcasm. But he refused to let it pass so easily.

"That wasn't a compliment, Miss Winston. Frankly, I think your articles have been less than impartial."

"To return, though, Cardinal O'Brien, to my question: why won't you describe the details of the procedure to me?"

"I'd prefer you spoke to the man who is responsible for it. He would be glad to answer your questions. He is Father John Tierney of the cathedral staff."

"Would it be fair to characterize this . . ." She glanced down at her notes. ". . . canonical procedure as a trial?"

"Yes, but only by analogy."

"Would you call it a 'heresy trial'?"

"That's a loaded term, as I'm sure you know, which is why I suppose you'd love to use it. But no, I would not call it a heresy trial. There is no question of heresy here. The question has to do with a specific act, an alleged violation of the law. It is a question of ecclesiastical discipline, not dogma."

"Would it be fair, Your Eminence, to characterize Father" — again she consulted her notes — "Tierney as the 'prosecutor' in the case?"

"Again, by analogy. But the analogy is limited. Church law does not take its structures from civil law."

"Who appointed Father Tierney?"

"I did."

"And he reports to you?"

"Yes."

"And who is the final arbiter of the case? Who decides finally the matters of," she paused, looking down, " 'fact and consequence'?"

"I do."

"Not Rome?"

"No."

"Would it be fair to say then, Cardinal, that ultimately you are both the prosecutor and the judge in this matter?"

"I know what you're driving at, Miss Winston. You want to demonstrate that Sister Dolores is being treated unfairly. First of all, comparisons with civil proceedings are misleading. The Church is not a court. It is much more like a family. Secondly, I can assure you on the basis of my own integrity as a fair man that Sister will be treated fairly."

"Cardinal, there's certainly no question in my mind that you would deliberately be unfair."

"I assume the word to be emphasized in that sentence is 'deliberately.' "

"Well, it is possible, isn't it, that, apart from the people involved, the procedure itself might be unfair?"

"What do you have in mind?"

"Will there be any women involved in making these judgments of 'fact and consequence'?"

"No."

"That's what I have in mind."

"Miss Winston, who makes the decision about the hiring and firing of reporters for the *Washington Post?*"

"Ultimately, Ben Bradlee."

"And is he a . . . ?"

"No, but his *boss* is, Katharine Graham. The *Post* has a woman *at the top*, Your Eminence."

"I was going to ask, is Mr. Bradlee a *reporter?*"

"No. He's the editor."

"I suggest the *Post* wouldn't be the paper it is, Miss Winston, if reporters hired and fired themselves. There has to be a structure of authority. And authority is not always and in every case unfair."

"Cardinal, a moment ago you compared the Church to a family. Now to the *Post*, which, I assure you, has nothing in common with a family."

"A good point. Obviously, the Church in many ways is a large, impersonal organization. But believe me, we strive to treat each other as members of a family would."

"Would it be fair to say that you are, by analogy, the father of the family?"

"Ah, and would it be fair to say that Sister Dolores will be treated like a child?"

"You read my mind."

"Miss Winston, would it be fair to say that you have a certain bias in this matter?"

"Yes, Cardinal, it would."

"Do you think you can be fair in spite of it? To all parties involved, including me?"

"Yes, I think so."

"Why?"

"Ah, nicely done, Cardinal." She closed her notebook and smiled. "Because I'm a fair person."

"That's good enough for me, Miss Winston."

"If I may speak for a moment outside my role as a reporter, Cardinal, maybe my personal fairness *shouldn't* be good enough for you. It may be that the news media, especially when they report a fairly sensational, controversial issue like this one, are inherently unfair. The point I tried to make before is that at times the structures of which we are part can be unfair, independent of the integrity of the people involved."

"I agree. As I said, I don't think the *Post* has been impartial in this."

"Even though I may be a fair person?"

"Yes."

"Well, the same may be true in your case. And Sister Sheehan will be the one who pays for it."

"Miss Winston, we are both subject, not only to the limits of the organizations of which we are part, but also to the limits of insight and courage that mark us as people. But we must both do what must be done, limits aside. I am charged with the pastoral oversight of this archdiocese. I do my best. In this case grave consequences that you wouldn't understand could befall the whole Church if I fail in my duty. Many more people than Sister Dolores have a right to be treated fairly by the archbishop. From where I sit, what's fair for the Church will be fair for her, even if difficult or painful. What's at stake here is the truth that there are consequences to behavior. Frankly, I don't think Sister Dolores appreciates that. I am fully aware that, as I face her with the consequences of what she did, I will be faced finally by God Himself with the consequences of what I do."

The woman had nothing to say. Somehow the discussion had turned out differently than she had expected. He was wrong, she was sure of that. He had no idea how impossible the Church was for women. And even his earnestness made him all the more unable to see what was so clear to her. He would do real damage, she was certain.

But she had nothing to say. No rebuttal, no further argument. She could only sit in the blast of what she knew was the man's own searing truth, searing for him, searing for others. But it was his truth, and he could articulate it.

She didn't know, leaving, whether to pity him, hate him, or envy him.

"From reports I've received, the F. O. was flabbergasted," the ambassador said.

"Well," Tierney replied slowly, uncertainly, "it's not every day one of the queen's own is raised to the papal Order of Saint Gregory the Great."

They were sitting in Ferris-Cogan's spacious and elegant office. From the center of the high ceiling a large crystal chandelier was suspended, and on the floor a pale blue carpet stretched like a pool's surface across the room to the bank of French doors. Through their windows one could see on a distant hill the Victorian mansion at the U.S. Naval Observatory that for decades had been the residence of the Chief of Naval Operations, but that in late 1974 became the official home of the Vice-President of the United States. It was one of Nelson Rockefeller's houses now.

The ambassador and the priest were sitting in wingback chairs the color of oyster shells by the huge fireplace that opened like a cave in the wall opposite the French doors and their vista of the mansion. Ferris-Cogan was wearing a dark pin-striped suit, highly polished black shoes, and an air of self-mocking good humor.

"No, really, Father, when word came from the Vatican that

a senior officer was to receive the pope's title, it caused a genuine flap. Is the Vatican a foreign power? Or is it merely the locus of Roman Catholic religion? Is a papal knighthood political or religious? It was dandy!"

"What happened?"

"Well, calling upon more ingenuity than usual, the F.O. asked me what I thought. You'd have to know these public school Anglicans to appreciate the grotesque — I mean literally 'of the grotto' — the grotesque imaginings they still have for Rome. I told them it had nothing to do with government and to forget it. They did."

"I had the impression, Sir Alisdair . . ." the priest paused.

"What, Father?"

"That there was some . . . government involvement."

"Oh? Of what sort?"

"The Irish situation."

"Where did you hear that?" All hint of amusement had left Ferris-Cogan's voice.

"I didn't hear it. I surmised it."

Neither of them spoke for a moment. Tierney decided that he'd been indiscreet. He could tell that the ambassador was disturbed.

But then Ferris-Cogan broke into a large smile, apparently genuine. "Well, Father, very astute of you. We've said enough already, haven't we? Why don't you tell me about the ceremony?"

"Certainly." Tierney took a folded sheet of paper out of his inside coat pocket, unfolded it, and reached across a small coffee table to hand it to the ambassador. "This is the order of service."

"Ah," the ambassador said, taking the paper, reading it.

"Basically, as you'll note, the service has the standard order of the mass — procession, opening prayers, scripture readings, and so forth. The actual investiture will take place at the point where, ordinarily, we would have the homily. After the investiture we will go on with the offertory and eucharistic prayer as usual."

"Now the investiture itself, who does that?"

"Archbishop Benelli, as the pope's delegate."

"I've met him."

"Cardinal O'Brien, as your ordinary, will present you to the archbishop."

"The cardinal, so to speak, sponsors me, testifies to my worthiness, and so on?"

"Yes."

"I wonder," the ambassador joked, "how he knows."

"I've told him."

"Ah, so you're the intelligence source."

"I suppose. It's not the CIA, but we manage."

"But what exactly happens in the investiture? You don't, of course, dub me with a sword or anything so . . . militaristic?"

"Not quite, though certainly several centuries ago there would have been a dubbing exactly as it was done in the royal courts."

"Yes, of course. When the pope *did* have his divisions."

"Now, the *matter* of the ritual — that's the technical word for it — comes when you are entrusted with the Word of God. Archbishop Benelli will hand you the large missal from which we will have just done the readings."

"And I take it?"

"You don't quite take it. You lay your hands on it. The archbishop actually continues to hold the book as he pronounces the formula."

"Do I say something?"

"You say 'Amen' after the archbishop."

"Is it in Latin?"

"No."

"Too bad. The quality of language in the Church now is so abysmal. I'm sure you won't agree with me, but I think the grandeur of our cult has been banalized by — what do we call them? — the reformers."

"Well, Ambassador," Tierney said good-naturedly, "it's important to recall that the substance of things hasn't been changed. Just some of the accidents."

"As Aquinas would have it."

"Yes."

"Ironically enough, Father, I agree with those contemporary philosophies which hold that if you change the accidents you've thereby changed the substance. In my opinion the Church should either have pronounced anathema on the first man to utter a vernacular word in the liturgy or should have, at that very moment, engaged Wystan Auden to personally supervise the translations."

"Well, you certainly have a point, Ambassador."

"But it's neither here nor there, is it?" He said it a bit testily.

"I wasn't saying that."

"Perhaps you'd understand what I mean, Father, if you had a daughter. Frankly, I do not think Catholicism as it is now will engage her imagination sufficiently to survive into adulthood with her."

"I think I do understand what you mean, frankly." Tierney's voice too had a sudden edge to it. "In a small way I do have a daughter. Yours. And the challenge of nurturing in her a religious, a Catholic imagination leaves me winded. You needn't tell me about the difficulty of that."

Sir Alisdair started to apologize, but Tierney went on, "I think she may surprise us both with a kind of Catholic adulthood we could not anticipate, but which we will need profoundly. In any case, she's the one who has to do it. We can't do it for her."

"Father, I'm sorry to have sounded snobbish and ungrateful. I've been unfairly venting at you emotions and opinions that have more to do with, well, my personal problem with the age we live in than with theology. I hope you know how appreciative I am of your work with my daughter. She couldn't be more fond of you, and I'm delighted with what she's learning."

"I know, Sir Alisdair. The Church is something like a lightning rod for a whole variety of anxieties these days, most of which have nothing to do with God."

"Let me risk one final arrogant layman's comment, Father, before we go into a lighthearted lunch with the ladies. I'd have thought that if they were genuine human anxieties, they'd have quite a lot to do with God."

At Dulles Airport Brigadier Cameron watched the Mobile Passenger Unit carrying the arrivals from BOAC Flight 924 ease into the docking ramp at the U.S. Customs area, on the ground floor adjacent to the main terminal. He was standing in the main concourse and looking through the huge window at its north end. From his place on the second level, Cameron could see the passengers filing from the mobile lounge into the hall where they would retrieve their baggage and pass through the visa check and luggage search.

Cameron turned and walked casually to the stairwell in the center of the spacious, nearly empty concourse. He went down to the ground level and took the left corridor, which brought him to the reception area outside Customs.

He walked slowly across the terrazzo floor to the bank of phone booths on the wall opposite the large doors that closed the inspection area off from the reception area.

"Everything set?" he asked.

"Yes, sir." Captain Mitchell was pretending to make a phone call. He spoke without taking his face from the receiver. "Two men outside, one at the car rental, one at the newsstand, two with baggage carts. Wills has a taxi."

Cameron said nothing, but turned away from the phones and sauntered across the area toward the wall nearest the large doors. He moved through the small clusters of relatives and friends who were gathering, chatting, eyeing the doors. Here and there was a lone man or woman, lover or spouse. There was one uniformed chauffeur. Cameron reached the wall and turned his back to it, but did not lean against it.

Janus was patient. She lined up with the others beside the conveyor belt waiting for it to move, to bring the bags. So many cattle, she thought, waiting for slush in the trough. She let her eyes drift around the low-ceilinged room. There were a dozen counters at the far end, ten feet long, low, like chutes for the livestock. Customs officers, all men, she noted, were standing idly in several groups waiting for the stampede that would begin when the bags arrived. There were no other officials in the big room, no police. That's to the good, she thought. Security would be lighter here than in London.

The Customs process and the possibility of a luggage search had forced Janus to the one decision she hated making, to the one thing she did not like about this operation. She could not risk bringing a weapon through, which meant she had to have a contact on this side.

The council had set it up, even with the short notice. O'Rourke assured her that the Washington agent would be competent and totally secure. But the likes of O'Rourke said that about everybody, and she knew that nearly everybody was either a liar or a fool. Janus trusted no one.

In London she had considered using the specially designed Swedish Gevar 42-B, which, when dismantled, looked nothing like a pistol and could be hidden inside a phony typewriter. But she had decided against it. If there were a drug alert on, or if the Customs man had the rare instinct, the risk was too great. What, given her cover, would she be doing with a typewriter anyway?

No, there was no way to avoid it. All she could hope for now was that the contact could be made swiftly, that he wouldn't try like a fool to nose in, and that he'd obtained the weapons she'd asked for.

A bell sounded. The conveyor belt started to move and all the passengers stepped closer to it, as if on command. Most of them seemed harried or nervous. The young woman near Janus seemed particularly distraught.

Janus let her eyes move again to the far end of the room. The Customs officers were filing to their stations. Janus knew that this was the easy part. For once she was traveling on her own passport. That could complicate things later, she knew. This action could well cost her the obscurity she had won and protected. But if it went smoothly the payoff would be enormous, and it would have been worth it. Assuming that her cover would be blown before she made her escape, she had a second complete set of papers taped to the inside of her thighs, a one-way airplane ticket to Mexico City, and the near-native Spanish she'd spent the better part of two years perfecting. She had not expected to need it so soon, but she was ready.

She watched the bags slide by. Hers was smaller than most. It held two dresses, one completely unlike the other, a raincoat unlike the one she was wearing, and the odds and ends of makeup and toiletry, all quite ordinary but for the bottle of hair dye that would complete her transformation, if need be, into a blond Argentinian archeologist.

Bridgit Connor was visibly nervous as she approached the Customs officer. She put her canvas floral-patterned suitcase on the low counter and waited for him to speak. He held out his hand. She gave him the declaration form that she had filled out on the airplane.

"Ireland, miss?"

"Yes, sir."

"I'm Irish myself. My folks, that is."

"Are you, sir? What part?"

"Cork on my mother's side. My father I don't know. You're from Londonderry?"

"Yes, sir."

"Here for a visit?"

"Yes, sir. My aunt, my mother's sister. And my cousin, he's a priest."

"Is that so? What parish?"

"The cathedral."

"Oh, downtown."

"Yes, sir. I suppose. I mean I don't know."

"Yes, it's downtown. Well, have a fine visit."

He kept the form. He smiled at her. He seemed to be finished.

"Is that all, sir?"

"Yes, indeed, miss. Go right on through."

"Thank you, sir."

Bridgit picked up her suitcase, tried to smile at the man, to thank him for being so polite, but she managed only a kind of nervous grimace. As she moved toward the large doors she chided herself for her awkwardness. After all, she wasn't a smuggler.

Cameron was watching the passengers coming through the doors. A short man in a loud checkered overcoat maneuvered his two suitcases through. He was perspiring. A heavy woman struggled behind him with a large suitcase of her own.

The tidy clusters of waiting people had broken as they had pushed toward the doors, looking, waving, rushing up and hugging arrivals. The quiet chatter had been replaced by squeals of recognition, laughter, loud talking.

"Hey, Barney!" a man called. "Welcome to the home of the brave!"

Cameron was eyeing the passengers carefully. He looked at them all. Customs slowed them down enough so that they came through the doors in a gradual, broken stream. He was looking especially for unaccompanied males who were not met and who seemed to be between the ages of twenty-five and fifty. There were many. None looked likely. None set off the signal of his instinct, which he had learned over the years to trust absolutely. But as each passed, his eye shot imperceptibly across the area to Mitchell, who returned the contact with the barest nod. Mitchell would approach the man thus designated holding out a dollar bill, saying, "Excuse me. Do you have change for the phone?"

Since none of them did, none having American currency, much less loose change, each encounter was brief. But each was long enough to get a sense of the man, to hear his accent, to watch for the telltale defensiveness or fear.

There were seventy-seven passengers on the plane. Of that number fifty were unaccompanied males, of whom two-thirds seemed of the age group. Of that number, seventeen were not met by anyone. Of the seventeen, four spoke with Irish accents. They were followed. Six others spoke with indeterminate accents. Four of them were followed. Of the other two, Cameron could have followed one.

He decided not to. His instinct told him that either Janus wasn't on the plane or they had missed him.

After exchanging twenty pounds for exactly forty-eight dollars at the currency window, Bridgit Connor found a telephone. A man bumped her as he asked another man for change. She would like to have helped him, but she hadn't enough coins. He didn't ask her anyway, so she didn't have to turn him down.

"Hello, Aunt Nell?"

"Yes. Bea?"

"It's Bridgit. Yes, Bea."

"Hello, Bea! Where are you?"

"I'm at the airport, Aunt Nell."

"Oh good! I'm delighted!"

"I just got in."

"How was your flight?"

"All right. I had a bit of a stomach, but I'm fine now."

"Was it rough?"

"No, surprisingly smooth. But I'm not used to flying, you know."

"Did you ever fly before?"

"To tell the truth, no. Here I'm thirty years old and my very first flight was this morning from Derry to London."

"You came from London?"

"Yes. That's how you do it. Seems a bit of a waste, doesn't it, going back to England to come to the States. But this way I've been to England too."

"Yes. Well, I'm glad you're here. Come right out."

"How shall I do it?"

"There's a bus from the airport. I checked. Every thirty minutes, you get it at the main entrance. That'll take you to the Holiday Inn on Thirteenth Street. Then take a cab. I live in an apartment house on Wisconsin Avenue, the Woodner, apartment thirty-four, eleven seventy-one Wisconsin Avenue, Northwest. Got that?"

"Yes. I'm writing it. Eleven seventy-one Wisconsin Avenue, Northwest."

"It shouldn't take an hour and a half, all told."

"Aunt Nell, is the Holiday Inn near the White House?"

"Yes, why, dear? A few blocks."

"I'd love to see where President Kennedy lived."

"Well, it's President Ford now, of course."

"I know. But, well, you wouldn't mind if I just went over there for a minute? To look at it, you know?"

"Of course not, darling. But I'm sure Father John is going to take you sightseeing. He's coming to dinner. He wanted to meet you at the airport, but he's so busy. We'll all go sightseeing later. We'll have a wonderful time."

"I can't wait. Meantime, on my way, I'll just take a quick, you know, gander, and then catch a taxi to your house."

"It's an apartment, dear, not a house."

"Right, eleven seventy-one. Thanks, Aunt Nell."

"It's a lovely day, your coming to visit, darling. We love you."

"Well . . . I . . ."

"See you soon."

"Yes. Good-bye."

The food at the embassy was always excellent. Tierney was regularly amazed at the expert care with which the simple dishes of the midday meals he took there were prepared. They were never elaborate. The menu was usually spare and light. On this day the meal had consisted of a thick lentil soup, fresh dark bread, a variety of continental sausages and cheeses, fresh fruit, and a Chablis. Tierney had been raised on the overdone meat and boiled potatoes that was still the typical fare of the rectory table. The Irish spent their imagination on what came out of their mouths, not on what went in. And so he enjoyed the embassy lunches with the gusto of a man who only lately had discovered that even the simplest food can be laid out like a work of art.

"That was fine," he said, touching the napkin to his lips.

"More wine, Father?" The ambassador was holding a crystal ship's decanter toward him.

"No thank you, Sir Alisdair."

"Nancy?" The ambassador turned toward his wife.

"Yes, dear, a touch." She held her glass to the wine as her husband poured it.

Melissa held up her glass. "May I, Daddy?"

Ferris-Cogan feigned surprise, then tilted his head at the girl. "You know the rule, one glass for little girls."

"But it wasn't even full," she protested in a half-whine.

"One's glass," the ambassador said, playfully pompous, "is not to be *filled* until after the sacrament of Confirmation. And you haven't even made your First Communion yet. Actually, you're not legally entitled to get *any* wine until then."

The girl's eyes flashed then, because she thought she had him when she declared, "But Mother hasn't made *her* First Communion yet, have you Mother?"

Nancy blushed slightly and replied, "That doesn't count, Melissa."

"Why?"

"Because I'm not a Catholic. You and Daddy are."

"But if you haven't made your First Communion," she persisted, "why can you have all the wine you want?"

Tierney and Ferris-Cogan sat in amused silence, watching Nancy summon up all her reasonable patience. After ten years of asserting her religious independence from her husband, she found herself having to do it more and more recently with her daughter.

"Wine is for adults, Melissa. Children may have a bit with meals if their parents think it a good idea. If one is a Catholic, the way one becomes an adult is through First Communion and then Confirmation, and that's why they are very important moments in your life. I became an adult without First Communion and without Confirmation because I'm not a Catholic. You see?"

"How did you do it?" This was no longer playful banter. A change had come over the girl. She seemed worried.

Ferris-Cogan and Tierney both sensed the sudden serious-
ness of the exchange. They remained silent, but they were not
amused anymore.

"Darling, when I was growing up, since Nana and Grandpa
weren't Catholics, I became an adult in other ways. For example, when I was your age, I went away to school. You see,
that helped me to grow up. And then, when I was a teenager,
which is when you will make your Confirmation, I started going
to movies and things with boys. And *that* helped me to grow
up. Do you see?"

"No," she said, without any hint of stubbornness. She seemed
genuinely perplexed.

"Catholics have their way of doing things, darling. Other
people, like Protestants and Jews and people like me who aren't
religious, have other ways of doing things. What's important
is that, however one does things, one does them as well as
possible and with as much kindness as possible."

"But I want to do it the way you do it, Mommy." The girl's
eyes were filled with tears, and panic had fallen like a shadow
across her face. Nancy moved her chair back from the table
and held her arms out. The child went to her without speaking,
but, as she buried her face in her mother's breast, she could
be heard sobbing. As Nancy closed her body around her daughter, her eyes went to her husband. He rose, came to her chair,
and stooped by it. He put his left hand on his daughter's
shoulder and began rubbing it in a slow, soft circle.

When Melissa's sobbing ceased and she straightened herself
in her mother's lap, Nancy pushed the child's hair back from
her face and said, "Darling, when people love each other it
doesn't matter what religion they are."

"I know," the girl replied.

"You do?" Ferris-Cogan asked, still stroking her.

"Yes. That's what Father John says." She turned in her mother's lap and looked at the priest. He nodded at her and winked.
She turned back to her parents and continued, "Father John
says God loves everybody, even if they don't go to church."

"That's right, darling," her mother said.

"Mommy?" Melissa put her head on her mother's breast. "Why don't you go to church?"

"Darling, sometimes, for me, when I'm painting a picture, it's like being in church."

The little girl pulled quickly up then, looked in her mother's eye, and said with a mixture of relief and excitement, "That's what Father John said!" She turned and looked at the priest. He winked once more. Now Melissa was smiling broadly.

As if to signal the completion of the event, Melissa slid happily from her mother's lap, transformed again into the carefree child. She scooted back to her chair, pushed it up to the table, grabbed her napkin and pulled it through its silver ring. "May I be excused, please?" she asked with studied politeness.

"Where are you going?" her father asked, having resumed his place at the head of the table.

"Out to play."

"You may," Ferris-Cogan said.

Melissa dashed around the table and kissed each of her parents in the casual manner of habit. But she hugged the priest especially hard, and Tierney returned her hug, feeling more affection for her than he had ever felt before. And, he realized, more pain. After she had bolted from the room, a silence settled on the table.

"Well," the ambassador said at last, "wasn't *that* something?"

"Yes," Nancy said, slamming her napkin down on her plate, "wasn't it?"

Tierney and Ferris-Cogan were both surprised at her obvious anger.

"What's wrong?" her husband asked.

"What's wrong? Damn it, Alisdair!" She buried her face in her hands, trying to get hold of herself.

"Nancy, really!"

"Yes, Alisdair, really!" She whipped her head up to face him. A deep wound of pain and fear opened in her breast. "That child thinks our love is in jeopardy because *I* don't go to church! She thinks I'm en route to hell!"

"Nancy!" Alisdair was amazed and embarrassed at his wife's

outburst, but she continued, ignoring him, turning to the priest.

"*That's* what comes of your religion, Father: terror and suspicion!"

"Terror and suspicion! God's teeth, woman, what in the bloody hell are you talking about? The girl is a Catholic because I am, not because she's been kidnapped by Irish gypsies! Am I riddled with terror and suspicion?"

"Your Church is — speaking of the Irish!"

A furious anger tightened Alisdair's mouth. He glanced incredulously at the priest, as if in alliance with him. For an instant, beneath the current of his anger, he had the odd, complacent peace of the victim who is long accustomed to being attacked. But his rage choked this off. "Woman, I refuse to have you demean my faith with your sterile, Waspish stereotypes. Our daughter is damned lucky to have the Church and its priest."

Ah, yes, they were together against her. Nancy trembled, her throat clotted with emotion. If she had had a glass in her hand at that instant she'd have smashed it to the floor. She shifted her glare from her husband to Tierney, who immediately looked away from her.

He was himself in the grip of an irrational fear. At one level he felt like a child surreptitiously witnessing a sudden wrathful exchange between his parents. It was as if he had caused it, as if they were arguing about him, about something he had done. When he returned his glance to Nancy, it seemed that she was looking at him with loathing. The pain of that set his heart to beating so rapidly he could feel it in his fingertips. It was almost unbearable.

When Nancy spoke then her voice had become cold and even. Her anger had become an instrument of her own defense. "Neither of you has any idea of the position I'm in. My daughter is slowly and surely being taken from me. And when the estrangement is total, I will be blamed for it as an impious person."

"If you lose your daughter," Ferris-Cogan said while fiercely pulling his napkin through its ring and standing, "it will be through your own arrogant bitchiness." With great deliberation he pushed his chair under the table, glared steadily at his wife for a moment, and walked out of the room.

Tierney was stunned and at an utter loss to know what to do or say. Beneath the miserable embarrassment that was turning him red in the silence, he understood what the woman had said. He knew the uses to which piety could be put. God loves Catholics more than other people: it was one of the unspoken tenets of his religion, and he knew it. And he knew the bitter energy that that faith could release against Paisleyites or Jews. He had never understood that that same energy could work its havoc on a family. Oh God, he thought, what had happened? And had he done it, somehow? Unable to bear the silence or to remain in the woman's sullen and accusing presence, the priest pushed away from the table. He was looking at Nancy warily, searching for a friendly look that would ease the deep hurt he felt.

The woman moved in her chair slightly. She was aware of his gaze and knew instinctively that she had wounded him. She resolved to hold her ground, and though she felt it rising in her throat, she would not let him see her shame at the outburst.

With a quiet, expressionless voice she said, "Now you can consider yourself one of the family."

Tierney returned her look with an expressionless gaze of his own, but behind the surface of his face was a crush of conflicting emotions. He was drawn to her, wanted to support her, but her bitterness frightened him and her willingness to sit calmly now against his own transparent frustration made him want to leave.

He stood. He wanted to say something sharp and half-witty in reply like, "It's quite an invitation into quite a family." But the sounds wouldn't form in his throat. He said good-bye and left.

Someone was parked in Cameron's space when he wheeled into the embassy lot.

"Goddamnit!" he said, slamming his open hand down on the top edge of the steering wheel of his Austin. It was the sort of inconsequential peeve into which he could channel the anger he felt at missing Janus. It needn't have been a problem. He could have parked in any of half a dozen other spaces. But Cameron got out of his car, leaving the engine running, and walked around the trespassing vehicle. It was a '69 Ford Maverick, dark blue and slightly battered. He had seen it before, but he didn't know whose it was. On the dashboard in front of the driver's seat was a white cardboard sign with the word CLERGY.

"Judas priest! Christ! You might know!" Thus muttering to himself, he turned back toward his own car.

Just as he had his hand on the door he saw the priest coming around the corner from the direction of the ambassador's apartments. Cameron watched him. He had seen him before. It was Ferris-Cogan's priest. They had never met, which was fine with Cameron.

"Am I in your space?" the priest asked, with no hint of apology.

"Yes," Cameron glared at him.

"I didn't see the sign. Sorry."

The sign, lettered BRIG. F. CAMERON, M. A., was a foot long, six inches high, and hung prominently on a post at the far edge of the space.

"You didn't?" Cameron wanted to add, "Fucking liar!" but he checked himself. He said it with his tone of voice, his eyes. The priest looked at the sign and shook his head. "No, I really didn't. I guess I was late arriving, distracted, you know? I'm very sorry."

The priest got into his car, started it, and waited for Cameron to move. Cameron got into his Austin, put it in gear, and squealed forward twenty feet. The Maverick backed out of the space, and, as it turned toward the driveway, the priest waved. Cameron ignored him, slammed his shift into reverse, squealed back into first, and shot into the space as if he parked cars for a living.

Seven minutes later he was sitting at his desk. The magnum was back in its drawer.

He smashed the button on the intercom.

"All right, Stone, bring it in."

"Sir!"

The office door opened smartly. Sergeant Major Elias Stone strode across the room to Cameron's desk. He was upright, stiff. He wore the perfect blue uniform of Her Majesty's Special Branch. He carried a large sheaf of typescript.

"Well?" Cameron said.

Stone handed the bulk of pages to Cameron, saying, "Draw your attention, sir, to the clipped page. The relevant passage is bracketed in blue pencil."

Cameron opened the stack to the page that had a large metal paper clip on its top edge.

"The entirety, sir, is the transcript of the telephone tap on Shannon's Public House beginning the second day of this month, ending this morning, sir."

"What am I looking for?"

"The bracketed section, sir, may be something. Note the clip, on page . . ."

"I have it."

Cameron read silently:

"Hello, give me Murray."

"This is Murray."

"You've been expecting me. I'm here."

"When did you arrive?"

"This morning. Look, they're really . . ."

"All right. Fine. We'll talk later. Where can I reach you?"

"No place. That's the problem."

"Okay. I'll see you in an hour at Gusti's."

"Where's that?"

"Ask a bobby, arsehole."

"Okay."

There was a blue line across the page at this point. Below it someone was ordering two hundred pounds of ground beef from someone called Wolfie.

Cameron looked at Stone.

"Who's Murray?"

"He's the barman, the day-shift barman."

"What do we have on him?"

"Borstal Prison, 1954–1957; Birmingham bombing with Goulding, sir. Nothing since. He's been here since 1959. Probable connections with the Officials."

"But Shannon's is a Provo hangout."

"Yes, sir. Surmise they don't know, sir."

"Murray plays it both ways?"

"Perhaps so, sir."

"Money?"

"Don't know, sir."

"This came through" — Cameron looked at the date on the page — "a fortnight ago. Why was it missed?"

"It seemed insignificant then, sir."

"Does it now, Stone?"

"No, sir."

"Get out."

"Sir!"

Janus entered the public library at Ninth and New York Avenue. It was a jolt to go from the bright afternoon sunshine into the musty old building that was still dank with the aftermath of winter. Just inside the revolving doors that creaked with age and poor maintenance was the information booth. An old man with rimless spectacles sat staring at the ceiling. Janus had the impression he'd been sitting that way for a long time.

"Excuse me," she said.

He started. It took a moment for his eyes to focus on her. When they did, he smiled benignly.

"Yes, may I help you?"

"Can you direct me to the section, please, in which I might find a map of the city?"

"Of the city?" He turned the phrase over on his tongue slowly, as if he didn't comprehend.

It seemed a simple enough question.

"Of Washington," she said.

"Oh," he said, his eyes darting. *"This* city."

"If you please."

"I would think . . ." He paused, turning his silence over on his tongue. "Yes, that's right, it certainly would be . . . the Social Studies Resource Room."

"Could you point the way for me?"

"You know, you can't check it out if it's from there."

"I needn't discharge it, thank you."

"Discharge it?" He paused again, mulling over the unfamiliar phrase.

"I needn't take it out, thank you," she said patiently. "Could you point the way for me, please?"

"You're a foreigner, aren't you!" he said, like a Greek saying "Eureka!" Janus looked at him. She did not reply.

He shrugged. "Just go up the stairs and to the right."

"Thank you," she said and started toward the elaborate but faded stairwell.

But he saw her suitcase and hollered after her, "Miss, miss." When she turned back toward him, he went on, "I'll have to look at that bag of yours when you leave."

Oh, shit! she thought, how stupid of me! Of course, a library, the checkout.

"You can leave it here if you like. With me." He made the offer as if it were exceptionally generous.

She considered it. There was nothing in the bag to hide, but all of her instincts rebelled at the unnecessary exposure, the unplanned-for search. They rebelled even more, however, at the prospect of leaving the suitcase with the old fool.

"No thank you. I'll keep it."

He shrugged again, and she thought she could hear his bones crack.

Janus turned and mounted the staircase, cursing herself and wondering if she were slipping.

The Social Studies Resource Room was dark, high-ceilinged, and cluttered beyond description. Large bureaus lined the walls.

Old tables of a height to stand at, instead of sit, ran the length of the right aisle. A relic of a man leaned on one, reading a newspaper. Ten feet above the floor a cast-iron balcony made a circuit of the room. Stretching thirty feet from the balcony floor to the ceiling, the walls were all books. Here and there a narrow ladder hung from the top edge of the shelves.

To the left as Janus entered the room was a desk. An antique gooseneck lamp illuminated the chaos of piled books, papers, ancient magazines. A woman sat hunched in the circle of light, writing on an index card in tiny script. All that Janus could see of her was short cropped red hair, the exceptionally pale skin of her thick neck, and the curve of her broad back. She was wearing a dark sweater.

"Excuse me," Janus said.

The woman looked up. Her face was alert. She was not old, younger than she herself was, Janus guessed.

"I'd like to see a map of Washington, D.C., please."

The woman nodded. Without speaking she rose and led the way down the aisle on the left side of the room. Janus fell in behind her. She was a short woman, a bit on the heavy side. She wore a dark wool skirt that was too small for her, obviously so from behind. Her shoes were unstylish, practical, thick-soled. The only sound when she walked was the faint *hiss-hiss-hiss* of her heavy nylon-covered thighs rubbing together. The woman stopped at a bureau in the far-left corner of the room. She pulled a large, flat drawer out. It was filled with folded maps. The woman rifled through them, then found one marked "District of Columbia and Environs."

She unfolded it before handing it to Janus, saying, "I'll just check it."

Janus noted her accent with some surprise. The map fell open. It was a yard and a half by two yards. Both women noticed that a piece of the map four inches square was missing from the lower right quarter.

The librarian said, "Seems to be torn."

Janus opened her purse and took out her billfold. She opened it, as if for currency, and withdrew a folded piece of paper.

She unfolded it. It was four inches square. She held it to the hole in the map. It matched.

"I didn't expect a woman," the librarian whispered in an Irish voice.

"I didn't either," Janus replied. "You're MacNeil, then?"

"Yes. Oona MacNeil. And you?"

"Doesn't matter. I'm in a hurry."

"I don't get off for several hours."

"I have to pick the stuff up for my friend immediately."

"You mean, you're not . . . ?"

"Of course not. You don't think he'd risk this, do you?" The lie came to Janus automatically.

"There's no risk. I'm untouched."

"There's always a risk. Did you ever hear of Cameron?"

"Hear of him! He killed one of my brothers, put the other on ice at Kesh. He's here now, at the embassy."

"He was at Dulles to greet our friend."

"No!"

"Yes. You see, there is a risk."

"How did Cameron know?"

"I was going to ask you." Janus stared at her, deciding.

"We can't talk here. I'll get off. Wait for me outside."

In the broad daylight a few minutes later, Janus followed MacNeil to an old Volkswagen in the parking lot across New York Avenue from the library. They did not speak until they were headed north on Ninth Street.

"I told her I'd be back in an hour," MacNeil said. "I told her my apartment house was on fire."

"That was bloody stupid."

"Why?"

"They can check."

"It's not like that here."

Oh, Christ! Janus thought to herself.

"She doesn't believe me anyway," MacNeil went on.

"Who?"

"Mrs. Crane, my boss. She thinks I've a drinking problem."

Oh, *Jesus* Christ! Janus thought, then asked, "Do you?"

"Of course not."

"What about Cameron?"

"He's the attaché. Mostly diplomatic stuff. They put him here to get him out of the way when the MRF was under scrutiny. He runs their stateside network, but there's not much action for him. He keeps a count of the money raised by the Aid Committee. His men are at the occasional rally. Quite obviously, too."

"Intimidation?"

"Attempted. He only frightens the Irish-American pups who play at IRA."

"But not you?"

"Look, Miss Whoever-the-hell-you-are, I don't like your attitude. I'm not a pampered housewife with a warm roof and a cozy fire and a flock of parochial school kids. I'm not a part-time member of the Ladies' Auxiliary. I'm here on a fucking assignment. They sent me here. I didn't ask for it. I've done my share of crawling through the tunnels beneath Falls Road. Don't you come here running errands for a hot-shit gunman and condescend to me!"

Janus liked her. "What hot-shit gunman would that be?" she asked coolly.

"You know damn well what I mean."

"Tell me!" It was a command from a ranking officer.

"The one who's to hit MacCree."

"And who's MacCree?"

"The big ear and bigger mouth who's been blowing the Official pricks in Belfast for the last eighteen months."

"And how do you know all this?"

"It's my fucking job to know it. Where do you think your friend got his information? Who do you think found the bastard?"

"All right." Janus's voice changed, a signal of minimal acceptance of the other as comrade. "You seem to do your job. Let me clarify some points on my friend's behalf."

"What?"

"You report that MacCree is hiding in a one-room flat?"

"Yes."

"That someone brings his food and supplies in several times a week?"

"Yes. The barkeep from Shannon's, an old-time Official named Liam Murray."

"This Murray, I take it he's — "

"He's a fool that lives in the past. Plays games with the cowboy-Irish at Shannon's, reports the pub gossip to his cronies in Dublin, thinks he's a spy. As if a real Provo would set foot in the place. Goulding's just using him now to nursemaid MacCree."

"So Murray is harmless."

"Totally."

"Is there a back way into MacCree's building?"

"Yes. An alley runs behind it, off M Street. Why? Who besides us would be watching it?"

Janus didn't answer the question; it seemed pointless to explain what was so obvious. Instead she said, "One other question," then paused. MacNeil had stopped the car for a light. Janus was watching a pair of black children crossing the street in front of them. Janus went on absently, "Has MacCree had a woman?"

"Not to my knowledge."

"You should know definitely."

"I don't, but I'd say it's unlikely."

"And he's been here . . . ?"

"Almost three weeks."

Oona MacNeil was looking at her companion. The light changed, and she gave her attention to the road again. Silence fell between them.

MacNeil coaxed the spitting VW up the hill at Lincoln Road where it branched off North Capitol. They drove past the large stone shrine at Catholic University and out Michigan Avenue.

Finally, MacNeil said, "May I ask you something?"

"Yes," Janus replied.

"Are you recently over?"

Janus considered what to say. There was no reason to tell the truth. The less the other woman knew the better. But something in MacNeil's voice made Janus nod.

Then MacNeil asked, "Are you . . . close to the network?" Janus tensed. It was the sort of question one didn't ask.

"Why do you want to know?" She eyed the other woman carefully.

"My brother: it's been a month since we had news. He was very sick."

"The one in Kesh?"

"Yes. I was hoping you might have heard something."

"What's his name?"

"Danny MacNeil."

"Never heard of him."

"Also, he went by . . . Dangerfield."

"I knew him. I didn't know his name."

"You *knew* him?"

"Yes. He's dead."

"Oh, God."

Janus expected her to weep. She didn't. Her pale, round face became paler. Her eyes clouded a bit. She let up on the accelerator for a second. But that was all. She focused her attention and energy on driving.

Janus sensed the shock, the instant power of her grief, even through the control with which she held it in check.

Janus said, "I'm sorry," and she touched the woman lightly on the sleeve. Janus felt herself hovering on the lip of the dread abyss again. Eternal life; eternal loss; the ravenous despair of her kind . . .

"One gets used to it."

"No," Janus replied, "one doesn't. A brother is always a brother."

At that the woman looked at Janus. The pain was all over her face. "Would you mind if I stopped for a minute? There's a chapel near here. I . . ."

Janus looked at her watch, but it had stopped. She looked at MacNeil again and said, "Of course."

They entered the small chapel together, the Franciscan Sisters Chapel of Perpetual Adoration on Twelfth Street near Monroe, Northeast. It was the redesigned first floor of what had been a large private residence. There was room for perhaps forty people in the pews. In the sanctuary two nuns in the long brown Franciscan habits, belted at the waist with a white cord, knelt in prayer before the exposed Sacrament. Along each wall were banks of devotional candles, most of which burned in vigil while the nuns prayed for the intentions of the people who'd lit them.

MacNeil knelt down in the rearmost pew, and Janus joined her. Both women blessed themselves. Their lips moved almost in unison as they uttered silently the same memorized prayer for the dead. MacNeil got up and walked awkwardly across the width of the pew, balancing in the small space between the kneeler and the seat. Janus raised her head and watched the other vacantly. She felt an immense emptiness, as if she were kneeling in the void itself. It was a feeling with which she had grown familiar, if not comfortable. The ravenous despair of her kind, she repeated to herself, eats nothing but God.

At the end of the pew MacNeil crossed the aisle to the nearest bank of candles. She opened her purse and her wallet, took out a dollar. A small, neatly lettered sign by the money box read DONATION: TWO DOLLARS. She took out another dollar, folded them both, and squeezed them into the slot. She took a long wax taper from the sand-filled tray beneath the candles, lit it from one already burning, and then touched it to a fresh candle near the top of the bank.

She then took the pencil and pad that were provided on a small table and wrote, "May the angels carry him home to his Father in heaven." She ripped the page off the pad, folded it, and put it in the basket under a small sign lettered INTENTIONS.

Outside the chapel MacNeil said, "Did you make your wish?"

"What?"

"Your wish. Whenever you go into a church for the first time, you say the Hail Mary and make a wish."

"Oh." Silly as it seemed, Janus began to think about it.

"I know what I'd wish for," MacNeil said.

"You do?"

"Yes. Vengeance." She said it dully, without any apparent emotion.

"I'd probably wish for something sentimental," Janus said, "like an end to it all."

They went from the chapel to MacNeil's flat, about two blocks away. It was a small, sparsely furnished basement. The two windows were at eye level, and, even on that bright afternoon, the apartment was dark and chilly. MacNeil offered Janus a cup of tea, but she refused it, having resumed a brusque, hurried manner.

MacNeil pulled a medium-sized footlocker from under her bed. She opened it and stepped aside for Janus.

Neatly laid out on a folded blanket were a Luger automatic with two ammunition clips by its side; the silence cylinder that would muffle its shot; a thin, black switchblade; two boxes of bullets; and a second, smaller pistol, a flat Beretta automatic.

Janus took the knife, the Luger, the two clips, and the silencer. She thanked MacNeil on behalf of her friend, wished her luck, and left.

Cameron was blinded for the instant it took his eyes to adjust to the darkness of the pub.

When his vision returned, he saw that half a dozen men were on stools along the far end of the bar. Another pair sat in a booth halfway to the rear wall.

Cameron slid onto a stool at the near end of the bar.

"Yes, sir." The bartender stood with both hands on the counter. He seemed not to notice the conspicuous difference between the dapper, tweed-suited gentleman and the other patrons, who were uniformly dressed in working clothes, caps, windbreakers.

Cameron came right to the point. "Are you Murray?" There was no one within earshot of his careful voice.

"Who's asking?" the bartender replied evenly, softly, wiping the bar.

"I am." Cameron stared at him.

"In that case, no, I'm not Murray. Are you drinking or not?"

Cameron recognized the cocky lie. "A glass of seltzer, please."

"Soda without whiskey is two dollars."

"Fine."

When the bartender brought the glass of soda water, Cameron said, "I owe him some money."

"Who?"

"Murray."

"I know Murray pretty well, and I don't think he counts any fancy gentlemen among his chums."

"I'm not a chum. It's strictly business. Five hundred dollars."

"What did he have to do for that?" He asked it softly, wiping the same spot on the bar.

"Two minutes of frank conversation."

"I doubt it. Murray's not the sort. They've a name for that, you know."

"There was no betrayal of trust. It happened that Murray's interest and mine coincided."

"How so?"

"In preventing the execution of a mutual friend."

The bartender looked at Cameron. He ran his tongue over his lower lip. He touched the back of his right hand to his chin. He said, "Liam Murray has no mutual friends with any fucking Englishman! Two dollars, Mac!"

Cameron stood. "Whatever you say, my friend." He took a glove-leather billfold from the inside pocket of his coat, withdrew two bills, and put them on the bar. "Whatever you say," he repeated as if it were true.

In the back room, Murray made a phone call. "Stay put," he said. "I'll be over later. Cameron's on the snoop. Something's up."

"Oh, my God," the voice replied.

4

4:50 TUESDAY AFTERNOON

John Tierney was trying to make a decision. He was standing in the middle of his cramped room at the rectory, looking at the clock on the bedtable. It was almost five. He had an hour and a half before going to his mother's apartment for dinner. He was trying to decide whether to take a quick nap or go for a jog.

He hated to sleep in the daytime because he loved it so much. He loved pulling down the shade and, in the artifical darkness, crawling between the cold sheets of his bed and hugging the pillow in the crook of his elbow.

He never enjoyed getting into bed late at night the way he did in the middle of the afternoon. But waking up was dreadful: that's what he hated. He hated the hint of an overpowering laziness that he feared would overtake him as it overtook so many of the priests he knew. It was a laziness that built a life out of sleep and drink and golf and the track and, finally, the oblivion of daytime television. And he knew that the laziness he detected in himself and abhorred in others was finally nothing but a disguise for the most awful fear.

Tierney was terrified of looking back on his life from old age and saying, "I had a good life, but it wasn't mine. It was someone else's: my mother's, my father's, the Church's, the people's, God's — they all had a piece of it, but I didn't." It was a fear he almost never looked at. But sometimes in that moment of waking in the middle of the day, he opened his eyes, and it was there like a face above him.

He decided to go jogging.

Twenty minutes later he turned back toward the cathedral. He had run as far as Hayne's Point, about two miles. Now he circled around Main Avenue and over to the Tidal Basin. The cherry blossoms were just beginning to fall. He dodged between the cars that were oozing out of the city toward the Fourteenth Street Bridge in the slow crush of evening traffic. He cut across the grass to the sidewalk that bordered the basin and he slowed his pace somewhat as he entered the beautiful archway of pink and white blossoms.

Suddenly the world changed. The gold of twilight was beginning to wash the air with color. The sparkles of the sun's rays on the water flashed up at him from the basin on his left, signals of the day's glorious demise. On his right, the gnarled bark of the old trees testified to the real cost — year in, year out — of spring's pleasures. The canopy of leaves hung over him, and every ten feet or so he had to weave and duck to avoid being slapped by the petals, to avoid knocking them down from their clusters prematurely. They were already on the verge of going from ripe to rotten; he didn't want to hurry the grim underwork of spring.

He remembered reading that certain influential congressmen had wanted the cherry trees cut down during the Second World War, since they had come originally as gifts from Japan. But even as he remembered that, he thought he understood it, because war is war. As he cut across the grass again, through the traffic and toward the Monument, he glanced over his shoulder once more at the blooming trees, and he was moved to thank God for them, even in their fading. And he thanked God for whatever it was in his people that had let them, finally, spare the sad and lovely trees their hate.

At the cathedral a basketball game was in progress on the back lot, which had been emptied of cars by the day's end.

Tierney watched the black kids madly rushing up and down the court. The hoops and backboards were still almost new; Tierney had bought them the previous autumn. When the other priests on the cathedral staff had objected to his idea of combining the parking lot with a basketball court for the neighborhood, they made the mistake of basing their argument on the state of parish finances. They didn't expect him to pay for the baskets himself.

He couldn't resist a game. It happened that one of the teams was short a man and, without being asked or asking, and so observing the code of street ball, Tierney slid into the game after a basket.

He was good. He was taller than all but one of the players — the opposing center.

"Pick, man! Pick!" shouted the short, peppery guard at Tierney. He wanted him to stand at the top of the key and hold his position while he, the guard, ran his opponent into him.

Tierney obeyed. The guard fired a pass to the left forward, who drilled it back to him. Then the guard made his move, deftly dribbling, faking, hesitating, and suddenly driving for the basket. The guard's covering opponent, trying to stay ahead of the drive, backed into Tierney, ramming him. But Tierney was set; he didn't budge. The guard was around and free, the opponent blocked and stopped for the crucial two seconds. The guard was up for his jump shot. The opposing forward couldn't reach him in time. He floated the ball off his loose right wrist into its slow high arch: swish!

"Baybee!" The black kid took five from his fellow guard and then crossed in the run upcourt to give skin to Tierney.

"Aweraht!" he said.

Tierney played for ten or fifteen minutes. He scored eight points, four for five. His team was losing, though, and he was bushed. And he had to shower and get over to his mother's. He decided to quit, and so slipped out of the game as he had joined it. Several new kids were waiting to play now. One of them took his place. Everyone on the court relaxed some, as Tierney knew they would. The new kid wasn't as good as

Tierney, but he was one of them. He wasn't from the cathedral. He was their age. And he was black.

"Good game."

"Thanks." Tierney hadn't noticed the attractive, well-dressed white woman who had been watching. She was standing by a car on the edge of the lot. She made her comment as Tierney passed her on his way toward the rectory. He had replied without thinking, not wondering who she was and certainly not expecting her to step in his way and say, "You're Father John Tierney, aren't you?"

"Yes, I am. Who are you?" He didn't want to talk to her. He was still breathing hard and perspiring heavily. He did not want to stay out in the evening chill.

"I'm Roberta Winston. I'm with the *Post.*"

Oh, great, he thought, groaning inwardly. He knew it would happen sooner or later. He forced himself to smile. "Nice to meet you. I think I've seen your name." He started to go by her, but she stayed with him, blocking him.

"May I ask you something?"

"Sure, but this hardly seems like . . ."

"I know. Forgive me." She seemed to mean it. "But it won't take long. I'll be glad to wait for you, though, if you prefer."

"No. I'm on a pretty tight schedule. Why don't you ask me now."

"Just a couple of questions. Actually, I'd like to talk to you at length later, but there are a couple of points I'd like to confirm for tomorrow's story."

"Shoot."

"I understand you are in charge of the ecclesiastical case against Sister Sheehan."

"I am. Yes."

"Can you say briefly what you think will happen to her?"

"I was only appointed to the matter this morning. I'm not in a position yet to know much one way or the other right now. When I am I'll be glad to talk to you. Very glad."

"That's fine. Thanks."

"You're welcome." Tierney smiled at her and started to go by again. But again she stopped him.

"May I ask a question about yourself?"

"Certainly."

"Why did the cardinal appoint you to this case?"

"I don't know, to be honest. I wouldn't have expected to be, shall we say, chosen."

"Do you want to do it?"

"Not particularly, no."

"Why are you doing it, then?"

He looked at her, weighed his answer. "I do a lot of things I don't want to do. Don't you?"

"Is it a matter of following orders, as, say, in the army?"

Tierney wondered what she was driving at. He could feel his heart pumping; it hadn't eased off at all since he'd left the court.

"No. I do what I do because, finally, I believe in it even if, on occasion, I don't like it."

"Weren't you in the army, Father?"

"I'm sorry?"

"You served in Vietnam. Isn't that correct?"

Tierney couldn't believe it. Why was she bringing that up? His heart resounded in his ears.

"How did you find that out?" he asked.

"It's a matter of public information. I checked your service record."

"To what purpose?"

"Well, I'm doing a profile on you for tomorrow's paper. Man in the news, that sort of thing."

"Oh."

"You had quite an outstanding career."

"Not quite a career, actually."

"Four years."

"Yes."

"Head of the Military Advisory Assistance Group in Pleiku from 'sixty-two to 'sixty-four."

"Yes."

"I read the citation that came with your Distinguished Service Medal."

"You did?"

"Yes. You killed four men with your hands, it said."

"Did it?" Tierney's calm exterior gave no hint of the turmoil he was feeling. The woman had found her way inside his secret.

"What is your position on the Vietnam war now, Father?"

"Is that relevant?"

"I'm sure our readers will be intrigued by your background. They'll want to know how you feel about it now that you're a priest, now that it's drawing to such a grisly close."

"I think, if you don't mind, I'd rather not discuss it with you."

"Would you say your experience with the Special Forces was good preparation for your duty now of prosecuting Sister Sheehan?"

"You people don't mess around, do you? Excuse me, please." He said it almost politely. He walked away from her slowly, with composure, giving no sign of the fact that the wolf under his shirt was about to chew through to his heart.

Nancy Ferris-Cogan was still at her easel. She was racing against the fading light of the day. The painting was nearly complete, but not quite. The fine hair brush moved against the canvas ever so slightly. It was an exquisite exercise of control. She was stroking in the shadow, cobalt blue, beneath her husband's left eye. The marks she was making were each no bigger than a fleck of dust. The brush jumped and danced in a tiny staccato that was the merest hint of the frenzy Nancy felt. It was the channeled frenzy of the creative fit in which her hand tried desperately to keep up with her eye, which in turn tried futilely to keep up with her mind. It was as if an outburst of artistic energy would make up for her anger at lunch. Her earlier rage had functioned to shut off her husband. Now she sought out his image, gave herself over to it. As if she were healing some hurt she herself had inflicted. She had been in this state of controlled tension most of the afternoon, and the small section of the canvas that had troubled her had been transformed finally. She had seen the face she wanted; she had seen its eyes, and she had painted them.

She stopped. She stepped back from the easel and looked at what she had done. It was her husband mounted as before, frozen in the moment just before striking the willow ball with his mallet. Still there were the strain, the fury; the celebration of blood, muscle, coordination, effort. But there was something new planted in the very center of the painting in the middle of the man's face. She looked at it. She tried to find a word for it. In addition to the power, the strength, the toughness that distorted the mouth slightly and gave the eyes their edge, there was — what to call it? — a delight, a gentleness, something tender.

It was what she had seen in her husband's face that morning when he cantered toward her from the broad lawn on the large black horse with his daughter in his arms. She had seen it again at noon when he had joined her in caressing the girl during her brief misery, and before her own angry outburst.

When Nancy returned to the painting after lunch, she remembered a phrase that he had used once years before in the middle of a furious polo match on the green in Essex. He had yelled it at a teammate who had fired a shot wide of the goal: "Don't kill it! Kiss it! Love it! Love it in!"

That was the difference. She stood looking at what she had done. Yes, that was the difference. She had caught her husband in the split second before his mallet head caught the running ball and kissed it toward the goal. What she saw in his face now she had seen in him on the field years before, in that first season when he rode Gandalon. In the midst of the brutal charging, checking, dangerous swinging of clubs, wailing of frenzied beasts, men on the edge of a kind of madness, she had seen, watching him, an act of love.

"Hello," he said.

"Oh!" She jumped. She was totally startled. Ferris-Cogan

was standing inside the solarium door. He was wearing a brown cardigan and smoking the thin Peterson she had given him for Christmas. He was holding two glasses.

"May I come in?" He was being polite. As she looked at him from behind her easel, she remembered the outrage that had poured from her at lunch.

"Yes. Do." Her voice was soft.

"You're hard at it, eh?"

"Have been."

"I came down when you weren't dressing for dinner."

"Oh, my God, what time is it?"

"There's time."

"What time are they coming?"

"Not till eight. You know the Ramseys, though. It'll be more like nine. Wouldn't do to have Canadians show on time. Might be mistaken for deference. I brought you a drink."

She came from behind the easel and met him in the middle of the solarium. Both hesitated, caught momentarily in the embarrassing aftermath of their argument. Awkwardly, she offered her cheek. He kissed it, and she took the glass he held out for her.

"Thanks. God, I need it."

She turned to face the windows. The sun was below the wooded ridge in the distance, but the sky was a brilliant final red.

Ferris-Cogan moved to the chaise longue and sat on it, stretching his feet along its side to the floor. He looked at the darkening sky and at his wife's figure against it. After a moment he said, "It's lovely."

"Yes." She hugged herself, unconsciously covering what was still raw inside her. She would not open herself to another of his blasts, or to another of her own. She sipped her drink. It was Scotch cut with a bit of water, no ice. She deliberately continued to stand facing away from her husband. His silence weighed on her. She wondered if he was thinking of her exchange at lunch. She wondered if *he* was afraid of *her*.

Alisdair ran his eye along her back and thought about waking in the morning, when it was usually the first thing he saw. He couldn't make out the lines of her muscles and bones through the black smock that hung loosely on her, but he could imagine them: strong, clearly defined, flesh tight across the spine. He'd often thought her back elegant, but it was, as he'd thought more often, so very mute. It told him nothing. As he sat looking at her now he wondered if the spark of anger they'd struck on each other earlier had ignited something. He thought it likely. That's probably why, he realized, he'd come down with drinks.

"How's your drink?" he asked. There was a hint of remorse in his voice.

"Fine." She turned to face him. "Fine,' she repeated warmly. The smile she gave him then made him feel the way he always felt on those mornings when she awoke at last and rolled toward him, showing him her face and its signal that, no, the night had not destroyed her love for him.

"Busy day?" she asked.

"Not very. Could have been, though. Word came through early this afternoon that Thieu was shot and Saigon had crumbled this morning. Kissinger called. False alarm."

"If not today . . ."

"Exactly. Also, I just learned that our friend Viscount Thompson — you remember, Malaysia? Guerrilla war expert? — announced that Saigon's fall is blood on the hands of America, called it the worst surrender since Waterloo, *and* implied that he was speaking for the queen."

"Oh, God."

"Everybody here knows he's a fool, of course. Except the press, who always take him seriously. Bigger fools."

"Did you get a statement out?"

"Yes. 'Ladies and Gentlemen of the Press, Her Royal Majesty wants it understood that, as is her long and firm-standing policy, she has nothing to say about everything.' "

"Alisdair!"

"Or was it 'everything to say about nothing'?"

"How unlike you to mock the queen!"

"How unlike you to defend her!"

"Are we both trying too hard?" As she asked it, she laughed, and he joined her in laughing.

When they were quiet again, he asked, "How's the painting?"

"I had a good day," she replied.

"Good. When will you admit the public?"

"Tomorrow."

"Really?"

"It's for a special occasion."

"A special occasion? What?"

"Think about it."

He did, then said, "You don't mean . . . ?"

"Well, you could hardly have thought I'd let the pope outdo me."

She could see that he was moved. She had planned to unveil the painting, even to her husband, at the reception following the ceremony the next evening. But she changed her mind. "Would you like a preview?"

"Yes," he said without hesitating.

"All right." She took her weight from the door against which she'd been leaning. She put her whiskey on the stereo speaker by the easel and stood there gesturing him toward the canvas.

He put his drink on the floor by the chaise longue, stood, and walked the four steps to the easel. He looked at his wife as he slipped between her body and the tripod, brushing her frankly. Then he turned to face the work. There was just light enough remaining for him to see the painting, and for her to see his face.

"Oh, my God," he said. "Nancy . . ." His eyes hung on the painting. His face was brilliant with feeling. "It's . . . beautiful."

"That's because you are." She spoke without a curve in her voice, feeling the warm weight of her affection for him.

He turned and took a step toward her; she flowed into his arms. As Alisdair closed on her he saw an image of her long white body naked, spread-eagled on their bed. She took him, slitting her eyes at him, filling his mouth, holding fast gratefully, fiercely.

Across the room and down on the long chair. Their strong tumbling embrace reflected everything they could not utter. Night was coming, but the day's strange fury had not opened its great space between them. It was all right.

And she was strangling him everywhere but at the throat.

Liam Murray never saw them. He was turning the corner at M Street, his shift at Shannon's having just ended.

He was walking quickly when the blow came. It seemed to melt his skull. As he fell, it seemed to him that warm and loving arms were taking him.

Almost the arms, he thought, of a woman.

"What can I do to help, Aunt Nell?"

"Hello, Bea. You're up."

"Yes." Bridgit stood blushing in the threshold of the small kitchen. She looked at the thin, wiry old woman who limped toward her, favoring the leg in which her vein was swollen.

"Nothing, darling, nothing." The woman nudged her back into the living room. "Are you rested now? You had a good nap?"

"I should say. Two hours' worth. I can't imagine why I was so tired." Bridgit was mortified to have slept so long, having just arrived.

"Jet lag, darling, they call that jet lag."

Bridgit thought that jet lag happened when you went the other way, when you lost hours. She had gained them. But she wasn't sure. All she knew was that she was exhausted. She had never been so tired. And even after her nap, she was still listless, empty of energy. "Isn't jet lag if you go the other way, Aunt Nell?"

"You know, I couldn't really say, Bea. We'll ask Father John when he gets here. He'll be over any minute."

"You're very proud of him, aren't you?"

"I am. Don't breathe a word to Johnny, but Father Stevens, the pastor here at Saint Teresa's, tells me he's on the new list for monsignor."

"Isn't that grand?"

"He'll be a bishop, I'm sure. I only hope I live to see it."

"That's what my ma says. We're all very proud of him back home, you know. It's a blessing to have a priest in the family."

"Just let me turn down the gas on the potatoes . . ." The older woman disappeared into the kitchen. Bridgit moved to the couch and sat down. Her eye fell on the table photograph of a smiling young man with wavy black hair. When her aunt came out of the kitchen, Bridgit said, "This is Uncle Mike, isn't it?"

"It is."

"He was a handsome fellow."

"He was indeed. But, to tell you the truth, we fought like banshees."

"How old was he when he died?"

"Thirty-seven. Johnny was just four."

"Oh."

"Your Peter was twenty-six, wasn't it?" Her aunt was looking at Bridgit closely, carefully. Her relatives almost never mentioned her dead husband.

"Yes. Twenty-six." Bridgit said it easily, with the calm acquired over eight years of widowhood. Peter Connor was a memory to her, cherished, dear, but no longer the center of dreams, pains, or life.

Mrs. Tierney's eyes filled, as if the sight of her niece were the sight of her own youthful bereavement. But she shook off the emotion. Bridgit's attention was back on the photo, which reminded Mrs. Tierney of the album.

She crossed to the small desk in the corner of the room, saying, "You never saw the pictures of Johnny's ordination." She was at the desk, opening a drawer, withdrawing an album.

"I did, Aunt Nell. In fact . . ." Bridgit hesitated, wondered if she should go on, decided she could, and proceeded to tease her aunt. "You've brought them over with you every year."

"Oh?" The older woman sounded disappointed, almost embarrassed.

Bridgit hastened on, "But I'd love to see them again. They're wonderful photos."

"All right. I'll show them to you."

They sat together then, turning the thick black pages. Tierney's mother explained, commented, identified, and bragged.

"That's Cardinal O'Boyle. He did the ordaining, of course. He retired a few years ago. He was a bit stuck up and he had all that trouble over birth control. Cardinal O'Brien is much nicer, though he's a bit old, too."

"And the ordination was in the cathedral, was it? Where Johnny works now?"

"Yes. We'll see it tomorrow."

"I've never been in a real cathedral, Aunt Nell. Just in the pro-cathedrals in Derry and Dublin."

"Oh, Bea, you'll be so impressed. And I'm sure Father John will introduce you to His Eminence. It's the next thing to meeting the pope himself."

"I'll be thrilled. I'm so glad I came. My Ma told me it'd be the perfect occasion for my visit. You know, I admire your son quite a lot."

"And he does you, dear. He was just delighted when I told him you were coming. Let me go check those potatoes. Where is that boy?"

She got up and limped toward the kitchen. Bridgit turned the pages of the album, looking at the photographs interestedly, almost studiously.

When her aunt came out of the kitchen she had her head cocked toward the door. "I hear the elevator."

Bridgit heard nothing, but, sure enough, within a few seconds there was the sound of a key being inserted into the lock. Before it could be turned, Mrs. Tierney had the door open.

The priest was standing there, wearing a blue blazer and a red checked shirt open at the neck.

"Aren't you the one," she was saying, "to be taking your time?"

"Hi, Mom." Tierney kissed his mother on the forehead and then handed her one of the two long-stemmed roses he was carrying. She was delighted. "Why, son!"

He passed her then and crossed the room toward Bridgit, who stood nervously by the couch. She was taken aback by the warm energy of his greeting. He hugged her, saying, "Bridgit, Bridgit, what a great surprise!"

"Hi, Johnny," was all she could manage. Since they were children he had been like a hero to her: five years older, always wise, and ever ready with the familial affection that made her feel special. Even though, in growing up, they had seen each other only every few years, he had come to occupy in her life the place her only brother might have had if he hadn't died an infant. And in recent years, since Peter's death, Tierney's visits with his mother to Derry were more frequent, almost annual, and their youthful attachment had grown into a friendship they both cherished.

He held her at arm's length: "You look good!"

He had never noticed her eyes before; now they seemed a richer, livelier blue than any he had ever seen. His look made her feel pretty, and she was.

He handed her the second rose and said simply, "Welcome."

"Thanks, Johnny. Oh, thank you." And she hugged him again.

"Darling," his mother said, "maybe Bea would like some sherry, and you can fix yourself something."

"How about you, Mom?"

"No, go ahead. I have to finish dinner. I'll pop in and out."

"Bridgit?" he asked. "There is sherry. There's also Scotch and gin and . . ." He faced the kitchen. "There's beer, Mom, right?"

"Yes, left over from your friend last week."

"Right," he said to Bridgit. "There's beer, too. What would you like?"

"Sherry, Johnny. That would be lovely."

"Okay." He went to the buffet at the end of the living room, opened one of the panels, and took out two bottles. He went into the kitchen, but came out immediately, shooed by his mother, who was saying, "Use the good glasses, Johnny."

"What, the Waterford?"

"Of course. What's it for if not this?"

Sheepishly he shrugged toward Bridgit, who smiled broadly and nodded at him. He took the good glasses from the lowest shelf in the buffet, poured sherry for Bridgit and Scotch for himself, just as his mother arrived with a bowl of ice, put it down, and returned to the kitchen. He dropped several cubes into his glass, looked at his cousin as if to ask whether she wanted ice. She shook her head. He brought the drinks across the room and sat by her on the couch.

"How are you?" he asked.

"I'm fine, fit as ever." Actually, her stomach was beginning to feel a bit queasy again.

"You must be wiped out after your flight."

"I had a nap. Your mother and I were discussing the meaning of jet lag."

"Well, by your clock right now it's" — he looked at his watch — "quarter to twelve."

"I've been up since four."

"No wonder you were bushed!"

"I didn't sleep at all last night with the excitement. I felt like a child again. It was wonderful."

"Don't you love to travel?"

"I haven't done that much of it, you know. I hardly believe I'm here. I only decided to come day before yesterday."

"That's what Mom said."

"I didn't know what to do with my leave. I was just going to sit around, you know? Then Ma got her letter from Aunt Nell about you and His Honor and everything, and she thought I should go. And plus the air fares go up for the tourists next month, you know, so it seemed a good idea."

"A *great* idea. About time! Although the ceremony tomorrow, Bridgit, well, it may not be as big a deal as you think." He lowered his voice. "Or as our mothers think."

"To tell you the truth, Johnny, I'll love to go, and I'll be honored to meet your important friends, but mainly I'm just glad to see you and be visiting finally. I was glad to have the excuse."

He winked at Bridgit as his mother came back into the living room.

"Johnny, you should have worn your collar." She said it as if she had just noticed his blazer, his shirt, as if his manner of dress didn't dawn on her until just then in the kitchen.

"What?" he asked, though he knew what was coming.

"For Bea. So you could look the proper priest when you welcomed her."

"I'll look proper tomorrow, Mom. Very proper."

"He looks fine," Bridgit defended.

"Well, it's not every day you come to visit."

Tierney was determined not to let his mother get to him. He took her elbow and shook it playfully. "Don't mind Mom, Bridgit. Her memory's slipping. She thinks I'm twelve years old."

"Oh, you," his mother said, matching his playfulness, shaking her arm free of him. "Come into the dining room, the both of you. Dinner's ready."

The dining room was a space at the end of the living room near the kitchen, set off by a low divider. Tierney and Bridgit sat at the small but formal table as Mrs. Tierney insisted on serving them.

When the food was out the priest offered the traditional grace, and the women blessed themselves when he made the sign of the cross over the table. They ate heartily, and all three of them enjoyed the easy talk of family gossip and old stories through the meal.

When they had finished their tea, Mrs. Tierney said, "Johnny, Bea is dying to see the sights. Why don't you two go for a drive so she can see the splendid monuments all lit up at night?"

"Oh, I'd love that," Bridgit said.

"You come too, Mom," Tierney said.

"No, darling. To tell you the truth, my leg is acting up. I need to rest it. I'll just clean up here and go to bed, I think. You don't mind, Bea, do you?"

"No, of course I don't, Aunt Nell. But I'll certainly help clean up." Bridgit started to clear the table.

"I won't hear of it." Bridgit stopped. She heard a hint of her own mother's voice. It was a voice not to be disobeyed.

Bridgit got her coat as Tierney stood and watched his mother scrape the plates. When Bridgit returned, Mrs. Tierney crossed to the desk and got her keys. She handed them to Bridgit.

"This one is to the door downstairs, dearie. This is to our door. Now when you come in I'll probably be out like a light. I take a little pill, you know? But I'll have the hideaway . . ." Here she gestured to the couch they had been sitting on earlier. ". . . all made up for you."

"Fine, Aunt Nell, but just leave the sheets out. I'll make it up."

"Don't be silly. Now you two go off and have a grand time."

"You sure you won't come, Mom?"

"No, really, dear."

"I was just thinking we might run into the cardinal."

"Johnny! You just tell him it's your cousin, that's all."

"No, no. I meant . . ." At this Tierney was laughing and pulling the door behind him. ". . . then we could be a foursome. You could be *his* date!"

Mrs. Tierney put her head into the corridor after them and said in a stage whisper, "You see, Bridgit, what happens to them when they stop dressing like priests."

At the elevator, Tierney put his hand briefly on the small of his cousin's back, ushering her ahead through the doors. He was still laughing at his mother's chagrin, and an intangible, fleeting joy filled him. But as the elevator began its descent, their eyes met. The space was suddenly all too small. An abrupt awkwardness fell between them as each became bodily aware of the other.

And Tierney was thinking of the banter he'd exchanged with his mother. Was this a date? What did Bridgit think? Did she know he was joking? Was he?

"Jefferson designed it himself."

He was pointing through the windshield at the Jefferson Memorial, which passed slowly on their right. "It's modeled on the home he built at Monticello about a hundred miles south of here."

"It's a grand monument, Johnny, isn't it?"

Tierney swung the Maverick north on the Washington side of the Fourteenth Street Bridge. He thought the stretch of road along West Potomac Park was the most beautiful part of Washington at night. He pointed out the various buildings and monuments, speaking with the pride and affection for the city that he felt as one of its few native residents.

On their left the illuminated Pentagon sat strong and squat across the river. On their right the great obelisk in memory of Washington soared into the night sky. Tierney pointed up at it, helping his cousin to see the faint line a third of the way up its five hundred and fifty-five feet where the hue of the stone changed slightly, the one benign scar left behind by the trauma of the Civil War, which had interrupted the Monument's construction for a dozen years.

They circled the Lincoln Memorial, where Bridgit asked if they could stop for a minute. They sat in the great man's gaze, not speaking, following the Doric gesture along the axis of the Monument and the glowing Capitol at the far side of the Mall. Tierney drew his cousin's notice to the light burning in the Capitol dome and told her that meant that one of the Houses was still in session; probably the Senate, he said, debating the emergency appropriation for the evacuation of Americans and refugees from collapsing South Vietnam.

They resumed their circle of Lincoln then, and, at the foot of Memorial Bridge, Tierney pointed to the small, constant flame on the dark hill across the river.

"That's John Kennedy's tomb, Bridgit." He said it almost tenderly, anticipating the effect it would have on her. She leaned across him to see the flame more clearly. He could hear the catch in her breath.

"Oh, dear God, Johnny, we loved him."

"Yes. I loved him too, like he was . . ." He spoke softly, letting his words trail off. His left eye quivered with a rush of the old anguish. He knew without seeing them that the flame had drawn tears from Bridgit's eyes.

Bridgit's easy lightheartedness was singed in the flashing of the sadness that smoldered in her, waiting. She could never have uttered it, not even to her cousin. Kennedy was from that other world that had turned on her own youth, her innocent happiness, her vast expectation of love and good living. None of what she had hoped for had come to pass; all that she valued had been sullied or utterly destroyed. Ordinarily she lived without grief, as without dreams.

"I hate what killed him."

He was surprised at this expression from her. She had an unfamiliar weariness as she spoke, an almost jaded tone. He looked at her more closely. The thin trickle of her tears shone on her cheeks. He wanted to touch them, to put his hand on the skin beneath her eye.

"Bridgit, so do I."

He brushed her left cheek with the back of his hand and took it away. He put his hand to his mouth, touched the moisture of her tears with his tongue.

"I marched in his parade, you know," he said, vaguely proud. "His inaugural."

"You did?" She matched his light tone, but a corner of her mind remained in the cold shadow where the immense disappointment nursed its ache.

"Yes. I was on an honor guard drill team at the time. We

marched right behind a contingent of cavalry. Ruined our shoes."

They both laughed at the image of crack cadets striding through horse dung the length of Pennsylvania Avenue. Their laughter cauterized their grief. Tierney thought that he and Bridgit had overcome some similar private pains, and, but for that corner of her mind, they had.

When he resumed driving he turned north again on West Potomac Drive. Ahead they could see the spires of Georgetown's Healy Hall, where Tierney had lived as an undergraduate and which had been the scene of several stories of youthful mischief that kept them laughing.

"At freshman hazing I refused to wear the blue-gray beanie and the stupid tie. I said I was a sophomore. It nearly worked."

"What happened?"

"The real sophomores caught on, caught *me*, coming out of religion class. I ran, of course, thinking they could ruin me for life. I hid in the ladies' room of the gym, stooped on a toilet so my legs wouldn't show."

"Oh, John," she said, sparkling, "how dreadful!"

"Actually, after that, I was a class hero briefly. After the freshman mixer a girl named Janet said she loved me, proved it with her bra, homage to my courage. She wouldn't quite sleep with me."

"Silly girl," Bridgit said, laughing, giving him a sharp, coy look that made Tierney regret what he'd said immediately.

At the imposing Watergate apartment complex, Tierney mused that the *real* scandal was the Vatican money that had built it in the first place. Bridgit responded with counterfeit horror, and they both agreed jokingly that you could expect corruption everywhere these days, even in the Church.

Across the river from the Kennedy Center for the Performing Arts they could see the spotlit Iwo Jima Memorial, its five bronze marines who raised the flag into the night; the only flag, Tierney explained, aside from the one on the Capitol, that flew twenty-four hours a day.

"You were a marine," she said. It wasn't put as a question, but she was asking him something.

"Not quite. I was in the army."

"You don't speak of it much."

Tierney remembered his exchange with Roberta Winston and thought of what his cousin would be reading about him in the *Post* the next day.

"It was," he said finally, frankly, "a bitter experience, Bridgit."

"Were you . . . against the war?"

"No. I was in it early."

"It must have been . . . hard."

"You do what you have to do, you know? History might prove you wrong, but history doesn't get you off the hook."

"I know."

"I suppose you do. War has cost you and your people more than us."

"Yes." Bridgit paused as if deciding whether to go on. She was picturing her own corner of Derry. The ragged women were carrying their laundry in wicker baskets along Landown Street. The boys were running past in their short pants. The dull houses of cinderblock mirrored the gray skies. The skies and the houses had been there forever. It was a depressing place. She hated it.

"Johnny, it's more than the fighting makes it awful." She turned to face him directly. "If I say something a bit strange, will you understand me?"

"I'll try." Despite himself, Tierney was shocked at her tone even before she spoke. But he was attentive, anxious that she reveal herself to him.

"It isn't the war that kills, Johnny." She spoke evenly, seriously. "What kills is nothing. Day after day and week after week and year after year of *nothing happening* — that's what kills."

"Are you talking about your own life, Bridgit?"

"Yes, of course. And not only mine. Honest to God, the wrecked houses and the corpses on the road are little enough sorrow compared to the perpetual, never-ending dreariness of the place and the people. Shall I say something truly horrible, John?" She stopped, clearly deciding. She looked right through him. Even though the Maverick was moving slowly along Rock Creek Drive, he was having trouble concentrating on driving. When she spoke again her voice had the gentle sorrow that was the seal of confession.

"The sound of guns from the edge of town can be like a tonic sometimes. Shattered walls can become the lively center of a street when it's the others who are dead, blown to smithereens, even if you loved them." Bridgit stopped. Despite herself, she pictured her husband, Peter. His face shocked her, made her feel guilty, as though she were making light of *his* death. But she forced herself to finish. "Perhaps it's only then that you know yourself what it is to be living. Johnny, the truth is we *yearn* for the war. Which is why if the British don't force it on us, we force it on each other."

Tierney was stunned by the palpable despair in her voice. It was as if she had admitted to the most repugnant perversion, though he knew she was articulating what the survivors and bystanders of war had always felt. He was blinking his, eyes, uncertain. He had nothing to say. His own part in the Vietnam war was not equivalent. That war had never caught him by the very bowels — he had mastered a soldierly detachment — while Bridgit was saying that the Irish war came out of hers. The montage of explosion, blood, smashed faces, wrecked bodies, children screaming, filled his mind. He looked over at his cousin. It was inconceivable that this thin and lovely woman had a place in it. It was too immense, too futile. His mind veered back, absorbed itself in her beauty. The profile of her face was stark and exquisite against the night lights.

"Bridgit . . ."

She looked at him.

"Would you like a cup of coffee or something?"

She looked away from him. She knew that he could not take in what she was feeling. Why, when no one else could, had she expected him to? There are despairs so vast they can engulf all who hear them spoken of. Even though she had lifted the cloth on the barest corner of what she felt, she would not speak so again.

"Oh," she said, as if startled out of some reverie. She hesitated.

"It's not nine-thirty yet," he coaxed. They were headed north on Wisconsin Avenue toward his mother's apartment.

"Johnny, to tell the truth, my stomach hasn't been right since the airplane. I'd like to get to bed, I think."

"Oh, sure. You must be bushed. God, it's the middle of the night by your clock. I forgot." Tierney knew that something had become confused between them. He wondered what.

"I really am tired." She spoke with an unfeigned fatigue.

"Sure. We're almost back to my mother's."

"You give a great tour."

"I love this city, Bridgit." This expression of a simple, true emotion relieved him.

"It shows. Looking at it through your eyes, anybody would love it." She had retreated from the gloom and spoke with genuine pleasure too. She touched his arm.

"Well, it's a pleasure to have somebody nice to share it with." He took his eyes from the road and looked at her, laughing easily.

"Thank you." Bridgit's wretchedness — mysterious and transient — had been dispelled.

"Tomorrow we can see some more of it. I think Mom is planning to bring you down for lunch."

"She has an appointment with the hairdresser in the morning. I'm going to town with her, and she's going to show me some good stores while I wait for her. I love to look in the windows."

"Tell her I'll expect you a little before noon."

"Okay."

At the Woodner there were no obvious parking spaces, and

Bridgit insisted that Tierney not worry about accompanying her inside. Tierney would have double-parked, but she was adamant. The building was safe enough, and the doorman was still on duty, so Tierney relented. Even the women in Ireland were claiming their independence. Tierney reminded himself that chivalry is just a disguise for oppression.

He kissed her on the cheek she offered When she leaned toward him he could hear the sound of her clothing against her skin. Only after she got out of the car was he aware of her body's pleasant smell. It seemed to hang in the air for a minute.

He watched Bridgit until she had crossed the lobby of the apartment building and entered the elevator. When the doors had closed on her, he put his Maverick into gear and drove back to the cathedral. In his room, Tierney undressed, climbed into bed, and read the latest issue of *Commonweal*.

When he finished, he turned out the light on the table next to his bed and slid down into the sheets. It was early, but he never had trouble getting to sleep, especially if he'd been jogging during the day.

But on this night he lay awake for a long time, listening to the city and wondering what was bothering him.

MacCree didn't want to answer the telephone.

He was lying across the width of the rumpled bed looking at the woman. He thought she was the most beautiful thing he had ever seen. A little on the lean side, especially her tits, which had just bleeding disappeared at one point in the middle of things. In fact, her breasts had been pulled taut and flat by the arching of her back just as she went into orgasm above him. But MacCree was not complaining, small tits or no: she was the first lay he'd had in over a month and the best since he didn't know when. He'd rarely had it before with the woman on top. It was terrific.

He was enjoying the sight of her now from his place at the foot of the bed. They were both naked, and, for some reason,

MacCree wasn't self-conscious about his nakedness the way he usually was; at least not until the damn phone began to ring.

"Should I answer it?" he asked her.

She shrugged and smiled at him. He almost decided not to. But then he remembered the phone call he'd gotten that afternoon.

"Hello."

"MacCree?"

"Murray, that you?"

"Yeah."

"Hey, you don't sound right. What's wrong?"

"They fucking burned me."

"Who?"

"Fucking goddamn Cameron."

"Who's Cameron?" MacCree didn't notice the woman sit up, listening.

"Fucking Englishman! Fucking burned my feet with his fucking cigarettes."

"Your feet? Oh, fuck! The soles of your feet?"

"Yeah."

"Oh, fuck, Murray, why?"

"They want *you!*"

"Jesus Christ! Me! What do the fucking English want me for? I'm not on the lam from them. Jesus Christ, I used to *sell* shit to them."

"You bastard, you never said that!"

"Well, shit, Murray, not a lot. Nothing important."

"You fucking bastard! Put me through this! I hope they miss him!"

"What do you mean?"

"Cameron thinks you're going to be hit tonight."

"By who?"

"Janus."

"Janus! Christ, no!"

"Good riddance, you scum!"

"Hey Murray, Murray, don't be like that. Come on, Murray."

"I called you to tell you something. I'm going to tell it to you, and then I'm through. I don't want to ever see your fucking face again. You hear?"

"Yeah."

"You got about ten minutes before Cameron gets to you. He just left here. I told him where you are."

"Fuck!"

"Fuck you! I got holes in my feet, you bastard. What do you got?"

"Money, Murray! Don't chuck me! I'll give you more. I'll double what I gave you, Murray. Please, Murray, please."

"I'm through, MacCree."

"Look, I'll get it to you right now. I'll have the woman that you sent bring it over, wherever you say."

"What?"

"I'll get it right to you. One thousand dollars cash."

"No, what'd you say about a woman?"

"The woman you sent over with the whiskey . . ."

MacCree looked up. The woman had circled around from behind him. She was standing six feet in front of him now. She was still naked, but all he saw was the pistol in her hand. It had a long barrel with a fat snout: a silencer, he knew.

"Oh, Christ," he said softly. "Mother of God."

She didn't say a word. He knew when she fired because her shoulders tensed momentarily and he was sure the muscles of her chest stretched her tits away into nothing just as she pulled the trigger.

He dropped the telephone when the bullet, true to his heart, killed him.

Murray's voice could be heard saying, "Good-bye, MacCree, you bastard."

Janus put a second bullet through his left kneecap, the Provo signature, so that MacCree's friends and those who were tempted by like impulses would know who killed him. So that they would know what treason pays.

Then she dressed quickly and slipped out of the building. She was thinking that Cameron's pursuit was making it all the more interesting; the old excitement had returned. It was her own private war again. She would take on the best of the bastards and beat them all.

Janus was ready, after MacCree, for something serious.

II

WEDNESDAY APRIL 23, 1975

The gentle first light of the hour after dawn filled the ambassador's office.

Brigadier Frank Cameron and Reg Parsley were seated in the plush oyster-white chairs by the fireplace. Both wore dark suits and striped ties. Ferris-Cogan was standing, leaning on the mantel, filling his pipe. He was wearing a Pendleton robe over trousers and slippers. He was not looking at Cameron while the military man made his report. But he listened intently even as he stuffed the flaked tobacco in the blackthorn bowl of his Peterson.

"By the time we arrived MacCree was dead. Janus had made him strip. He was naked, awash in blood, bullets in his chest and knee. We couldn't have missed him by more than a matter of minutes."

"What do you know about MacCree?" Ferris-Cogan asked it without looking up from his pipe. There was the barest tremor in his voice. In twenty-six years of service, including a tour in Kenya during the uprising, he had never dealt directly with violence.

"M.I. should have a full report back to us this morning. Apparently he was the Official plant in the Provo Action Council. If it's the same MacCree that Mitchell remembers, he had been of some small use to us on three occasions year before last. We expect confirmation on that."

"So . . ." Ferris-Cogan straightened, withdrew a silver lighter from his robe pocket and lit it. "A mid-level informer whose number came due, would you say?"

"Yes, sir, exactly."

Ferris-Cogan drew in on his pipe as he held the butane flame to its bowl. Smoke rose around his face, obscuring its expression. Cameron couldn't tell what the ambassador's response to his report would be, but he had noted the initial tremor in the man's voice.

"And Janus?" the ambassador asked.

"As I said, sir, we know almost nothing in detail. His name is linked — it's a code name, of course — to perhaps half a dozen IRA slayings. We know that he has had a training function for IRA snipers. We believe him to be one of the Provisionals who has undergone training himself with the Palestinians in Algeria. We assume he was involved in the Parliament bombing in seventy-three, and he was probably a central figure in the terror wave launched in Birmingham and London in the early months of last year."

Ferris-Cogan turned to Parsley, who had been sitting silently across from Cameron. "Reg, what do your people have on this Janus?"

Parsley blushed. "Nothing, sir."

"Nothing?" Ferris-Cogan saw the satisfied smirk that came briefly across Cameron's face but ignored it.

"No, sir. I spoke to Cambridge Circus this morning . . ."

"What?" Cameron interrupted, edgily, haughtily.

"By secure transmission, of course," Parsley went on, not looking at Cameron, who muttered under his breath, conveying his contempt for the inept and careless methods of civilians.

"And," Parsley was saying, "there is no such name in our files. Apparently the activities of the person so designated have been limited to the war zone."

"Is Parliament the war zone?" Cameron asked.

"Brigadier!" Ferris-Cogan said, tamping his pipe. "If you please."

Parsley went on: "A threat not political in character, appropriately covered by Military Intelligence."

"Well, gentlemen, here the military and the political converge. This is not the time to indulge in pointless rivalry, is it?" Ferris-Cogan spoke sternly.

"No, it isn't, Ambassador," Cameron said. "As long as Janus is at large in this city we have a potential military emergency on our hands."

"And," Sir Alisdair said, "a political one. Washington will not welcome bloody backwash from Ulster. Especially not now, with Indochina coming apart at the seams."

"If I may, Ambassador," Cameron said tentatively.

"Yes?"

"Washington need not know."

"What do you mean?"

"MacCree is nothing to this city. The police report filed early this morning describes another itinerant robbed and murdered in a disreputable boardinghouse."

"Was he robbed?"

"We took the liberty of making it seem so."

"How?"

"In point of fact, sir, we robbed him. Took some of his clothing, his timepiece, his billfold, which contained a considerable amount of cash."

"On whose authority did you so act, and to what end, Brigadier?" Ferris-Cogan spoke without overt alarm, but there was an unmistakable note of increasing urgency in his voice.

Cameron, on the other hand, couldn't have been cooler. "On the authority of my orders from Whitehall, sir. This is a British matter, Ambassador. We have the resources with which to handle it. And, as you say, sir, Her Majesty's interests will not be served if the war in Ireland seems to be spilling over into America."

Parsley leaned forward in his chair and said, "Cameron, there are procedures for matters of this kind. We do not have the resources required to deal with an assassin on the loose. State must be brought into this."

"You summon State, Parsley, what you'll get is the FBI."

"This is not Ulster, Brigadier," Parsley rebutted. "You can't indulge your fondness for army-sponsored acts of kidnapping and murder here."

"Parsley!" Ferris-Cogan interjected. "That's enough!" He turned back to Cameron. "All right, Brigadier, obviously you have a *modus operandi* in mind. Let's hear it."

"Yes, sir. To review certain points of fact. First, Janus is an officer of a secret terrorist army with which Great Britain is at war. Therefore, counterterrorist procedure, even involving apparently extralegal methods, is fully appropriate. Second, the procedures of American criminal justice, hypnotized as they are by civil libertarianism, are incapable of either preventing terrorist activity or keeping counterterrorist planning secret. Therefore, we should not inform local authority unless and until it is absolutely necessary to do so. If possible, we should apprehend Janus and deliver him surreptitiously to the queen's justice. Third, Intelligence suggests the likelihood of 'high intensity operation,' a technical phrase reserved for serious military activity. Therefore, we must assume that Janus has a further mission beyond the killing of one IRA turncoat. Fourth, the targets of potential political and military significance for the IRA in Washington include: one, the British Trade Board on K Street, Northwest; two, the BOAC U.S. head office in the Seagram Building; three, Barclay's at L'Enfant Plaza; four, British American Petroleum on Capitol Hill; five, the Commonwealth Culture Institute at — "

"For God's sake, Cameron," Ferris-Cogan interrupted with the impatient gestures of a waving hand and a shaking head, "how do you know the man isn't in New York by now? Maybe he's after our U.N. consulate. There are a hundred possibilities. We can't guard them all."

"Which," Parsley interjected, "is why we must inform State and the FBI."

"If I may finish what I was saying, sir," Cameron continued unflapped. "I was merely outlining the obvious potential targets for terrorist activity. Some security precautions must be taken locally and in New York. But I have one final and separate point to make."

"Make it." The ambassador was losing patience.

"In my judgment, there is only one operation of sufficient, as we say, intensity, to warrant Janus's presence in this city."

"What is it?" Ferris-Cogan demanded sternly, but the tremor, audible now, ominous, was back in his voice.

"An assassination. Possibly a political kidnapping."

"Of whom?"

"Of yourself, sir."

"How did you sleep, darling?"

"Oh, Aunt Nell, I slept wonderfully."

"Look here, it's going to be a wonderful day." Mrs. Tierney was standing by the window in the apartment living room. Bridgit got up from the large double bed that had folded out of the sofa. She wore a gray, floor-length nightgown that was utterly lacking in frills. She stepped to the window and looked out on the clean, broad avenue, the buildings across the way, the tops of the trees beyond. It *was* lovely. The sky was crisp and blue. The sun was very bright, though, since it was still below the buildings opposite, she couldn't locate it exactly. She could even hear birds chirping.

"It's going to be lovely indeed, Aunt Nell."

"Well, it's only fitting. God wouldn't want His Honor's day to be ruined by bad weather, now would he?"

"Indeed not."

Mrs. Tierney turned and moved around Bridgit's bed toward the kitchen. Bridgit noticed that her limp was considerably more pronounced than it had been the evening before.

"Aunt Nell?" She didn't know quite how to ask it.

"Yes, darling?"

"Is your . . . leg . . . worse?"

"In the mornings. It takes some doing to get the blood flowing properly. My blood sleeps later than I do, dearie."

The older woman was laughing to herself then, and Bridgit took comfort from the ease with which she carried her pain.

Mrs. Tierney said, moving to the kitchen, "The bathroom's all yours, darling. I'll have your breakfast ready when you come out."

"Don't go to any trouble, Aunt Nell."

"And why shouldn't I?"

"Well . . . all right." Bridgit blushed. Her aunt was so patently fond of her that she was nearly as embarrassed as delighted.

Bridgit withdrew the flowered canvas suitcase from its place under the bed and opened it. She took out her toothbrush and her comb, went into the bathroom, closed the door, and stood before the mirror.

She leaned across the sink and looked at her face carefully, running her fingers along her right cheek because the first lines of age were concentrated there. Bridgit made a habit in front of mirrors of looking at her facial lines, watching them, trying to see them grow. She couldn't.

She put the fingers of both hands in her hair and rustled it vigorously, shaking out the contours of sleep. She should let it grow, she thought, and maybe dye it. Her hair was a dull but authentic brown. When she was a child it had been auburn, nearly red. She had thought it would always be pretty, but it wasn't. Bridgit knew that her nondescript hair was the one feature that kept her from being a beautiful woman. She wondered if her aunt's hairdresser could fit her in that morning. Maybe he could make it red again. Not flaming. Not obvious. Red highlights, perhaps. A shade of auburn.

"Oh, such tribute to vanity!" she said to herself, aloud, still stroking her hair, letting her hand fall to the back of her neck and stroke her flesh.

She remembered Peter, tried to think of his touching her neck there — her long neck; it was what made her pretty — but he never had, not that she could recall. So much about him had faded with the years, so much about him gone like color from her all too ordinary life.

When Bridgit had washed and dressed and joined her aunt

in the small kitchen, she said, "Aunt Nell, do you suppose your hairdresser would have time for me?"

"What, Bea, this morning?"

"Yes."

"I don't know, darling. We could ask her."

"Her?"

"Yes. Annette's her name."

"I thought hairdressers in America were men."

"Some of them are, dearie, but they tend to be, you know . . ."

"Queer."

"Yes. They make me nervous. Annette's a wonderful hairdresser, though you'd never know it from the look of me now. But later you'll see. What were you thinking of having done?"

"A rinse, perhaps. Something to bring out the red."

"You did turn darker, didn't you? As a little girl you had the reddest hair in the family."

"Yes."

"I think a rinse would be lovely. You're a very pretty girl, Bea."

"You know I'm not, Aunt Nell."

Mrs. Tierney looked at her. Was it modesty, or did she really not know?

"I know nothing of the kind."

"Well, *you're* kind to say it."

"How do you like your eggs? Where is that pan?"

"Any way. Whatever's easy."

"It's all easy. Scrambled?"

"Lovely."

"Bea, do you have a fella?"

"No, I don't, Aunt Nell."

"You ought to have a fella, darling."

"Easier said than done, Aunt Nell. Where are the plates?"

"In the cupboard there. And silver here."

"Right. I'll get these napkins."

Bridgit set the table in the other room, then returned to the kitchen and watched her aunt in silence for some moments.

As Mrs. Tierney dished the eggs and bacon onto the plates, Bridgit said, "Aunt Nell, you never married after Uncle Mike died."

"No, Bea. I was about your age. But I wasn't alone. I had Johnny."

"Yes. Well, you were lucky."

Mrs. Tierney put her pan down on the stove and looked quickly at her niece. The pain and sorrow and deep loneliness that she saw in Bridgit's eyes caught her by surprise. Suddenly, the old woman moved to the younger and took her into the ancient embrace.

But Bridgit stiffened instantly, held back, was afraid of being stifled by her aunt, smothered in pity.

"I'm all right, Aunt Nell, really."

Bridgit stepped back and out of Mrs. Tierney's arms. She was feeling the resentment that her own mother often sparked in her, the anger at the overwhelming arms that would hold her and imprison her and keep her the pitiful young widow for whom everyone would feel sorry.

"Darling," Mrs. Tierney said with perfect tenderness, "you don't seem all right."

"But I am, Aunt Nell."

"You seem sad and distant."

"I'm tired of people feeling sorry for me."

"I don't feel sorry for you, Bea. Not a bit. Don't you know by now the difference between love and pity?"

Bridgit moved away from her aunt, into the other room, where she circled the small table to the chair in which she had sat the night before. She took her place as Mrs. Tierney put the food on the table and began to eat the eggs and bacon in silence. Mrs. Tierney went back to the kitchen and came out carrying an electric coffeepot.

"Coffee, Bea?"

"Yes, please."

The older woman poured coffee into Bridgit's cup and then into her own. She returned to the kitchen, then to the table again. She sat down and she too began to eat in silence. They ate in misery.

Bridgit immediately felt waves of remorse. The old woman was simply being kind to her, she thought, and she had gone stone cold at her touch. Had her life come to that? Was she so pathetic to herself that she mistook common gestures of affection for pity? Was she so consumed with sorrow and loneliness that she had become incapable of the smallest delight in herself? Bridgit ate quickly, efficiently, trying to focus her attention, her energy, on the movements of her hands. But it was impossible to fend off the panic that closed in on her, tightening like a noose around her neck.

Mrs. Tierney wanted to weep, but gave no sign that she felt that way. Her hurt feelings, her sense of failure at having done the wrong thing, her sudden worry about the emotional health of her beloved niece, all went into hiding behind the curtain of neutral good humor that had fallen instantly across her face. She ate slowly, politely. She had the habit, perfected over a lifetime, of taking refuge in manners. She cut the scrambled eggs with a knife. She placed her left hand in her lap as she brought a dainty morsel to her mouth. She chewed the bacon elaborately. She touched her napkin to her lips before sipping her coffee.

The noise of silverware against china was deafening. Bridgit felt that if someone didn't speak she would scream.

"Aunt Nell?"

"Yes, dear?"

"I'm sorry."

"Darling, it's not a matter for being sorry."

"It is. I was rude."

"I was prying. I shouldn't have asked about a fella. It's none of my business."

"That's not why I was upset. It has nothing to do with men."

"Why you're upset is your affair, darling. But you said you didn't want me feeling sorry for you. I don't. You've your youth, your health, your mind, your looks, and the fondness of your family. How you put it all to use — or how you don't — is up to you. I think, if there's anyone feeling sorry for you, Bea, it's yourself."

"Aunt Nell, back home I'm everyone's idea of a Greek tragedy: the young bride whose groom is blown to smithereens; the dull bookkeeper who spends her days in musty corners, nights in a dreary flat with the shades drawn. I'm the woman the children point at, the woman the old ladies are kind to, the woman the men look twice at but never presume to call."

"It's what you think of yourself that matters, Bea. The children and us old ladies and the young gentlemen all learn to look at you from how you look at yourself."

"I know that. And I'm trying to change. I've been *my own* idea of a Greek tradegy, as if I were Mrs. Onassis, but without any money. The part of me that's trying to break out of the gloom is what brought me here, though I was only half-invited."

"You couldn't be more wanted."

"I know."

"And not just by me. By Johnny. He's very fond of you."

"I know, Aunt Nell. And I am of him. And . . ." Here Bridgit hesitated, searching for the right way to say what she felt. "Even though he's a priest and my cousin, John makes me feel . . . well . . . attractive. Do you know what I mean?"

"I do, Bea. John is every inch a man, no matter what else he is. And he looks at you with love."

"Well, both of you put me in touch with feelings I haven't had in a while."

"Good ones, I hope."

"Very good." She smiled at last. "Like the wonderful moment of waking up this morning and saying to myself, 'By God, Bridgit Connor, you're in America!' I mean, I did it, Aunt Nell, on a whim, an impulse. I went against all the stuffiness and caution and need for planning that had been taking over my life. I went against it all and just came. Three months ago I made reservations for this week at the strand in Port Rush, and I up and canceled them. I came, Aunt Nell, and I'm so glad."

"Oh, Bea, good, good."

"And I would truly love to get my hair done if your Annette could fit me in."

"Maybe she can. We'll ask."

"I hope so, Aunt Nell. I think it's time I took my place once more among the redheads of the world!"

John Tierney lay in bed staring at the crack in the ceiling. In his dream he had lost control of himself in a way that had so frightened him that he woke with a start.

He had been playing basketball with a bunch of black kids who had no faces. They were all very fast, but he was very slow. Still, at one point, he had stolen the ball from his opponent and had begun his dash downcourt for the far basket.

But the faster he ran the more distance did he seem to have to cover. It was as if the basket receded at his approach. It actually seemed to back away from him. He dribbled and dribbled, ran and ran, faster and faster, until the ball was bouncing wildly under his hand, until his legs were churning like engines. Finally, the basket stopped moving away. He began his drive, cutting at an angle in from the top of the key, a clean shot at the hoop.

But just as he left the ground for his lay-up, someone appeared out of nowhere to slap the ball away. A perfect block! Tierney came down in a rage, turned on his opponent in what suddenly seemed like slow motion, and began the long swing of his arm that came back to him from somewhere in the dark past. His right hand was stretched stiff and nearly touching his left ear. Slowly and certainly it moved across his face and away, as his elbow straightened and the muscles in his forearm contracted. His eyes were fixed on the promontory of the thorax above the Adam's apple of his enemy's throat. He was throwing the side of his hand at it, as he had been trained to do. Once he took aim and set himself, he never missed. Slowly, certainly the blade his hand had become flew toward its target, the pale flesh of a person's neck.

Tierney struck. The bony edge of his rigid hand smashed

the thyroid cartilage of his enemy through the wall of her windpipe, killing her instantly. It was Roberta Winston. Her head rolled off her shoulders. He woke up.

He lay still, concentrating on the crack in the ceiling. He was breathing hard. Where did that come from? he wondered. Then he thought of that morning's paper and the story it would carry about him. The story by Roberta Winston.

He rolled his body toward the clock: seven minutes to eight. He rolled the other way, flipping the blankets off his body. He swung his legs over the edge of the bed and sat up. He didn't have much time — he had the 8:15 mass — but he sat there for a moment, elbows on his knees, looking down at his feet.

"All right, come on, get up!" It was an order he gave to himself. Tierney stood and went to the window. He looked out at the roofs of the buildings that backed away from the cathedral. The sun was bright. It was going to be another nice day. His eyes drifted down to the asphalt lot directly below his third-floor window. It was the lot on which he had been playing basketball the evening before and, presumably, in his dream. He looked at the spot on the edge of the court where he had exchanged words with the *Post* reporter. He thought of going downstairs to get the paper to see what she had written, decided against it, and moved instead to the bathroom.

By the time he arrived at the sacristy at twelve minutes past eight he was shaved, dressed, and composed. He had put the dream out of his mind. He wasn't thinking about the newspaper or the trial of the nun or his own part in the horror of Vietnam as it wound down like a worn-out machine.

He was thinking about the mass. He filled the cruets with wine and water, dressed the chalice with its square white veil, found the tabernacle key, and carried them all deftly out into the sanctuary and to the altar. Back in the sacristy, he flicked the appointed switches that threw on the lights over the body of the church. He donned his amice, alb, cincture, and chasuble, saying as he did so the prayers for vesting.

When he was ready he stood before the full-length mirror

on the back of the closet door. The white underrobe fell in neat folds to the tops of his shoes. He adjusted the raw silk chasuble so that it sat squarely on his shoulders and draped elegantly to his knees. He turned sideways and saw that the vestments were perfect from behind.

And then he caught his own eyes in the mirror: no hint of the fear with which he had wakened. He was himself again, John Tierney, priest, preacher, celebrant. He was about to call down God once more. He was ready.

He turned and walked through the door, tugging as he went, on the thin cord that rang the bell that announced the beginning of mass. It was 8:15 exactly.

Janus had no appetite for breakfast. She was preoccupied with the events of the day ahead. There were still uncertainties to be resolved, questions to be answered, checking to be done. She would review her planning and finalize routes for access and escape. Her mind was whirring.

But there was another reason she wasn't eating much. On mornings after nights like the one just past she was always slightly nauseated. Her stomach churned with the sour, curdled fears of the damned.

She didn't know why: whether it was the killing that made her feel that way. Or the sex.

Nancy Ferris-Cogan was reading the paper. She was wrapped in a blue velour robe, sitting alone in the breakfast room off the kitchen in the ambassador's quarters. Her coffee was steaming and untouched.

She had read the story about the nun. Now she was reading for the third time the last half of the boxed columns entitled "Person in the News." It was a background profile of John Tierney, presented in a format the *Post* had only recently copied from *The New York Times*.

Father Tierney served as a member of the Special Forces in Vietnam from 1962 to 1964 where he was commander of the Military Advisory Assistance Group headquartered at Pleiku in the Central Highlands, a city which fell last month in the first wave of the current North Vietnamese offensive. According to the Army Public Records Office at the Pentagon, Father Tierney was awarded the Distingished Service Medal in 1963 for "valorous conduct before the enemy."

The citation which accompanies Father Tierney's medal reads in part: "Captain Tierney was responsible for saving the lives of seven men in his commnd when, having been attacked unawares by a superior number of NLF militia, and two of his men having been killed, and having been disarmed himself, he did at grave personal risk engage a number of armed enemy soldiers in combat. Captain Tierney single-handedly and without arms routed the assault force, killing four of their number in an exceptional effort of courage and military skill above and beyond that required by duty."

When asked about his Vietnam experience, Father Tierney had no comment. But Peter B. Hatcher, a Washington garage-owner and former member of Tierney's commando squad, remembered the officer-turned-priest when contacted by the *Washington Post* yesterday. "A very hard man," Hatcher said of the priest. "He was bigger and faster and better at it than anyone." When the *Post* asked Hatcher what Tierney was better at, he replied, "Unarmed combat. It was a different war then. It was very personal. We often had to be quiet, couldn't shoot you know? Tierney was the only man in the unit who could do it with either hand. Deadly hands. 'If it moves,' he used to say, 'hit it!' And then he'd say, 'If you hit it, kill it.'"

When asked how many men Tierney had killed, Hatcher said that he couldn't remember.

Nancy put the paper down.

She gathered the skirt of her robe around her legs. There

was a chill in the room. When she picked up her cup and sipped her coffee, it was cold.

"Your Eminence, the ambassador is here."

"Thank you, Dora. Show him in."

Cardinal O'Brien stood up, adjusted his red skullcap, tugged once at his broad cincture, and walked around his desk. By the time the door opened, he was halfway across his office, moving to welcome his visitors.

When the embassy had called an hour before, he had canceled his weekly meeting with the Archdiocesan Personnel Board. He couldn't quite imagine why the ambassador wanted to meet with him on such short notice. "Urgent," the embassy had said. The cardinal assumed the ambassador wanted to discuss the investiture, but it hardly seemed urgent that they do so. Tierney had been handling the preparations. Everything should have been in order.

"Good morning, Sir Alisdair." As the cardinal warmly reached out toward the ambassador, he noted the man's elegant but somber clothing: dark blue suit, Oxford shirt, the maroon and blue rep tie. The cardinal thought him a stunningly handsome man. Ferris-Cogan's trim, articulate posture conveyed the sense of self-assurance and authority that O'Brien associated with successful diplomats and politicians. The ambassador had the combined gifts of male beauty and physical power. He was, the cardinal thought as he went to him, like Kennedy. Kennedy was the measure against whom Cardinal O'Brien held every public figure, against whom he found almost all of them wanting. But not Ferris-Cogan.

Dora was standing by the door, holding it open. Two other men followed the ambassador into the office.

"Your Eminence." Sir Alisdair Ferris-Cogan took Justin Cardinal O'Brien's hand and, with easy grace, fell to one knee, bowed over the episcopal ring, and kissed it. For the diplomat it was like greeting the queen. He relished the prescribed and defined etiquette of royalty, whether of the court or of the church. As his knee touched the carpet and his back arched carefully over the cardinal's hand in the precise posture of obeisance, Ferris-Cogan was conscious of the ancient tradition of the gesture. By such rubrics human beings claimed their station in, and articulated their conviction about, a world in which everything, however minor, was jealous of its meaning. As the Englishman brushed his lip against the green jewel it was as if he were kissing his own past, the pride of it, the pain. As long as there was this ring to kiss, the gesture seemed to say, the crazed and bloody mind that would curse what was left of God would not have its way.

Cardinal O'Brien had his left hand on the ambassador's shoulder, was pressing it affectionately, receiving the man's perfect enactment of the ritual greeting with modest grace of his own. O'Brien knew that it was not to himself as a man that Ferris-Cogan knelt, but to the symbol that the Church had made out of the clay of his own life. It was a symbol of God's faithful love for his people. The cardinal withdrew his right hand from the diplomat's grasp and, enacting his own ritual, made as if to lift him to his feet. Ferris-Cogan rose as gracefully as he had knelt.

"Your Eminence," the ambassador repeated, "allow me to introduce" — Ferris-Cogan turned toward the two men who accompanied him — "Brigadier Francis Cameron of Her Majesty's Special Guard."

Cameron stepped forward formally, took the cardinal's hand, and imitated Ferris-Cogan's greeting, kneeling easily, kissing the ring and rising with the studied manner of one who knew the value of etiquette. But Cameron kissed the cardinal's ring with exactly the same hollow show that would mark his salute of a general officer in a rival army.

"And," Ferris-Cogan was saying, "Mr. Reginald Parsley of my personal staff."

Parsley was carrying a thin leather valise, which he shifted to his left hand. He bent over the cardinal's hand awkwardly, not quite genuflecting, not quite knowing what to do. The cardinal received his embarrassed gesture as warmly as he had the more precise and confident greetings of the other men.

"Please, come in, gentlemen," Cardinal O'Brien said, ushering them toward the Catalonian refectory table and its dozen monk's chairs that sat in quiet dignity beneath the gaze of Archbishop John Carroll.

The cardinal turned back to the woman who was still standing at the door. "Dora, would you bring coffee, please?"

"Certainly, Your Eminence," she replied with practically a curtsy. She started to move off, but he stopped her with an upraised hand and turned to the three standing by the table.

"Or should it be tea?" he asked.

"Coffee would be splendid, Your Eminence. Thank you," the ambassador replied.

"I thought perhaps, since you're English . . ."

"No," Alisdair said lightly, "never in the morning. Everything in its place."

"Indeed," the cardinal said, waving Dora off. She closed the door behind her without a sound.

"Please be seated, gentlemen," the cardinal said, as he himself moved to the ancient table's head. The Englishmen pulled out their chairs and sat. Cardinal O'Brien gathered the folds of his red cassock, pulled out his own chair — unlike the others, it had carved armrests; it had been the abbot's chair — and sat. His hand shot involuntarily but discreetly down to his left knee, which suddenly jerked with pain. He began to rub it, soothing the ache, and continued to do so for some moments. The others did not notice.

"Your Eminence, I apologize for disrupting your schedule." Ferris-Cogan pronounced it *shed-yool* in the British manner. His tone was serious, weighty, and Cardinal O'Brien guessed at once that something unexpected had happened. His mind raced ahead, trying to imagine what was coming. He saw a picture of himself explaining to Benelli that the ceremony had to be canceled. He could hear the Italian protesting that it would be immensely embarrassing to His Holiness.

But one thing at a time: he forced himself to concentrate on what the ambassador was saying.

"To get immediately to the point, Your Eminence, we have

reason to believe that there may be an imminent terrorist assault of some kind against my person, and we are here to discuss the implications of that possibility as they bear upon the ceremony this afternoon."

"I beg your pardon, Sir Alisdair . . .?" The cardinal was shocked. He could not grasp what the man had said.

"Inconceivable as it may seem," Ferris-Cogan repeated, "there is a real possibility that an IRA terrorist, in all probability acting alone, will soon attempt either to kidnap or assassinate me. Today's investitute is the only public function I am scheduled to attend outside the embassy compound over the next three days. Considering the risks involved, I did not want either to cancel the ceremony or to proceed with it without frankly discussing the matter with you."

"I appreciate that, Ambassador." The cardinal's heart was pounding. His knee was throbbing more than ever. But he had regained his even tone and he spoke calmly, deliberately. "Of course, I am prepared to see that whatever you decide will be implemented from our end faultlessly."

At that, there was a faint knock on the door. O'Brien said to the men, "That will be the coffee." Then to the door he said, "Yes, come in, please."

Dora entered the office carrying a tray laden with a sterling Victorian coffeepot, creamer, sugar bowl, silver spoons, and four Wedgwood cups and saucers. She placed it without speaking at the vacant foot of the table.

As Dora poured and served the coffee, Cardinal O'Brien said, "Sir Alisdair, it occurs to me that Father Tierney might appropriately participate in this conversation."

"By all means, Your Eminence. I intended to ask you if you thought his joining us would be in order."

"Yes. He might be useful."

The secretary was about to leave. Cardinal O'Brien caught her eye and said, "Dora, ask Father Tierney to step in here, please."

"Yes, Your Eminence," she said, leaving the office, once more closing the door without a sound.

A silence fell over the table. Cameron stirred sugar into his coffee, swirling the spoon without touching it to the china. Parsley had taken a blank notepad from his valise and was busily straightening it against the edge of the table and aligning a gold Cross pen alongside it, prepared to take notes.

Ferris-Cogan said finally, "We might wait then, before proceeding, for Father Tierney's arrival." He spoke with the respectful but undeniable authority of a man who found himself presiding at another's table.

"Yes," the cardinal said, falling silent.

They waited. No one spoke. There was the noise of the coffee. Cameron could hear the low hum of a furnace pumping warm air. Parsley stared at the notepad. Ordinarily Ferris-Cogan would have made easy conversation, but now even the suspicion of a fit subject eluded him. There was an overt tension in the room, a curious, troubled anticipation. The cardinal noted it.

At last, a knock on the door.

"Come in, please," the cardinal called. Tierney opened the door and entered. Surprise registered visibly on his face when he saw the ambassador and the two other Englishmen at the table with the cardinal.

"Good morning, Your Eminence," he said, crossing to the table. Without waiting for an explanation of their presence, he greeted each of the men as they stood. "Good morning, Ambassador," he said, then nodded at Parsley and Cameron, whom he remembered from the parking lot.

Tierney reached across the table to shake hands with the ambassador, and then all of the men resumed their seats. Tierney took one of the vacant chairs on the outside of the table, not presuming to sit opposite the cardinal at the foot.

"Coffee, Father?" the cardinal asked. Tierney noted that there were no remaining cups: another would have to be fetched.

"No thank you, Cardinal."

"Well, we were just discussing a matter that has to do with the ceremony this afternoon. Sir Alisdair?"

"Yes. Father, I was just explaining to His Eminence that a

potentially troublesome factor has arisen quite suddenly. As you may know, Mr. Parsley is chief of security at the embassy, and Brigadier Cameron is military attaché." Ferris-Cogan was speaking without a hint of feeling.

"We know without question that a dangerous, indeed, notorious, IRA terrorist arrived in Washington yesterday. Last night he murdered an informant for a rival IRA faction. Presumably he is still at large in this city. We are here because of the distinct possibility, if not likelihood, that he intends to disrupt the cathedral ceremony this evening."

"For what purpose?" Tierney's tone betrayed his surprise, his shock, the difficulty with which he was taking in the ambassador's dispassionate report. What the Englishman was saying seemed so dramatic, so impossible, so unreal. And Sir Alisdair himself seemed to Tierney to be strangely vacant of emotion.

"For the purpose," Ferris-Cogan said coolly, as if to underline Tierney's impression, "of either kidnapping or assassinating me."

"Oh my God! You can't be serious!"

"I couldn't be more serious, Father."

"But why?"

Ferris-Cogan turned toward Cameron. "Brigadier?"

"Yes, sir." Cameron had been sitting perfectly upright in his chair. As he began to speak he drew himself even straighter. He spoke with the precision and confidence of an experienced officer briefing his seniors. His hands were folded in front of him on the table. They did not move.

"The terrorist is known by the code name Janus. He is a skilled assassin, having personally killed at least four men and, after last night presumably, five. The man he killed was being hidden by Official partisans associated with a local pub called Shannon's. We know also that he has participated in wide bombing activity, including the bombing of Parliament in 1973.

"General intelligence leads us to believe that the Provisional Wing of the Republican army is about to launch a major new terrorist campaign directed primarily against the persons of senior government officials of the United Kingdom. That general assessment of current Provisional strategy, coupled with particular intelligence about the grave nature of Janus's mission in the United States, leads us to the conclusion that the most likely and dramatic assault on the symbolic authority of the Crown will be an assault on the ambassador."

"Excuse me, please," Tierney interrupted.

Cameron stopped speaking as if ordered to, but he fixed his harshest glare on the priest, as if rebuking his junior.

Tierney was made instantly uncomfortable by Cameron's stare, and he thought for a moment that questions were out of order. But the priest went on anyway. "The Provisionals, as I understand it, tend to be almost fanatically committed to their Catholicism, unlike the Officials, who tend to be Marxist in orientation. Isn't that so?"

"Yes." Cameron's response couldn't have been more brusque.

"Wouldn't that make an assault against Sir Alisdair most unlikely, since he, alone of the senior officials of Britain, is a Roman Catholic?"

"No, Father, it wouldn't. In point of fact, the reverse is true. If you could assume the mind-set of a Provisional for a moment — admittedly difficult to do, but essential if one is to understand this enemy — ask yourself this question: who would be the most enraging public figure of a government with which you were at war? Why, precisely the one who shared your most precious identity, the very identity you were claiming to protect *against* that government with your vicious acts of killing and maiming. From your point of view . . ."

As Cameron said this he spoke with such undisguised venom that Tierney wondered if the brigadier remembered that he was speaking hypothetically, that he, Tierney, was not an IRA Provo.

" . . .the *Catholic* Englishman, the *Catholic* consort to the queen's husband, the *Catholic* envoy stands in the hated company of traitors. If the Provos are fanatical about their Catholicism, Father, they are even more so about what they consider to be treason."

"Brigadier!"

It was Ferris-Cogan who interrupted him now. He was looking at the attaché sternly, displeased. "We must not under-
estimate the sophistication of the Provisionals. We make a
serious mistake if we assume that they are simply ideologues
blinded by fanaticism. Let me explain the likely rationale for
this turn of events, but I must do so in the strictest of confidence."

Ferris-Cogan paused. He let his eyes drift around the table,
collecting the full attention of each man.

The cardinal interjected, "Sir Alisdair, Father Tierney and I
know the meaning of confidence."

"Indeed, Your Eminence. Indeed so. Therefore, let me explain. In addition to the authentic religious observance involved in the ceremony of investitute, there is a political
significance to my having been so honored by Pope Paul."

The ambassador assumed once more the air of a classroom
professor. In part, it was a pose in which he took refuge from
the dread that was building inside him. And, in part, he pre-
sumed to instruct the others now because he understood exactly
what the Provisionals were up to.

"Let me review, first of all, a point of history in the British
government's recent attempt to find a solution to the strife in
Northern Ireland. The chief obstacle to reconciliation in that
province is the inability of local government to maintain the
confidence of both of the two antagonistic populations. Therefore, the Northern Ireland Parliament was suspended by London in 'seventy-three, and direct rule was imposed under a
secretary of state. That effort failed because, while the bulk
of the Loyalist population had confidence in London's admin-
istration, the Catholics were suspicious.

"Last year Prime Minister Wilson abandoned the effort at
direct rule, and Parliament created a single-chamber Assembly
to replace the old two-chamber Protestant-dominated Stor-
mont. It was designed to ensure Catholics a share of political
power. But because the Loyalists were suspicious, the one-
chamber Assembly has never worked, and in all likelihood it
will vote itself out of existence at its session early next month.

Wilson is even now preparing to recommend at that point the reinstatement of direct rule under a secretary of state.

"But with a difference: the new secretary of state will be a Catholic. Wilson hopes both groups will have confidence in him. Obviously, I am to be the new secretary. When the prime minister had an audience with Pope Paul six weeks ago, he discussed the plan with him. His Holiness at that time was good enough, and astute enough, to suggest that my effectiveness among my Catholic brethren might be enhanced by the honor of the Order of Saint Gregory the Great. Prime Minister Wilson agreed, and the process was set in motion that will culminate today. Unfortunately that process, involving as it does a variety of offices, also made breaches in normal secrecy inevitable, and we must assume that the prime minister's plan is known outside of Whitehall.

"Since the extremists on the Catholic side abhor above all the connection with London, they have ample reason to try to derail this new effort to win the support of the Catholic population. At this point in history, an attack on myself by the Provisionals makes excellent political sense."

Ferris-Cogan fell silent. Parsley looked up from the notepad on which he had been writing furiously. Cameron coughed. The cardinal clasped and unclasped his hands on the table in front of him.

Finally, Tierney spoke. "And an attack on you during the ceremony itself would be a stunning repudiation of what the Provos surely regard as an English attempt to co-opt Catholic sensibilities."

"Exactly," Ferris-Cogan replied.

"And in a perverse way," the priest said, "it would show a pretty good sense of ritual."

"Yes. Ironically enough, a *Catholic* sense of ritual." The ambassador paused. "Which means, of course, that we are not talking about kidnapping. We are talking about a — in liturgical language — bloody sacrifice."

"Hence," Brigadier Cameron interjected, "Janus, their best man."

Ferris-Cogan nodded, his controlled aloofness intact.

"Well, Sir Alisdair," Cardinal O'Brien said, stifling a spasm in his voice, "for the sake of your well-being, we must cancel the ceremony." Even as he spoke, the cardinal saw again a picture of himself trying to explain the cancelation to Benelli.

"Your Eminence," the ambassador replied slowly, "I am here to discuss this with you because in the course of such events there are dangers for others. You have a right to know what is possible. As for my own position, however, I believe it is more important than ever that the ceremony be held as scheduled. There is no tradition, either among my countrymen or among members of my family, that would encourage us to shrink from danger.

"But neither am I a fool. Brigadier Cameron and Mr. Parsley assure me that sufficient security precautions can be taken to reduce the risk to myself and to all bystanders to a level of reasonable acceptability. If you assent to my proposal that we proceed as planned, they are prepared to outline procedures that should protect the well-being of everyone in the cathedral."

"Sir Alisdair," the cardinal began, then hesitated before going on, trouble in his voice. "Are you asking me to make the decision?"

"Your Eminence, I am prepared to bow to your authority in this." Ferris-Cogan said this somberly, with a slight nod of his head. It was the first time he'd ever knowingly lied to a man of God.

"It is hardly a decision for which I feel prepared," O'Brien said, feeling the old terror, not of physical harm but of making a bad mistake. "For all our conflicts, the Church is a tame and not particularly dangerous place."

"Today that may not be so," Ferris-Cogan said, the barest hint of condescension in his voice.

The cardinal looked across at Tierney. Help me, his eyes said. Tierney returned his look blankly.

"John, what do you think?" The old man's use of his first name nudged Tierney. He felt a rush of sympathy.

"Sir Alisdair," he said, turning to Ferris-Cogan, "what is lost if the ceremony is canceled.?"

"Father, we have a rare opportunity to let the terrorists know that their threats won't stop us from doing what is right. Frankly, I'm afraid that if we appear to cower behind locked doors, we will be feeding their appetite for blood. There appear to be risks in whatever we do."

"It's one thing for us to accept those risks for ourselves, Ambassador . . ." Tierney paused and glanced at the cardinal, who was writhing with anxiety. "It's quite another to make a decision that involves grave risks for others."

"Yes. But isn't that exactly the burden of responsibility?"

"Perhaps so."

"Look," the ambassador said a bit impatiently, "we learned a lesson in the Blitz. If somebody bombs your house, you'd better risk putting out the fire on the roof before you run to the basement. Otherwise you won't be safe down there for long."

"I see your point," Tierney said.

Brigadier Cameron sat forward then, looking at the ambassador. "May I interject something, sir?"

"Certainly."

"It is my conviction," Cameron said to the clergymen, "that we will not only succeed in assuring the safety of those who attend this ceremony, but also, if Janus does attempt to disrupt the ceremony, we will seize him. We will *have* him, and such is his status that we will have delivered an extraordinary blow to the morale and terrorist capability of the IRA. We are therefore not only talking about preventing bloodshed today, but about reducing it indefinitely. We have been offered a rare opportunity, since the man does not know that we will be ready for him. The chief weapon of terror is surprise, and for once the weight of surprise is tilted in our direction. If we proceed with the cermony as planned, the war in Ireland will be, I assure you, shortened considerably."

Tierney had no argument. Why should the Church be exempt fom the madness? What should he say to the ambassador:

"Go get assassinated somewhere else"? What should he say to Cameron: "Go trap your fugitive in a ball park, in a theater, on an airplane"? No. There was no question of choice now. The cathedral had already been chosen, if not simply by the terrorist, then by the fates or by God. Tierney looked over at the cardinal. "I think we should do it, Your Eminence."

O'Brien stood up abruptly. "One moment, please," he said, turning from them and walking across the oriental past his desk to the window. He stood with his back to the room, gazing at the new leaves on his oak. He wanted a night with his decision, to wrestle with it the way he wrestled with all his problems. Then he would wake up at dawn and know what to do. The leaves are wild, he thought. And they could care less. He touched his hand to the bridge of his nose. "Oh, God," he began softly, but he didn't complete the prayer. Not in words. A picture flashed before him of a crowd of people screaming, bleeding, trying to escape. He saw the executioner drawing his sword in *The Martydom of Saint Matthew*. He knew that no matter what he decided, his cathedral would never be the same. He was fearful and sad. The pain was loose in his leg like a brood of furies. Finally, he knew what he would do. As he turned to face the room and the men, he offered his decision to God Almighty.

"Yes," he announced. "We should proceed with the ceremony as scheduled."

Reg Parsley noted the cardinal's words on his pad of paper, then lifted the Cross pen off its surface an inch and waited.

Brigadier Cameron sat impassively, stiff, ready. He did not react to the cardinal's words.

John Tierney saw in the cardinal a capacity for fright, a palpable weakness, he would never have guessed was there, and he felt an immense pity for him. Tierney's mouth was set. He pressed his hands together, as in isometrics. He was in.

"Fine," Ferris-Cogan said, standing. "Cameron, I want you to brief Father Tierney on security arrangements."

"Sir!" Cameron said briskly. Parsley inserted his notepad into the valise and stood.

Ferris-Cogan walked across the room to the cardinal, who, by then, was standing at his desk.

"Your Eminence . . ." he began. There was a deliberate note of the respect equals have for each other. The ambassador intended to warmly reinforce the old man's resolve. But before he could, O'Brien interrupted him.

"Sir Alisdair," the cardinal said emotionally, his eyes glistening, "I have been entrusted with a gift for you from His Holiness. Considering the . . . circumstances, I'm sure he would want me to convey it to you now."

Ferris-Cogan was surprised. The muscles behind his eyes tightened, and he had an impulse to protest. The cardinal was lifting from his desk a rectangular cardboard package, flat, eighteen inches long, twelve inches wide. It had been lying by the telephone. O'Brien opened one end and withdrew a framed and matted parchment that was covered with careful, cursive minuscule.

"I had intended to present this at the reception, but perhaps now is a more propitious time."

"Indeed? Your Eminence, I hardly expected . . ."

But before Ferris-Cogan completed the sentence, the cardinal had unceremoniously handed the neatly framed parchment to him. "Sir Alisdair, this is a page from a personal letter written by Pope Paul the *Third* in 1534. His Holiness, Paul the Sixth, would like you to have it as a token . . ." Cardinal O'Brien had to drop his eyes from the ambassador's face. He looked at the parchment. His own voice had threatened to break when he saw an involuntary tremble around the diplomat's mouth.

Ferris-Cogan's eyes rushed up and down the page. It had the venerable brown hue of an ancient manuscript, but it was clean and perfectly preserved. It was mounted under sealed, nonreflecting glass, edged with white matting, and framed in a tasteful, inch-thick wormwood.

The cardinal continued: "The letter of which this is a fragment was addressed to Sir Thomas More . . . *Saint* Thomas More . . ."

There was a gasp, it seemed almost of pain, from the ambassador. O'Brien could not look at him, but rushed on. "It was a letter of gratitude and affection to More at the time of his conflict with Henry the Eighth. The letter remained in the archives of the Vatican, having never been dispatched, since Saint Thomas was . . . of course . . . imprisoned in the Tower . . . and soon to be . . ."

The panic in Ferris-Cogan was acute. At that moment, after the wrenching effort to maintain his poise and to let nothing of terror in or out, an emotional torrent was loosed within him. Thomas More was *dead!* They *killed* him! Who the bloody hell have you been *kidding?* This is *death* you are dealing with! Your *own* death!

To his horror Ferris-Cogan could feel his legs beginning to quiver at the knees. He felt a spasm in his bowels. He felt tears forming in his eyes, which he crushed closed in an effort to stop them. *This will not happen! You will not feel any of this!*

"Your Eminence, I'm . . . honored . . ." The act of speaking stifled the rush of panic. He would not faint, but his hands were visibly trembling and the parchment was unsteady. Ferris-Cogan looked around at the other men. They were staring away from him, studiously, purposefully, as if aware that he was on the brink of losing his composure.

"His Holiness appreciates all that you've done for the Church."

"I've done nothing . . . to merit this . . . relic . . ."

Ferris-Cogan could feel his emotions ebbing. He had withstood the seizure, though still he felt a bit lightheaded and would have preferred to sit. He wanted to be alone. He looked at the cardinal. The old man had surprised him with a simple act of affection, and on the very pope's behalf. That expression of regard, together with the associations More had for him, had almost been his undoing. Sir Alisdair suddenly wanted to embrace the prelate, whose eyes were wet and full of worry. But he knew if he did that he would be finished altogether.

Besides, Ferris-Cogan thought, resuming his dry, ready mind, ambassadors don't embrace cardinals. If they were French and Italian, perhaps; but certainly not English and Irish-American.

Ferris-Cogan inwardly shook himself, stood up straight, smiled elegantly, and said, as if in tutorial, "Your Eminence, it is the proudest boast of my family that More once took refuge at our estate in Surrey. According to a family legend, More and my ancestor, a Cogan, coined the motto of Northumberland: 'Ever English, Ever Cartholic.' They spelled 'Catholic' with an r in those days."

"Is that so?" The cardinal's exhausted mind grasped at the trivial item as a swimmer does a log.

"Yes. Some, like the duke of Norfolk, still affect that old spelling even now."

"I didn't know that."

"Well." Ferris-Cogan's recovery was complete. "I want to say that I will prize this page not as a possession but as a trust. I shall prize it above all that I own. Thank you."

"Thanks are due His Holiness." O'Brien hadn't quite banished the crack from his voice. "It was my privilege merely to act as courier."

"Of course. I shall convey my thanks to Pope Paul forthwith. I am deeply honored. But I know that thanks are due you as well."

With that Ferris-Cogan made as if to leave. The cardinal took his arm and insisted on escorting him to the street. Parsley followed them from the office respectfully, a little to the rear.

Tierney's stomach was churning. The momentary and barely perceptible break in Ferris-Cogan's composure affected him deeply. As he looked around the room, the priest's eyes fell on Cameron. The two of them were still standing at the ancient table. Their business was not complete. They were to review now the several ways the enemy might strike.

Nerves and fluids stepped up pace within Tierney. He was suddenly conscious of the stride of his breathing. He looked at Cameron. Yes, the brigadier would know that turning of gut, the recognition of fear in the air. Yes, the brigadier gave off the faint but certain signal of total alert that makes a master technician of every animal that lives off the bloody deaths of other creatures. Tierney and Cameron alone of that group were men who had nurtured, attended to, honed the fine animal instinct to which most human beings have long since become oblivious.

Tierney was remembering. His stomach was reminding him. Cameron knew the feeling, and Tierney knew it. Cameron and Tierney knew what it was to stand opposite another man, ready to match him in strength and skill or die. A primal moment: once you have it and survive you are never the same. You have made your acquaintance with death. Since you matched strength and skill with another and won, you have made, indeed, your partnership with death.

It was the feeling Cameron lived for. Whenever he saw the blade coming toward him, he sent his own blade on its journey out and upward, into the middle of a body and then up again. Cameron was a soldier: it was that simple. Sworn to defend the peace, yet — and this was the ancient irony of the profession — only in battle was he certain that he was alive.

It had been so for Tierney once. The rush of his revved-up thinking reminded him, took him back. He could feel the energy, blood sugar, adrenaline, racing through his body, preparing his eyes to see more sharply, his muscles to explode with new strength, his ears to hear leaves hitting the ground. It was the nerve rush before combat. It was the exact opposite of panic. Wild dogs had it. Panthers and grizzlies had it. The elite corps of every army had it. And Tierney, who had it, did not want it.

How far?

That was the question in Janus's mind as she knelt in the rearmost pew of Saint Matthew's Cathedral.

How far from front to back? From the theatrical yellow arch behind the high altar to the huge, brass-plated doors of the vestibule immediately behind her? How far from the scattered points of the glowing gold candlesticks in front of Saint Joseph's statue in the right front corner to the gothic doorway halfway down the apse toward her? But that doorway seemed to lead into the adjoining chancery building. It would not do.

How far from Saint Mary's altar in the left front corner to the mid-church side entrance that cut the left wall of the cathedral in half? That doorway led to the street.

Janus was calculating distances for two reasons. First, to determine the optimum angle and position for the single shot that she would fire. Since she was using a pistol, even the highly accurate Luger, she would have to be closer to him than she would have preferred. The Luger would provide reliable accuracy up to seventy-five feet. The silencer would cut that by a third: fifty.

Her second calculations were a matter of escape. Presuming that she could squeeze the shot off while the huge organ was filling the unclothed heights of the cathedral, and presuming that she had succeeded in taking up an utterly unobtrusive position, she would have up to twenty seconds to get out of the church. Without running, she could cover up to fifty feet in that time.

She concentrated her gaze on the middle area of the left aisle near the side door that opened onto the street. Yes, there. It would be suitable. But she had to have accurate measurements.

Janus adjusted the blue scarf that covered her head. She rose, slipped into the center aisle, and slowly, devotedly, walked the length of the aisle past the point where a cross-aisle bisected the width of the cathedral and forward to the point where the center aisle ran into the stairs that led to the sanctuary.

She rested her left hand on the communion rail and genuflected. She turned to face the left wall, blessed herself and began barely to move her lips. An observer would have thought she was beginning the ancient procession prayer through the fourteen Stations of the Cross. In fact, she was counting her paces. As she moved around the cathedral, genuflecting, blessing herself and moving her lips, she was transforming the mysterious depths of Saint Matthew's into the familiar terrain on which she would meet her enemy.

There was a strange emptiness to the place. Not like the pro-cathedral in Derry, not like Westminster even. No one joined her. There was no worshipers, no tramps snoozing, no old women lighting candles, no nuns sweeping and polishing. When she was adjacent to the confessionals that were halfway between Saint Mary's altar and the gothic side entrance, Janus thought of the queue of people who would be lining the wall in the middle of the morning at the cathedral in Derry. Priests would be bustling about. Workers would be stopping by for a short visit to the Blessed Sacrament on their way home from the night shift at the textile factory. There would be, in a word, life about the place. Not this dull and hollow mustiness. This loneliness.

Janus raised her eyes toward the high altar. Something like pity filled her suddenly. Pity for God, alone and forgotten in this alien place. Abandoned by everyone except one wretched woman who had long since sacrificed her holiness, her innocence, her untroubled conscience, to the grim effort to avenge a love and reclaim a land.

Abruptly her mind took her elsewhere.

She could feel the night releasing its grip on her. There was no sound in the ditch where she was lying, waiting. She was absolutely still. She did not shift her position or flex her cramped limbs. Her clothing had been dampened by the heavy night air. She was in a ditch by Amesbury Road. She was waiting for the army truck that would trip the wire that would blow the mine. It was her first solo mission. The truck was due. She was barely breathing. Then she heard it: the wet, singing sound of tires, the creaking, the groaning over bogholes. The noises grew louder. Together they made a mournful sound. She raised her head slightly. She tensed the muscles in her buttocks. Through the mist the truck rumbled toward her, whining at the top of a gear. She held her breath. There was a strange sucking sound, and then a flash, a loud noise, and a wind that stung her face. When she looked the truck was gone. For an instant she feared that it had passed safely, and she thought she would retch. But then she heard them, deep sobbing sounds, hollow groans, a voice lost in shrieking, a chorus of agonized noises. She knew she should flee, but she lifted herself to her feet and climbed from the ditch to the road. In the gray haze she saw figures and parts of the machine. But the panting was wrong, the sounds of weeping and groaning were too high-pitched. She stepped into the midst of the wrecked bodies. They were not soldiers. They were children. It was not a truck. It was a school bus. A tiny leg lay at her feet, severed from its body. She turned away feeling — to her own surprise — nothing, the core of nothing she would carry in the center of herself from then on. And she walked slowly out of the fetid stench.

Janus tugged nervously at the knot of the silk scarf at her throat. She forced a stop to her musing. She could afford not the slightest hint of remorse, not the barest sentiment. The church was empty — all right. God was alone in his own house — all right. The damned were inheriting the earth — all right. Before the Christ comes, the innocents are slain. But that was the way God Himself had made it. He is the One, she thought, who pressed silence down on the agony of His own Son.

His silence pressed down upon her then as she thought — even as she tried not to — how far she'd come from the easy love of her benign, almighty, and heavenly Father.

How far she'd come from God.

How far she'd come.

How far.

I t was almost as if the telephone were looking at her, asking her to do it. But Nancy kept deciding not to. It was not her affair. It would be an intrusion.

She concentrated on the task of cleaning her brushes. She had finished trimming the excess canvas from the painting and had mounted it in the burnished aluminum frame she had bought the week before at Nielsen's. The finished work sat on its easel in the corner of the solarium.

Now she was busying herself in the ritual procedures of cleaning brushes, reorganizing tubes of oil, and restoring a certain order to her work space. It was the way she always dealt with the melancholy that swept over her when she completed a work. She hated to finish a painting. Much as she squirmed under the driving passion that had her in its grip while she tried to get her vision down on canvas before it faded, the days and weeks after a painting's completion always left her feeling empty, lost, caught in an immeasurable sadness. It was like mourning the death of a friend. And this time a peculiar wheezing feeling at the base of her spine made those usual feelings worse. The cluttered studio seemed like someone else's closet.

She squeezed the last drops of turpentine from the number 3. It was her favorite brush. She stooped and carefully ran the fan-shaped horsehairs over the newspaper that was spread out on the floor in front of the worktable. An old headline caught her eyes: REDS PRESS DRIVE TO TAKE XUAN LOC — FIGHTING IS FIERCE. She looked at the date of the paper: April 14, the week before. The denouement of the war in Indochina, the closing parenthesis. There were pictures of children being rushed onto a huge American transport plane, the panic in their eyes, the desperate fear, the end of their world, the beginning of what?

Nancy stood again. She put the brush down on the table and pressed her fingers to her temples and began massaging the hollows behind her eyes. "Oh God," she muttered. "Oh God."

She was trying to press away the picture of those children when the image of her own daughter's face abruptly filled her mind. It was *Melissa* with her mouth awry, shrieking, and her body misshapen and her arms reaching out grotesquely. Long-robed figures, like death-dancers from a medieval woodcut, were chasing the little girl. Were they nuns? Priests? Was that Father Tierney? *What are they doing to my little girl?* And there was Alisdair, aloof, smirking, snatching Melissa away, dragging her into the open belly of a huge airplane. Melissa screamed. Alisdair was laughing.

"Jeezus Christ!" Nancy said, dropping her hands from her face, shaking her head, letting her hair toss around her shoulders. Enough! She willfully put the intense and awful images out of her mind. But they had frightened her. She was not an irrational person. She was not accustomed to having bats flash out of caves at her in the middle of the day.

She dropped her hands to her hips, looked around the sun-filled but cluttered room, and determined to clean it thoroughly. She stooped again and began to ball up the newspapers that were scattered at her feet. She crushed the page with the Vietnamese children without looking at it again. She moved quickly, attacking the papers as if *they* were the source of the ache. She stuffed them in the low barrel by the table, then crossed to the other papers that were still folded and piled against the glass wall.

She picked up the stack and, crossing back to the barrel, crushed the papers into it. She picked up an old coffee tin from the floor, and, from one of the stereo speakers, the top of a mayonnaise jar that was crammed with cigarette butts. She pushed them into the barrel on top of the papers. Bits of wood from a broken stretcher, an old magazine, discarded sketches that she had balled and dropped in a corner weeks before. She stuffed them all in the barrel until it would take nothing else. And then she pressed down on it again with all her weight.

She stood up straight, put her hands on her hips, and looked around the solarium. Light filled it. It seemed empty. It seemed naked. But in the order, in the sterile neatness, that awful irrational vision of Melissa in distress was gone. She crossed to the chaise and straightened the Black Watch blanket, smoothing it, running her hands over it. The feel of the cloth made her think of smothering under a pile of woolens while locked in a stranger's closet. She snapped her head, cleared her mind, cursed inaudibly. She pushed the chair firmly against the wall and sat down on it.

And still the telephone on the low garden table seemed to be looking at her, asking her to do it.

"If anyone says that bishops are not superior to priests or that they have not the power to confirm and ordain, or that the power which they have is common to them and to priests, or that orders conferred by them without the consent or call of the people or of the secular power are invalid, or that those who have been neither rightly ordained nor sent by ecclesiastical and canonical authority, but came from elsewhere, are lawful ministers of the Word and of the Sacrament, let him be anathema."

Tierney whistled softly to himself and read the decree again.

"Anathema sit!" he said aloud, thinking the Latin could also be translated "her."

He was sitting at his desk in his room. He had returned there as soon as the meeting with Ferris-Cogan and the others had ended. Almost as if to banish from his mind what they had discussed, he had immediately begun the task of organizing the first stage of the canonical procedure against Sister Sheehan.

He had called Harry Burke, head of canon law at Catholic University. Burke had already spoken to the cardinal and had done the required research. On the phone he dictated to Tierney the numbers of the relevant canons, the citations in Buscarin-Ellis, the official commentary on the *Code*, and the numbers of the various conciliar decrees that applied.

Tierney was spending the morning in another world, a world in which nothing was contingent, in which every possibility was anticipated, in which for every problem there was a clear, immediate, straightforward solution. It was almost a pleasure, but it didn't last.

"Although the sword of excommunication is the nerve of ecclesiastical discipline and very salutary for holding the people in their duty, it is, however, to be used with moderation and great discretion, since experience teaches that if wielded rashly or for trifling reasons, it is more despised than feared and is productive of destruction rather than salvation."

"The sword," it said. Tierney had never seen the phrase before. Whatever medieval monk had coined it, he had understood exactly what the seemingly benign and bureaucratic procedure was about.

Tierney's mind drifted to the scene of the ceremony that would occur later in the day. Images of swords flashing in battle over the cathedral sanctuary. Images of swords piercing people, piercing Ferris-Cogan, piercing Christ's side. But it wouldn't be swords.

Tierney forced himself to read: "With regard to judicial causes, all ecclesiastical judges, of whatever dignity they may be, are commanded that both during the proceedings and in rendering decisions, they abstain from ecclesiastical censures or interdict whenever the action can in each stage of the process be completed by themselves through their own authority."

Well, he had tried that. The cardinal had tried it. The woman insisted on the full-blown process. She would get the full-blown censure. Was there something else he could do to head it off? Perhaps if he talked to the nun's convent superior . . .

His concentration faded. He was thinking of the terrorist, not the nun. What could he do to head off the one they were calling Janus?

"It shall be lawful for the judge to make use of this spiritual sword against delinquents."

What about assassins?

"*Potestatem offerendi Missae sacrificium habent soli sacerdotes.*"

Tierney lit a cigarette. The power to offer sacrifice: he thought about it. What *would* he do to stop a madman from killing the ambassador?

The phrase from theology came back to him: the man for others. Oh, come on.

But what would he do? What sacrifice would he offer? His life? The risk of health? His innocence?

He remembered the dream with which he'd awakened. He could feel the edge of his hand in his enemy's throat. But it hadn't been the Viet Cong or the IRA. It had been a woman reporter from the *Post*. The bitch.

He forced his attention back to the decrees. "If anyone says that in the Catholic Church there is not instituted a hierarchy by divine ordinance which consists of bishops, priests and ministers, let him be anathema."

Let her be. Let them all be. Let the ambassador alone. Tierney smashed his cigarette out and slammed the heavy book shut. He couldn't keep his mind from racing: what the hell was happening?

He reached across his desk and, under other books and a half-empty carton of Pall Malls, he found the small black handball. He wrapped his hand around it and squeezed. He relaxed his hand and then squeezed again. He turned in his chair to face the wall. It was six feet away. He threw the ball at a spot on the wall four inches from the floor, a spot in the midst of the black scuff marks the ball had made before. The ball bounced at an angle, hit the floor, then rebounded up to his hand. He caught it and threw it again, harder. It thumped twice quickly and was back in his hand. He threw it again. Thump, thump, and back. Thump, thump, and back. He continued in this way, throwing, catching, refusing to think. He didn't *know* what was happening.

The phone rang.

He caught the ball and turned back to his desk.

"Father Tierney."

"Line two, Father."

"Thanks, Mrs. Wills." He pushed the button. "Father Tierney."

"Good morning, Father. This is Nancy Ferris-Cogan. I hope I'm not interrupting something."

"Nancy! Hello! Just a handball game with myself."

"Oh, my, I . . ."

"No, nothing. I'm delighted you called." He was.

"I'm delighted you're still talking to me. After yesterday."

"Oh, go on . . ."

"Well, I was just thinking of you."

"Of me?"

"Yes. Actually, of the piece in the *Post*."

"It was a beaut, wasn't it?"

"I just called to tell you I don't believe it."

"You don't?"

"I don't mean the facts of the matter. I've no way of knowing about that. I mean I don't believe what the article obviously intends to imply."

"Well . . ." He paused. "Thank you. I must say I don't like the implications much myself."

"She was trying to make you seem like an ecclesiastical John Wayne."

"At best. As if I was about to napalm the 'poor sister.' "

"I don't think many people will be convinced by it. It was awfully crude." There was a relief in her voice that Tierney noted but would not understand. Nancy was relieved to have overcome the strange irrational emotions that had gripped her while she was straightening up her studio and deciding to call him.

"Nancy, thank you."

"I hope you don't get caught in the middle of this, Father. It seems to be heating up."

"I couldn't be more in the middle, and it will surely get hotter. But, well, something very serious is at stake."

"I think you'd be wiser to leave it alone."

"That would certainly be easier, but . . ." He remembered the way her husband had spoken. He wondered if she knew. ". . . these are difficult days, wouldn't you say?"

"Father, the Church is going to come out of this badly. I wish that you were not in it."

God, she doesn't know, he thought.

"I *am* in it, my bad luck, Nancy. But I'm not going to garrote Sister Sheehan. She will be treated fairly, I'm sure of it. But if she insists on a spectacle she'll have one."

"Father John, I know that you are a fair person, but, well . . ."

"Nancy, I appreciate your support." He paused. "But . . ." He was considering whether to say it, then went on. "As your husband would say, one does what one must do."

"Just don't let them use you, Father."

"Who?"

"Any of them — the women *or* the clergy. You are surrounded by unkind people."

He didn't answer right away. He looked at the small black ball in his hand, squeezed it once, then threw it at the wall and caught the bounce.

"Nancy, thank you."

"Bless you, Father John."

"Who?"

"You."

"No, I mean who should bless me?"

A pause. Then, "God, I suppose."

"Why, Nancy!"

"Quit laughing."

"Listen, I'm delighted you called."

"Good. I'm on your side. Don't forget."

"I won't."

"I'll see you this afternoon, then?"

"You will?"

"Of course. The investiture."

He paused. Clearly she didn't know. "Of course," he said, and then added quickly, "Will Melissa be there?"

"Certainly. After all your patient explanations? Of course she will."

"Oh."

"What's wrong?"

"Nothing. Nothing at all. See you this afternoon."

He hung up the phone, sat looking at it.

"Jesus, Mary, and Joseph," he said, thinking of Melissa, thinking of Nancy, feeling his first real fear in thirteen years.

Nancy hung up the phone and wandered out onto the sunny lawn.

When she was well away from the house, she happened to look back at the windows of the master bedroom and was surprised to see Alisdair standing in it, looking out at her.

They waved at each other.

Nancy wondered what her husband was doing in their room in the middle of the day.

Alisdair moved away from the window and crossed hurriedly to the bathroom again. The sight of his wife and the sudden sense of what a terrorist's bullet could do to her beauty had set loose a whole new tide of panic. Ferris-Cogan was desperately trying to get hold of himself. But he was failing.

In the elegant bathroom he stooped over the toilet bowl

and vomited for the third time, vomited now until there was nothing left in his stomach but terror.

"Brigadier Cameron?"
"Yes, Stone, what is it?"
"Captain Mitchell is here."
"Send him in."
"Good morning, Brigadier."
"Hello, Mitch. What do you have?"
"We've traced the Provo local."
"Good work. Who is he?"
"Not 'he.' "
"A woman?"
"Yes."
"Christ. Who?"
"Oona MacNeil. No record. Librarian downtown, false work papers, here nearly the year. She's the courier for the money raised by Northern Aid, makes a trip back every three months. Very anonymous. None of the pub rats know her."
"How did you get on to her?"
"Seton in Boston. He had met her twice, his funds all channel through her. He says her brother's in the Maze."
"Named MacNeil?"
"Yes. Danny MacNeil."
"Never heard of him."
"Also called Dangerfield, as in *Ginger Man*."
"*Dangerfield!* Bloody Christ! I know him."
"You do?"
"Yes. I took him through 'in-depth' two years ago myself. He wouldn't break. He killed two of my best men, fucking sniper. He was one of a handful I couldn't break. Goddamnit, if she's anything like her brother, she's a vicious bitch."
"Shall we pick her up?"
"No. Let's pay her a visit. It's not likely Janus would be working with anyone, much less a woman, a messenger at that, but he had to get his weapon somewhere."
"Seton says if Janus has any contact here it's her."

"Let's try it."

"By the way, Brigadier . . ."

"Yes?"

"I had to promise Seton three thousand."

"Three thousand dollars?"

"No, sir. Pounds."

"Pretty goddamn generous, aren't you? With the queen's money. No matter. If it bears out, we'll pay him gladly. Seton will be more valuable than ever to us then. If not, fuck him."

"Yes, sir."

Oona MacNeil was shelving books in the rear alcove where the geography and oceanography stacks leaned on each other. She was aware of the motion behind her before the man spoke.

"Miss MacNeil?" the voice nearly whispered.

An English accent. She ignored him, as if she had not heard him. Later she would wonder how she knew it was Cameron even before seeing his face.

"Miss MacNeil?"

She turned and faced him. She would have recognized him anywhere, even out of uniform. His fucking RAF moustache, his dapper, slicked-down hair, the sinister bridge his eyebrows made across his face. Two years before, she had spent weeks watching him go in and out of the Special Guard Headquarters on Church road in Belfast.

"Good day, sir. May I help you with something?" She was smiling, pleasant, the perfect librarian.

"Yes, you may, miss." Cameron decided that a direct, frontal assault would be the most likely way in. "Tell me what you know about Janus."

"Janus, sir? Is that the author or the title?"

Cameron realized how he had to play it. He must maintain the soft, authoritative drone that the mood of the library had forced on his voice. "Miss MacNeil, I know who you are. I shall certainly have your brother Danny killed forthwith if you do not answer my questions. Do you understand?"

"Yes." MacNeil's voice was no longer lilting with false politeness. She was staring at Cameron, holding his eyes. He had the immediate impression that she was not afraid of him.

"I will tell you what I know," she said. "Janus. In Roman mythology, the god of portals, the god of beginnings. Hence January." She spoke like a reciting student, that detached, that bored.

Cameron did not alter the threatening monotone of his voice, but he felt instinctively that the woman was not going to yield. He wondered about her relationship with her brother, whether she cared about him. Perhaps he had made a mistake in assuming that would be the point of vulnerability. "Miss MacNeil, perhap you don't understand. My name is Cameron. I assume you've heard it before?"

She said nothing.

"I know your brother — Dangerfield — personally. Indeed, I had the pleasure on one occasion that lasted several days to interview him."

"I remember," she said, her eyes full of murdering hate.

"Good. Now, let me say once again that it is easily within my power to arrange for an unfortunate accident to befall your brother. Her Majesty's Prison, the Maze, can be a very hazardous place. Do you believe me?"

"Yes."

"Good. Now, tell me about Janus, the gunman."

"Janus. Also the god of endings. Usually depicted as having two faces looking in opposite directions. Hence Janus-faced; deceitful."

"Miss MacNeil, are you indifferent to the death of your brother?"

"No."

"Do you believe that I have the power to have him killed?"
"Yes."

"And are you willing to be responsible for his death?"

"I am not responsible for his death."

"If he dies tonight, Miss MacNeil, you will have killed him."

"He will not die tonight."

"I promise you, he will."

"So be it, then. I know nothing."

"All right. Thank you."

Leaving her, Cameron experienced an uncomfortable combination of anger and respect. It was what he felt on the rare occasion of confronting someone who, like himself, had total control over his emotional life. The woman was prepared to sacrifice her brother. It was not that she didn't care for him, he concluded. It was that she was hardened, tough, ready to pay whatever her meager part in the war cost. She was military. Her brother was military. "Military" was the noblest adjective Cameron could think of. All too few of the IRA were military. All too few — he had to admit — of his own army were. But he was military, and therefore, even though now it was pointless, he would indeed see that the woman's brother died immediately.

As they left the library, Cameron said to Mitchell, "Stay here, Captain. Don't lose her. She's in it up to her fat Irish titties."

Oona MacNeil resumed shelving books. She forced the tremble from her hands. She breathed in and out in the slow, disciplined manner of a Yoga practitioner. And she was thinking. One: she would be useless from here on in Washington now that the English had her made. Two: she would have to assume that she was under surveillance now and until she took elaborate measure to elude it. Three: she was not in danger, since she had no further part in the action, whatever it was. Four: Cameron was closing in on Janus, but she had no way to warn her. Five: Janus, of course, had posed the day before as the woman courier. Oona had realized that the woman was the feared killer.

Oona smiled, shelved a heavy book, and said aloud, "Burn them, sister! Burn them!"

The fire was in her hatred. The strength was in her love.

Bridgit loved Connecticut Avenue. She loved being surrounded by the display of opulence — jewelry, lace, French dresses — even if it was behind plate glass. She pretended to be a wealthy lady out for a late morning stroll. The sun was glorious.

Not like the impenetrable mist of mornings at home. The avenue was not like the forbidding roads of Derry's shopping district, where the air always tasted of moist dust, where the shops were all barred and battered like something out of Dickens. At home, walking the streets, even in the busy morning, could frighten you to death. No one *strolled* though Derry anymore, not even on Queensbury Street. They *strode*, to get to where they were going. At home, even the spiders had reasons, as her mother said, to die of fright. "But if I were a spider," Bridgit said to herself, "I'd die of boredom."

Bridgit waited in the middle of the block between U and V streets, outside Rene's Salon. Mrs. Tierney was to be finished by 11:15. Her beautician, Annette, had said she could give Bridgit an appointment that afternoon at three. When her Aunt Nell assured her it would be no trouble to anyone, Bridgit had said she'd take it please, and, while Mrs. Tierney had had her hair done, she had taken her stroll on the avenue, satisfied that the scheduling had worked out so well.

"Hello, dearie, am I late?"

"No, Aunt Nell. Just in time."

"Oh, good. How do you like it?" Mrs. Tierney carefully pulled the large white scarf back from her hair and turned her head bashfully. Her hair was teased and blown and sprayed with fixative, just the way Bridgit hated it. But somehow, on her aunt, it didn't look false at all. Indeed, the small old woman had a touch of elegance about her now. Her eyes shone with pleasure and self-satisfaction.

"Why, Aunt Nell, it's beautiful. You look wonderful."

"Do you think so?"

"I wouldn't say it if I didn't. You look like a real lady."

"Thank you, Bea. I think I'll just leave it uncovered for John." She put the scarf in her bag.

"I hope your Annette does as well for me."

"Oh, she will, darling. Just you wait."

"You're sure it's no trouble, Aunt Nell?"

"None at all. When you're through you can just go right to the cathedral, and I'll meet you there. It'll give me a chance to have a nap."

"Fine. I've been wanting to do something about this poor head of mine for ages."

"Today's the day. Shall we take a taxi, or would you rather walk?"

Bridgit would have enjoyed the walk, but John was expecting them by 11:30, and she knew that her aunt's leg had been worse than usual. "Oh a taxi, I think, Aunt Nell. Don't you?"

"Yes, dear. Look, there's one coming. Can you get it?"

Bridgit stepped into the street, right arm upraised, waving at the cab. It pulled over and the two happy women got in.

Tierney was waiting for them.

He was still mulling over the wrathful morning, walking up and down the sidewalk in front of the cathedral as if it were Brontë's moors. When the cab pulled up and he saw his mother's hair, how fine she looked, how radiant, his heart sank. Bridgit was excited and joyful too. And he was about to douse them with ice water. How to do it? How to tell them without telling them?

"Hi." He held the door of the cab for them, took each by the hand as they alighted.

"Good morning, John," Bridgit said warmly, squeezing his hand.

"Hello, son," his mother said, holding up her cheek so he could kiss it. He did so, not dutifully. "Did you sleep well?"

"Yes, Mom. How about you two?"

"Oh, we've been having a wonderful time, haven't we, Bea?"

"Indeed, Aunt Nell. Doesn't she look wonderful, John?"

"I should say so," he replied, feeling the sadness weighing down his voice.

"Indeed you *should!*" his mother said, noting the moderation of his compliment, misunderstanding it.

Tierney ignored her, reached inside the cab, and paid the driver. When he straightened, he took each of the women by the elbow and turned them toward the rectory. Walking between them, he said, "Let's go inside. I want you to meet the cardinal."

"Oh," Mrs. Tierney said, "I thought we wouldn't see him until this evening."

"Well," Tierney replied, "Let's just greet him now. I want to make sure Bridgit has a chance to meet him."

"Oh, my, Johnny, I've never met a cardinal."

"You'll be charmed. He's just like Mom."

"He'll be too busy, son."

"I've already checked with him."

Outside the cardinal's office, Dora greeted Tierney's mother with affection and familiarity and then welcomed Bridgit. While they stood at her desk, the secretary buzzed the cardinal, who ordered them all sent into his office.

"Well, well, well," Cardinal O'Brien was saying as he came toward them. "Nellie, what a sight for sore eyes! Where have you been? You promised you'd visit!"

The old man and the old woman limped together. When they met, she started to go down on her knee, but he prevented her from doing so, held her up, hugged her. She accepted his greeting with dignity of her own, and when he released her from his embrace, she seized his hand and kissed it, saying, "Your Eminence."

"Cardinal O'Brien," Tierney said, "this is my cousin, Mrs. Bridgit Connor."

"Hello, Bridgit," he said, instantly familiar. He accepted her genuflection and kiss without protest.

"I'm honored, Your Eminence," Bridgit said. Then her nervous mind played its trick on her: had she just said, "I'm eminent, Your Honor"? No, of course not. But suddenly she wasn't sure. She could feel herself blushing. She clasped her hands over her stomach. They were clammy with sweat. She was determined not to be flustered.

"I hope you're enjoying your visit."

"Oh, I am indeed, Your Eminence." That came out sensibly

enough, so she dared to continue, "Father John showed me all the sights last night."

"Good. Good. Did you see President Kennedy's tomb?"

"We did, Your Eminence. The eternal flame."

"The President was in this very office many times."

"Did you know him, Your Eminence?"

"Why, Bridgit, he was buried from this very church."

Bridgit was touched, awed. "I didn't know that. I saw it all on television."

"President Kennedy was very close to the Irish. Your people loved him well, Bridgit."

"We still do, Your Eminence." Bridgit could feel herself relaxing. The man was full of warmth and friendliness. He seemed very down-to-earth, not at all like Dr. Conway, who, having been Derry's religious superior for years, had come to think he was exactly that.

Tierney, his mother, and his cousin remained in the cardinal's office for nearly ten minutes, during which time they talked about how the best Catholics in the world are Irish, about the number of priests Erin gives the world, about the glories of spring in Washington, about the cherry blossoms, and about the glories of spring in the old country.

When Mrs. Tierney said suddenly that the troubles in the North could ruin spring even in Ireland, there followed a short devastating silence. Tierney and the cardinal exchanged an uncomfortable glance. Bridgit noticed and assumed they were ill at ease for her sake. She was, of course, wrong.

As the priest and the two women rose and began to take their leave, the cardinal took Tierney's elbow and pulled him a step away.

"Father, a question. Excuse us, ladies, for just a second."

Mrs. Tierney and Bridgit smiled and stood awkwardly by, listening as Cardinal O'Brien and Tierney had a brief exchange.

"What is protocol, Father, for the greetings this afternoon?"

"You mean . . ."

"Yes, all the diplomats arriving and so on. Do I do it?" The cardinal was perplexed, in the grip of an anxiety he was trying to smother with details.

"Yes, you should be at the entrance."

"But, who's with the ambassador then, in the sacristy?"

"I will be. I'll be supervising preparations back there, and I'll make certain Sir Alisdair is well taken care of."

"All right. Then I'll come back when they've all arrived. All the VIPs, I mean."

"Right."

"Good. That's what I wondered."

O'Brien turned to the women, and said with an affection that was, while not precisely false, designed mainly to override the agitation he felt, "What would I do without your Father John?" He squeezed Mrs. Tierney's shoulder with one hand, brushed the small of Bridgit's back with the other.

"Isn't he nice?" Mrs. Tierney asked when they left the building. It was a question put not so much to either of the two as to the air.

"Yes. You were right, John. I'm totally charmed."

"I rather admire him myself," Tierney said. "We're lucky to have him. These are not easy days in which to be a bishop."

They were all getting into Tierney's blue Maverick. Bridgit climbed in back. Mrs. Tierney sat down awkwardly on the front seat and eased her favored leg in after her.

"I thought," Tierney said after the engine caught, "that we'd go to Gusti's. Do you like Italian food, Bridgit?"

"Love it, John."

"Okay with you, Mom?"

"Fine, dear. I'll just have a salad."

The drive to Gusti's took less than five minutes. The restaurant was on M Street across Connecticut, just a few blocks from the cathedral. No one spoke. Tierney appeared to be concentrating on his driving, and the women seemed to take their cue from his silence.

At the restaurant, Tierney double-parked long enough to help his mother out and hold the front seat forward for his cousin. He left them briefly to park the car in the lot across the street, and then began jogging to where they were waiting.

But suddenly he felt quite conspicuous, dressed clerically and running along M Street like a boy. He slowed to a walk, trying to understand what was happening. He had the feeling that each hour of this day was taking a year off his life. What else could he do with a worry like that but somethig silly, like run? The question uppermost in his mind was how to tell them?

As they all went into Gusti's, he thought that at that moment he would rather be having lunch with the lunatic from the IRA.

He had a martini.

The women had vermouth.

Halfway through the drinks he said it: "I'm afraid something's come up, Mom and Bridgit, that will make it impossible for you to attend the ceremony this afternoon."

"What?" His mother couldn't believe it.

"I can't say any more than that, Mom, I'm sorry. I apologize especially to you, Bridgit. I know you were counting on it."

Bridgit didn't reply at first. She was looking into the conical glass, fingering its long stem. When she looked up, Tierney could see disappointment in her eyes.

"Don't give a thought to me, John," she said. "I'm sure there must be a good reason."

"There is. Please trust me," he said. "I'll explain it later. Perhaps tomorrow."

"Johnny." His mother's voice was stern, pointed. "Does this have something to do with that nun? With what was in the paper?"

Dear God, what could it have to do with that? But then — his second thought — why not let them think so? "I didn't say that, now did I?"

"No," Mrs. Tierney persisted, "but it does, doesn't it?"

"Well, we do expect . . ." He offered it tentatively, knowing they would be misled. "We expect a demonstration of some kind to start this afternoon."

"A demonstration!" His mother said it as if it were an obscene word. "And you foresee trouble, don't you?"

"There could be trouble, yes. But I won't say any more about it. I'm sorry, but the ceremony will be absolutely restricted to official guests. They will be checking at the door. I'm sorry: you just can't come."

"Johnny," Bridgit asked, "what is this business with the nuns?"

"Bridgit, you'd have to be able to decipher babble to understand. Briefly, a nun said, or is accused of having said, a mass last week. The cardinal asked her to resign. She wouldn't. Now there's to be a church trial. Some vocal and fairly militant women's groups have been bringing public pressure to bear on the thing. NOW is going to picket the chancery today."

"What's NOW?"

"National Organization of Women. They're still stinging because some bishops elsewhere have condemned them specifically for their pro-abortion effort."

"I don't understand." His cousin seemed perplexed. "Does Cardinal O'Brien dislike nuns?"

It seemed a trifling question to Tierney. "No, not at all. He loves nuns. But he wants them to be the way they always have been. He's sure that, once they started to wear street clothes and go modern, it was inevitable they would end up in arrogance."

"Well, I think I agree with His Eminence. I'm not much for the changes myself."

"Me neither," Tierney's mother chimed in.

And then they were launched on the old conversation: how grand things were before; the trouble with the youth today; the New Morality; poor Pope Paul; the way nuns dress. Usually Tierney found it all insufferable. But this time he joined right in, partly out of gratitude that the focus had shifted away from the ceremony, and partly because, yes, he did after all long for the dull and perfect turning of that other world — the one people always claimed to have been born to, but never lived in.

"The dragon sits by the side of the road, watching those who pass. Beware lest he devour you." Cardinal O'Brien was discreetly looking out the window of his office, watching the women assemble on the sidewalk. They were the first pickets arriving at the cathedral, college students, some women in their thirties, some nuns in lay clothing. He was muttering from memory the line from Cyril of Jerusalem: "We go to the Father of Souls, but it is necessary to pass the dragon."

This mysterious passage past the dragon, by his jaws, by *hers!* Nothing matters but that Jesus Christ was telling the truth and shares the passage with us.

The cardinal could tell instinctively which ones were nuns. He watched them in particular. None was familiar, but the crosses at their breasts, the way they dressed, wore their hair, carried themselves — he knew a sister when he saw one.

He wanted to holler, "Sisters, don't be foolish! Sisters, don't be taken in! Sisters, don't betray us!"

Who would have thought it possible? Sisters in alliance — the Alliance of Saint Joan, they called themselves! — with pro-abortionists and radicals and, probably, judging from the look of them there, lesbians; in alliance against their own, against their archbishop, against their spiritual father.

The cardinal was nearly overcome with sadness — the best disguise for the anger one cannot acknowledge. The poor women, he thought, they have already been devoured by the dragon.

Well, he wouldn't be! They could be sure of that!

He let the curtain from behind which he was peeking fall. He turned back toward the center of his office and limped the ten feet to his desk. His leg was killing him. Someone, the IRA gunman probably, had slipped into his room the night before, removed his knee, and transplanted a bomb that he could feel ticking. Or maybe it was the nun.

Ferris-Cogan was sure of only one thing: Nancy and Melissa must not be there. He recalled Tierney's words: "It's one thing to accept risks for ourselves, quite another to make a decision that involves risk for others." He recalled his own cocky reply: "Isn't that the burden of responsibility?"

No, he decided. It isn't.

He would not be responsible for exposing his wife and daughter to the terrorist. He would not allow them to be anywhere near the danger. He would not accept *that* burden. The thought of it was enough to turn his stomach — again.

"Here, here, Melissa, eat up!" Alisdair said sharply, but pushing away his own plate.

His daughter slouched at her place at the lunch table.

"I don't like it," she whined.

"It's soup. You love soup."

"Not this kind. Mommy . . ." The little girl turned toward her mother at the end of the table. "Must I?"

"Talk to your father, Melissa. I'll not be a referee between you." Nancy was chuckling visibly.

"Melissa, as a favor for me?" he said.

Nancy thought that ploy a mistake.

"Daddy, I don't like it."

"Will you eat some fruit and cheese, then?"

"Daddy, I ate some bread."

"Bread is hardly enough, Pumpkin."

"I'm not hungry then." She was determined. She meant her declaration to be the conclusion of the discussion.

"Melissa, I want you to eat that soup."

Alisdair could feel the perspiration on his upper lip. He was surprised at the edge in his voice, and he found himself being much more stern than he had intended to be, much sharper than the matter required.

But it was too late.

"No!"

"Eat!"

"No!"

"If you don't eat it, young lady, you will go to your room until further notice!"

"Alisdair, really!" his wife interjected.

"Stay out of this!"

"Sometimes, Daddy . . ." Melissa's eyes brimmed over. "I don't like you." And she began to sob.

"Melissa, that's quite enough. Go to your room!"

The girl dashed from the table. As she left the dining room she slammed the door behind her, thereby making the silence that remained all the louder.

"You've a quick tongue today, Alisdair," Nancy said at last.

"And you've a sneering eye."

"Just a moment. That is utterly uncalled for."

"It is," he offered miserably. "I'm sorry."

"What's wrong, darling?"

"She doesn't eat properly, and her confounded whine sets my teeth on edge."

"I don't mean about Melissa, Alisdair."

But he didn't reply. He was devoting himself to the soup, trying again to eat. He spooned it precisely, sipped it in silence.

Nancy withdrew into her own eating as well, and she joined him under the weight of the indifferent mood that fell on the room.

Finally, she said, "Did you see the paper this morning, Alisdair?"

"Yes, of course."

"I mean the *Post*. Did you see the *Post*?"

"Yes, Nancy, I did." He broke a piece of bread in two and wondered whether to butter it. "They ran a follow-up piece on Viscount Thompson, used the statement I gave them. 'The Queen declines, et cetera.' "

"Did you read the thing about the Catholic nun?"

"What, the flap about the mass?"

"Yes."

"It disgusts me, frankly, Nancy. I didn't read it. I'm sure we disagree."

"We probably do, but that's not why I brought it up."

"It isn't?" Ferris-Cogan said it harshly, staring at his wife.

"No. I brought it up because the reporter makes quite a to-do about Father John."

"How so?"

"About his war record and its relation to the case against the nun."

"What's the relation?"

"None, really. But the piece is full of innuendo. You know the *Post*, their glee at the fall of Indochina finally. They're like jackals in the ruins. And they talk of Tierney as if he were personally responsible for all the Vietnamese dead. It's very nasty stuff."

"No doubt, they're setting him up as their villain in the story, the church's own Lieutenant Calley. They wouldn't dare take on the cardinal directly."

"Don't you think the cardinal is using him too, to hide behind?"

"Not at all."

"Why do you say that?"

"Father Tierney knows what he's doing. They are not Neanderthals, you know."

"Don't try to make me say something I'm not saying, Alisdair."

"I, for one, think the air would be clearer, Nancy, if you just said it out and quit this bloody hinting about like a schoolgirl."

"If I said what out? What *are* you talking about?"

"Your contempt for the cardinal."

"I wasn't talking about the cardinal. I was talking about John Tierney, and not with contempt."

"No, with demeaning pity, as if the poor bloke were surrounded by imbeciles. Well, the only imbeciles with whom he must contend are those pathetic, sterile victims of ecclesiastical penis-envy!"

"Alisdair, that's uncalled for!"

"Frankly, I'm fed up with your condescending attitudes toward my religion."

"Oh, are you? Well, I must say you are doing a miserable job of representing your noble religion to me and of practicing it toward your daughter."

"Well, at least now it's out in the open, Nancy." Suddenly he was very cool, his gaze fast upon her. "I'm sure you must be relieved now that you no longer have to pretend to respect my beliefs."

"I respect what is worth respect."

"Then," he said softly, intently, "be so kind as to spare me the hypocrisy of your presence in the church today. I couldn't bear it; frankly, your secular superiority fills me with disgust."

"As you wish," she said, stunned.

What had happened?

Deliberately, she placed her napkin beside her plate and stood. She looked at her husband and felt the pure cold rush of her anger. "As you wish," she said again, and then stepped away from the table toward the door.

As she moved away from him, Nancy Ferris-Cogan knew that when love fails there is always hate.

He watched her go, but before she had closed the door behind her, he said, "Nancy."

She stopped.

"Keep the girl home with you," he said. "You might as well. You've won her over already."

"Alisdair, you're pathetic."

She closed the door behind her without slamming it.

Ferris-Cogan sat in bewildered silence. What had he done?

His hands trembled almost uncontrollably as he filled his pipe and lit it.

As he sat desperately puffing on it, a gruff bastard's voice from somewhere in the back of his head said to him, "You're lucky all you lost is your wife and kid, war being what it is."

"Hello, Social Studies Reference."

"Good day. This is Professor Jane Wyath at Catholic University."

"Yes?"

"Can you tell me, please, do you have a current geophysical map of the District of Columbia and environs in your reference library here? Ours has been damaged up here."

"How current a map do you want, Professor?"

"The latest, 1974."

"I'm not sure of the date on the map here. It will take me some moments to check. Would you like to hold, or shall I call you back?"

"Would you be so kind?"

"Certainly."

"I'm at 267-9632. I'll be expecting your call."

"Fine."

"Thank you."

"Not at all."

Oona MacNeil tore the page with the number from her notepad. She stood and walked down the row of cluttered stacks to the door at its end. She went through the door lettered EMPLOYEES LOUNGE: NO ADMITTANCE.

Mr. Stanley was sitting on the shabby vinyl couch against the wall. That and a soiled, overstuffed easy chair were the only seats in the drab, bare room. Large, uncurtained windows at one end admitted too much light so that the room was harsh with a blinding midday glare.

Oona MacNeil almost never went into the place except to pass through to the toilet.

Stanley was eating his lunch, a cheese sandwich that looked overdry, a half-pint carton of milk, and a pickle. He looked at MacNeil as if she had intruded on his private space.

But she ignored him and walked directly to the old wooden phone booth in the corner. She closed the door firmly behind her and turned her back to the glass. She put her dime in its slot, waited for the tone, then dialed.

"Hello."

"Professor?"

"Are you on a safe line?"

"A pay phone. Yes, it's safe. Unless they've a tap on every phone in the block."

"One never knows."

"I'm glad you called, whatever the reason. I have something crucial to tell you."

"What?"

"Cameron was here."

"When?"

"This morning. An hour and a half ago."

"How did he get on to you?"

"I've no idea."

"Jesus Christ! What did he ask?"

"About you."

"What do you mean?"

"Well — sorry — about your friend."

"What does he know?"

"Not much I'd guess. He seemed desperate. He threatened to have my brother killed."

"Ah, stupid English bastard."

"Yes."

"All right. Listen to me carefully. I've no choice in this. I need your help. Are you willing?"

"Gladly."

"Can you get off immediately?"

"Yes."

"You must presume that you are being followed. Do you understand that?"

"Yes."

"There is a high level of danger in this."

"I'm ready."

"All right. You cannot risk going home. Your house may be watched, but we will need a second gun . . ."

"I have it with me. I had a feeling . . ."

"All right. Do you remember where we prayed yesterday?"

"Yes."

"Meet me there at three o'clock."

The candle burned between them like a votive light. Mrs. Tierney was away from the table at the ladies' room. John Tierney and Bridgit Connor sat silently, separately preoccupied in one of Gusti's dark corners. The meal was finished. The check was paid. They would be going out into the bright afternoon when the old woman returned.

"You know, John," Bridgit said finally, "it makes me laugh to come all the way to America and find that people are the same here as they are at home." She spoke easily, tugging absently at the thin velvet ribbon she wore around her throat. It drew attention to her long, elegant neck.

"What do you mean, Bridgit?"

"No one ever knows how to say what they want to say."

Tierney smiled.

The thin waiter appeared, gesturing with his coffeepot. Tierney raised his brows at Bridgit, who shook her head. The waiter moved off, slipping by the elbows of other patrons like a matador by horns. The place was still crowded and alive with a subtle but nervous bustle. The customers were intent on the aftermaths of their meals, their hushed conversation.

No one seemed to notice the priest and the attractive woman at the corner table.

"Are you talking about your difficulty," Tierney asked, "or mine?" He placed his fingertips together before his chin and looked directly at Bridgit.

"Both, I think." She was sweeping crumbs across the table-cloth with her nail, a bashful, falsely casual business. "It seems to me we're quite alike."

"How?"

She began tracing the squares of the red-checked cloth with her finger. "Perhaps, for all our adult independence — I mean, we both make our ways alone — maybe . . ." She cupped her hands around the water glass then. "We're just a couple of mere kids barely able to . . ." Her voice drifted off. When she raised her eyes from the glass she was holding, Tierney was still looking at her intently. He did not finish the sentence for her. He did not lower his eyes. He was watching the shadows that the candleflame was casting on her face. She met his gaze.

"I'm talking about being afraid, John."

"I know you are, Bridgit."

"Your difficulty or mine, eh?"

"Touché." He smiled at her. "I don't usually talk like this, not until a third martini anyway."

"We haven't the time, and I wanted to tell you something."

"What?"

"That I know, about your fear. I know all about fear."

Tierney's eyes fell, as if jarred. He lowered his fingers to his own glass in unconscious imitation of Bridgit. The two of them seemed to be holding on to the glasses for support.

"Bridgit, you're touching something I'd rather not . . ." He shrugged.

"An old wound?"

"Perhaps."

"Having to do with war?" She asked it very softly.

For a long time Tierney stared at a stain on the cloth. He held his head at a slight angle and his eyes abruptly took on a glazed, vacant quality. He seemed almost absent until the mumbled, half-finished conversation of the three men at a nearby table erupted into laughter. Bridgit and Tierney both looked toward the three men, who were immediately embarrassed and fell silent. When Tierney looked again at his cousin he seemed to be blinking something back.

"I thought it was over, Bridgit, buried, all the . . . but the last few days . . . every day, it's worse: the children, the refugees, the panicked soldiers, Thieu salting away millions in Swiss banks, Americans trying to get out before the ARVN shoot them. . . . It's like I'm still there . . . God!" Tierney stopped, his face set in a simple, rapt concentration. He had the water glass in his right hand and made a fist around it. "And then today, as if I needed the reminder, the paper drags *my* part in it all out of the past . . ."

"I didn't read it, John." Bridgit caught her left wrist in her right hand.

Tierney's hand was trembling. His mouth was stretched into a thin white line. He swallowed once. When he spoke, finally, his voice had dropped to a whisper, full-throated and slow.

"I killed . . . some men, Bridgit . . . the paper says four. But it was . . . nine. Over two years, nine. I . . . killed them."

Bridgit began to reach slowly across the table, but stopped short of touching him.

"It was war, Johnny." She said it vaguely, as if she knew it was a weak and sentimental statement that meant nothing.

"When a bullet goes into a man's skull . . ." He said, looking hard at her. Bridgit's eyes held his, did not falter, but made him stop. They were filled with tears. Tierney's eyes were harsh, direct, unyielding. Bridgit's mouth was twisted, wrenched with silence. Tierney's mouth became a thin line again. Bridgit said nothing. Still they were looking directly at each other. Tears fell down her face.

Suddenly Tierney released his grip on the glass, spilling a bit of water, and reached to her hands, pressing them together in his own.

"I'm sorry, Bridgit," he said desperately. "Forgive me. You've seen as much of it as I have. More. You've seen it in your own streets. Your own husband . . ."

"Oh Johnny . . . oh, John!" She clutched his fingers. Stifled by the effort to pass unnoticed in the restaurant, waves of emotion surged through their grasping, clinging hands.

"Bridgit . . ."

Before Tierney could complete his sentence, the three men at the next table rose noisily. They did not look toward the priest and the woman, but Bridgit pulled her hands away from John as if they had. She lurched abruptly back in her seat and pressed herself rigidly against the chair, as if to say with her body, *It's a restaurant! You're a priest!* Tierney was left hunched emptily over the table.

He glanced nervously around him. The three men were walking off into the darkness. When he looked at Bridgit, she drew his eyes into her own. For an instant their look acknowledged what had happened and, with the faintest of nods, it was over.

Bridgit opened her purse, withdrew a compact, and bent over the light to repair her eyes. Tierney lit a cigarette and looked about the restaurant. Though he leaned casually back in his chair, the lines of his body were rigid with tension. Now that the businessmen were gone no one was watching them. The waiter was nowhere to be seen.

Mrs. Tierney was making her way through the tables. She seemed to be having some trouble.

"It's so dark in here," she said when she arrived at the table.

"We're ready to go, Mom." Tierney was rising, bringing his mother's coat with him from the corner in the booth where she had left it.

"Well, it was a lovely lunch, darling. Wasn't it, Bea?"

"Indeed, Aunt Nell," Bridgit said, averting her eyes.

"I knew you'd like it," the old woman said.

As they left the restaurant and walked out into the brilliant afternoon, Tierney shook off what was left of the emotion. He stepped between the two women and deliberately put one of his arms on each of their shoulders, bashfully drawing them to himself, a pair of loved ones who filled him with joy. The world was warm and bright; the sky was blue; the city was alive with people hurrying to their places. The two women returned his one-armed embrace as they walked along M Street.

"Okay," he was saying, "so I'll pick you guys up after the ceremony. Then we'll go to the embassy for the reception."

"But John," his mother said, "if we can go to the reception, why can't we go to the ceremony?"

"The reception, Mother, is totally safe from any possibility of disruption. The cathedral is not. It's a public building, however much they control it."

"I think I'd still like to get my hair done, if you don't mind, Aunt Nell," Bridgit said.

"Of course not, dearie. Annette's counting on you. John, I think you should tell those women's-libbers to leave the Church in peace. This is a disgrace. What must His Honor think?"

"His Eminence, Mother," Tierney said patiently.

"I mean the ambassador."

"His Excellency."

"Well, it's a scandal. Bea, your mother won't believe it when you tell her."

"Ah, but she will. She thinks the Church in America has been taken over by lunatics or communists."

"When the truth is," Tierney said, "it's only been taken over by women."

"That's worse," his mother said. "Those awful nuns!"

"Not nuns, Mom. The Church has been taken over by the mothers of priests."

"Oh, you!"

"Come on, get in," he said, holding open the door of his car, laughing affectionately at his mother and not looking at his cousin.

After he dropped the two women off, Tierney sat behind the wheel of his car at the corner of Rhode Island and Dupont Circle, waiting for the light to change. He was giving careful thought to what he had decided to do.

It was not the sort of thing one should do impulsively.

Indeed, he thought to himself, it was probably not the sort of thing one should do at all. He had decided to go to Shannon's.

Not, of course, that he expected to find Janus, about whom he knew nothing. Nor that he could stop him if he did find him. Tierney knew that the terrorist Cameron had described would make limp hay of a middle-aged — well, early middle-aged — cathedral curate and part-time canon lawyer.

He was going to Shannon's because he had to go somewhere. He was going to Shannon's because he couldn't not go. He was going to Shannon's because he was going crazy.

He had been there before, years before, once. When Cameron mentioned it that morning in connection with the killing, it was as if he slammed the soles of his feet with a stick. He knew that the pub was a favored hangout for the local Irish romancers who gloried by long distance in the troubles of the North. He knew that young boys and old men would be wearing buttons that said SUPPORT THE IRA without the slightest idea of what the IRA was doing to the body of the land they claimed to love.

But going to Shannon's, if only to have a pint of stout, was *something*. It was a familiar place to him, and it was a link, however remote, with the brutal world into which he felt himself being dragged. If he was to go in at all, it would be under his own power.

Unless, of course, he got drunk.

He wouldn't do that. But could he spend the afternoon as if nothing was happening? Could he spend the afternoon worrying, for God's sake, about the canon law of menopausal nuns?

He was trying to take in the fact that the grotesque and tragic violence of Northern Ireland was about to pose a personal and immediate threat to him — whatever security precautions the English took. The chaos and absurdity of a guerrilla war were about to enter, if only potentially, the exempt precincts of his highly ordered life. No sanctuary in the sanctuary for once, he thought. The evil he read about daily in the papers could have its blade against his flesh. He couldn't believe it. It was like a bad dream.

Since the session in the cardinal's office that morning, Tierney had had the feeling that someone had shifted gears on the world's turning. Everything was slower. The short conversation with Bridgit just before they left the restaurant had seemed hours long to him. Her affection had been like the fond farewell of a family sending a boy off to war. Or was it the fond welcome of the boy returned?

At the rare times Tierney experienced such feelings, he looked for ways to dispel the uneasiness, to reassert the control he cherished. All right, maybe he couldn't stop the terrorist. But he could stop the panic from rising any further in his throat. He would go to Shannon's, a place that had been touching evil, find the panic's eye, and stare it down.

The light changed and he drove.

Eleven minutes and seven blocks later he was looking for a parking place. He found one on Columbia Road in the middle of the block between N Street and O. He locked his car. As he walked the block and a half to the Irish pub, he jangled the loose change in his left pocket as if everything were wonderful.

"Hi, Father."

The bartender was smiling broadly. Tierney was suddenly embarrassed and felt foolish. It was one thing to be seen dressed as a priest in a pleasant restaurant in a tony part of town, but quite another to be seen in midafternoon in what was, after all, a tacky little bar with a lot of faded shamrocks on the wall.

"Ah, look at that, will you?" Tierney could almost hear them. "The priest is on the juice in the middle of the day."

"Hi," he said, sliding onto a stool.

"What'll it be?" The bartender's breath was heavy with alcohol. He'd obviously been doing his customers the service of making sure none of his stock was poison.

"Guinness."

"A pint, Father?" Tierney noticed the barman's pained limp as he moved to the tap.

"No. Half," he said, giving his tribute to discretion. While the bartender unsteadily drew the thick foamy stout, Tierney chided himself for coming. The place was nearly empty. Nothing was happening. And, he knew, there was as little to do with the reality of the IRA there as at Saint Matthew's.

But what the hell.

"Cheers!" he said, raising his glass to the barman, who smiled drunkenly and said, "To your health," though he had no drink of his own.

"Can I buy you a drink?" Tierney asked, thinking again what the hell. The man seemed friendly and had not moved away from Tierney's place at the bar.

"You're kind, Father. I will join you." He drew a pint for himself. "But it's all on me. Yours as well."

"No, no," Tierney protested, hating the compulsion of the Irish to pamper their priests because he knew it for the sly contempt it often was.

"I insist," the barman said, raising his own drink. "To a death in Ireland!" Foam dripped down his chin as he tilted the mug.

Tierney drank. "That's a toast to keep you sober."

"Or to get drunk on, Father. To tell you the truth, I'm not myself just now."

"Oh?" Their eyes met, and something passed between them. Tierney knew what had happened. Even in the man's tipsy state the subtle but unbreakable pastoral bond had just been established between them. Even before the man spoke again, Tierney knew that he was about to confide in him, about to invest the remarkable trust that these people instinctively, and on occasion instantly, put in their priests.

"I recently suffered the death of a close friend, Father."

Tierney stopped breathing.

"Have you? I'm sorry." He was thinking of the murder to which Cameron had referred.

"Thank you."

"I hope," Tierney said, leading him on a bit, "that it wasn't a difficult death."

"I'm afraid it was. Very difficult."

"How did he die?"

The bartender looked at him carefully. Tierney's heart was

pounding. He felt himself to be closer to the mystery of the evil that had brought him there than he expected to be, than he wanted to be.

"Father," the bartender said heavily. He had decided there was no risk in talking to a priest, and he had to talk to someone. "My friend died a bloody death."

"I'm sorry . . ." Tierney felt a qualm that he was abusing the man's trust, but he ignored it. "And was it a car accident?"

"No." The man looked around. No one could hear them. When he resumed, his voice was barely above a whisper. "Can I talk to you as a priest?"

"Certainly."

"The Seal of Confession, I mean, Father."

"Of course," Tierney said, not lying.

"He was killed by the English."

"In Ireland?" Tierney was not playing dumb. If what Cameron had said was true, how could the English have done it?

"Here, in this city! Last night, Father! Father, I betrayed the man. The British soldiers burned me — I could show you my legs and my feet if you asked — with their cigarettes. And I told them what they wanted. They fooled me into thinking an IRA gunman was after the fellow, but it was them. Or it might have been them." The man grew frantic. He seized Tierney's arm desperately and pressed it. "Or maybe it *was* Janus! I don't know who it was, Father, but the man trusted me and I betrayed him to that bloody Cameron and now he's dead and I can't shake the feeling that I did it, Father, because I couldn't keep my mouth shut. Though I never did it for money, Father, honest to God I didn't. I didn't send no woman over there, honest to God. Who'd have thought a woman anyway? I'm sorry, Father. Oh, my God, Father, I had no idea somebody would die because of me. I left it all behind because I hated that, and now I've gone and done it myself. Oh, bless me, Father . . ."

The man was weeping out of control then. Remorse and guilt and a lifetime of disappointments poured out of him. He was drunk, yes. But a priest could not thereby assume that the man was not in the ruthless grip of his own truth. Tierney returned the press on the man's arm with his free hand.

"Father, will you give me absolution?" The man's face was wracked with tears and remorse. It was, the priest thought, the face of every derelict who ever confessed to him, the face that always shook him to his core, so pathetic, so powerful, so pure in its misery. It was, he thought every time he saw it, the face of Simon Peter.

"Bow your head," the priest said.

Tierney would have touched the man's head, caressed it even, but he didn't want to draw attention to them. He only increased the pressure of his grip on the bartender's arm, saying in a whisper, "May our Lord Jesus Christ forgive you, and, by His authority on behalf of the Church, I forgive you all your sins . . ."

As he said the words, their gentle, healing calm fell, not only on the crumpled Irishman, but on the priest as well. He had come to the pub in near panic, trying to recover his sense of things, an order to the chaos the day threatened. And he had come across, as if by grace, this piece of human refuse, this man whose life also had been caught up and hurled by the same winds that were tossing Tierney. If he could give this man the gift of God's peace, he would have it himself. If he could recall to this man's mind the good news that the Evil One has already been defeated by Jesus Christ, *no matter what*, then he would walk back out into the day with whatever he needed to do God's will, whatever it was.

Tierney lifted his right hand ever so slightly and, ever so slightly, signed the man with the cross: ". . . in the name of the Father, and of the Son and of the Holy Spirit."

The five-shot Smith and Wesson Airweight balanced uneasily across the heel of Parsley's hand. He had just cleaned it. It was the seventh pistol he had cleaned in a little over half an hour. It was, admittedly, most irregular for the chief of security to be cleaning weapons, but Parsley was a stickler, and he was channeling his nervous energy into the details of preparation. He was determined not to have any mishaps from his end of things. His men would be every bit as reliable as Cameron's, and their equipment would be faultless.

Parsley put the Airweight on the cloth that was spread on top of the file cabinet. He was in the vault in the sub-basement of the embassy, standing against the files in which his section's reserve weapons were kept. Ordinarily, only the five men assigned to the ambassador's personal bodyguard were armed. Today, all eleven of his men, six auxiliaries, and the four stenographers assigned to his section — all, of course, qualified marksmen — would be bearing guns. Of their number, twelve would be mingling with the other churchgoers, three would be stationed with him to supervise the brisk search of the guests as they entered the cathedral through its main door, and six would be posted at other entrances. Cameron's men would have the more military posts in the heights of the cathedral, on the roof and in the crawl space where a sniper might hide.

Parsley would still have preferred to have brought in the FBI. It was most irregular, ignoring the full police resources of the host country in such circumstances. But he had to admit that Cameron had been right on several counts. It looked to Parsley now as if security would be more than adequate. And, in addition to their own numbers, the District of Columbia Police would be outside the cathedral in force at his request. As far as they knew, their function would be to control traffic and oversee some bloody picket line that disgruntled Catholics were throwing at the cardinal. Also, the White House Executive Police, who were charged with the protection of the Diplomatic Corps, would also be in attendance since so many of the guests would be Ferris-Cogan's fellow envoys. Apparently security would be adequate.

Parsley knew further that Cameron had also been right about London's desire to handle the matter as discreetly as possible. His own headquarters at Cambridge Circus had dispatched orders for total secrecy, even and especially vis-á-vis the American government. The last thing Wilson wanted was American attention to what was happening in Ireland. If Janus could be caught and ferreted home without the complications of extradition and the attendant publicity, London would be highly pleased. That would mean, of course, that his career prospects, like those of Cameron and even Ferris-Cogan, would be considerably enhanced.

In all likelihood the terrorist, sensing the elaborate cathedral security, would be warned off and try nothing. Parsley dearly hoped so. Even if that meant not getting the bugger. Parsley was wishing the man would go back to Ireland and do his dirt there.

He reached into his left coat pocket and withdrew his key ring, heavy with keys. He selected one of the smaller ones, stooped, and inserted it into the lock of the lowest drawer in the file cabinet. He opened the drawer and saw that it was full of neatly folded gray cloth. But the cloth was solid to his touch. When he put his hands under the first layer of folds, it was very heavy. He picked up one of the lead bulletproof vests and held it in front of him. The things weren't nearly so cumbersome as they used to be. It wasn't pure lead; rather, an alloy with a titanium base or some such metal they invented for outer space. Heavy enough, though. Damned hot, probably.

Ferris-Cogan would complain. But he wasn't a fool. He'd wear it.

Parsley took some comfort from the vest. It would protect the ambassador from almost any pistol shot unless it was point-blank, of course, or unless it was, say, a .357 Magnum. It wouldn't do much good against a high-caliber rifle, but a vest like this, Parsley thought, would have saved Martin Luther King's life. Of course, there's no helping the shot to the head: the vest wouldn't have done either Kennedy any good at all, for example.

Parsley closed the drawer. He thought briefly of wearing the second vest himself. But that wouldn't do, would it? He imagined Cameron sneering at him.

As Parsley loaded the weapons and vest in the two attaché

cases he had brought with him, he could hear the vein thumping in his temple. It was a faint sound, like a steam engine off at a great distance, yet going *bang, bang, bang,* above his ear.

Closing the heavy vault door behind him, swirling the locking knob as he did so, he began reviewing in his mind the other details that had to be looked to. Ordinarily he delegated authority routinely. But on this occasion he was stingy with it. He — more than any other person — was responsible to see that Sir Alisdair Ferris-Cogan lived. Parsley's own life had come to that purpose. It was not just that he wanted to be certain of the equipment to be used and of the plans laid and of the instructions given and of the persons admitted to the cathedral. It was not just that he wanted everything to be executed perfectly.

It was also, and perhaps more, that Reginald Parsley had the primitive human conviction that when you anticipate an event, good or bad, with the most detailed preparations possible, it never happens.

When her eyes had adjusted to the dark after the bright afternoon, Janus saw MacNeil. She was on her knees in the same pew they had used the day before. No one else was in the small chapel except the two nuns, of course, who, with backs turned, maintained their vigil before the Eucharist in the sanctuary. Janus joined MacNeil.

"Hello," MacNeil whispered.

Janus nodded without looking at her, knelt silently for a moment, as if praying, then asked in a voice that was barely audible, "How many nuns are there?"

"Six."

"Where would the others be?"

"In the cloister."

"Which is . . ."

"Right through there . . ." Oona's eyes were fixed on the door to the left of Mary's statue. "And upstairs."

"Have you any coins?"

MacNeil nodded. Janus gestured with her head toward the

bank of candles at the base of the plaster Saint Mary. Oona stood, sidled to the aisle, and began noisily — it was her nylon thighs — making her way forward. Janus, still kneeling, slipped her shoes off her feet, secured her purse under her left shoulder, and, in her stocking feet, followed Oona without a sound.

The first woman waited by the candles, ready with several coins. Janus went to the door, tried it quietly. As she expected, it was locked: a simple snap lock. She opened her purse and withdrew a metal fingernail file, which she held at the lock. She looked at MacNeil, nodded once, and, as the other woman noisily dropped coins into the metal box at the base of the candles, she jammed the file into the lock and forced the beveled bolt back. The door swung open. The coins stopped clanging. Janus looked back at Oona and nodded. She closed the door behind her; Oona dropped another quarter into the brass box as the door clicked shut.

Janus was in a dark stairway. She did not move, but stood with her back against the door, waiting for her pupils to dilate.

There were between nine and thirteen stairs. At the top, the passage wound slightly to the right. Only a portion of the upper door was visible; the thin crack of light from under the door was barely a splinter from where Janus stood. There was no sound except for her own breathing.

She began to ascend the stairs silently. She waited for creaking noises. There were none.

At the upper door she found the knob and gripped it firmly. She had considered carefully what she would do next. Since she had no idea of the sort of room into which the door opened, she had no choice but to go through it boldly.

She opened the door quickly and walked through it as if in a hurry, still careful, however, to make as little noise as possible.

She was standing in a narrow corridor. No one was there. Other doors were closed down the hall. She stood quite still, listening. There were no sounds.

When she began to move she walked directly to the nearest door. It was seven paces away, on the left. She put her hand to the knob, turned it, and pushed the door open a foot. It was a tiny room, not larger than a good-sized walk-in closet. A narrow bed took up most of its space. Someone was in the bed, sleeping.

Of course. They maintained their vigil before the Sacrament around the clock. At least two of the nuns would be asleep.

Janus closed the door. The woman did not stir on her pallet.

At the next door Janus pressed her ear against it, trying to hear the breathing of a sleeper. She heard nothing.

She opened it. There was a low bed. It was empty. She went into the room and closed the door behind her. She saw what she was after: suspended in a clear plastic wrapper on a wooden hanger from a nail on the door was the nun's second habit, her special, her better, one. She would wear it only on feasts or to receive visitors from behind the grill. It was the brown wool, thick and rough, of the Franciscan Sisters of Perpetual Adoration. They were of the strict observance: no refined, smooth cloth for them.

Janus took the habit from its hook: the tunic, veil, and scapular were there. The white cincture and starched linen wimple that would frame the woman's face under the veil were not. She took the plastic off the habit and dropped it in the corner. She put the habit smoothly down on the narrow bed. Her eyes flashed around the floor of the room.

There. A pair of black nun's shoes against the wall by a small priedieu in the corner. Janus stooped and looked at them. They might do. She picked them up and put them on top of the habit.

She returned to the hall, empty-handed, still clutching her purse below her shoulder.

She continued down the corridor, then stopped.

Voices.

She tilted her head toward a door a few paces in front and to the left. A woman was talking. A second responded briefly. That was two. Two asleep. Two downstairs. Fine.

Janus took a deep breath and crept past the door from which the sounds were coming.

She was at the end of the corridor, the last door. It was open already. She looked into the room: an ironing board against one wall; a basket containing sheets on the floor; a sink. It was the laundry room. Perfect. Perhaps she'd find the starched linens, fresh cinctures.

She entered the room.

"What are you doing in here?"

Janus jumped, startled. She calmed herself instantly, however, and turned around. There, peering up at her from a stool in the corner behind the door, was an ancient gargoyle of a nun. On her lap was a pile of small linen altarcloths. She was holding a threaded needle. She had been mending linens.

"Hello, Sister." Janus looked at her carefully.

"Nobody is supposed to be up here. This is cloister."

"I know, Sister."

Janus's hand went rigid, ready to kill her.

But wait! She curled her hand into a soft, harmless fist. There was no need to kill in a convent, for God's sake. Janus's instinct never betrayed her like that before, never ran to carelessness or fright.

"Well, get out!" The old nun did not seem disposed to move.

Janus looked at her even more carefully. A white film covered the old woman's eyes. Janus realized that she was blind.

"This is Sister Phillippa, Sister. I've come to help out."

"Who?"

"Sister Phillippa. From the motherhouse."

"What do you mean, 'help out'?"

"You're so pressed here, all the sisters say so."

"Yes?"

"Mother sent me to help out."

"You're Irish?"

"Yes."

"My mother was Irish."

"Oh, was she now? What part?"

"Mayo."

"I'm from Mayo!"

Janus was moving around the room. She saw a pan filled

with liquid, presumably bleach. It held several coiled white cinctures, soaking.

"Are you, Sister?"

"Indeed. And what was your mother's town?" She lifted two cinctures out of the pan as quietly as she could. There were dripping sounds, but the old woman apparently didn't hear them.

"Don't remember."

"Well, I'm delighted to meet you, Sister."

"You shouldn't be talking."

"Of course not, but you asked me."

"Well, be quiet then."

"Yes, Sister."

Janus backed out of the room clutching the dripping cinctures.

In the hall again, she turned and moved silently back to the cell where she had left the brown habit and shoes. She went in and, wringing the moisture out of them, placed the white cords on top of the shoes. She sat down.

Janus knew she was at the far edge of prudence. She had only one habit: she needed two. She had none of the linen headgear. The old nun could call the others at any second. Janus was skilled enough, experienced enough, to know that she should leave. She should not push it. She should abandon the plan. She should forget it all. She shouldn't test the limit.

She decided to test it.

She went back to the laundry room.

"Sister," she whispered.

The old nun raised her head as if to look at her. Janus continued, "Where are the sisters' fresh linens stored?" She asked the question with authority, as if it were inconceivable that the old nun would not tell her.

"What?"

"The linens! Mother needs a fresh wimple at once!"

The old nun displayed a lifetime habit of docile subservience, raising an arm and pointing to a closet across the room. "On the shelves," she said, not comprehending, but not needing to. She knew authority when she heard it.

Janus crossed to the closet, opened it. The shelves were stacked with starched whites, cloths of all shapes and sizes. Janus quickly fingered several layers, but she could not tell which of them were the stuff of nun's facial garb.

"On the top," the old one said, having sensed Janus's hesitation.

"Yes."

Janus took the white bands and broad plaited wimples down. Two of them, yes, two pieces each.

Janus left the laundry room without speaking again. The old sister thought that this new one did not make the right sounds when she walked: she wasn't wearing shoes, and there was no soft rustle of the long robes, and the rosary beads were not clicking against each other. The old nun knew something was wrong. But she would keep it to herself. Her duty was to mend these finger towels. If Mother Rita had sent the new sister over, let Mother Rita worry about what was wrong.

Janus placed the starched linen on top of the habit, shoes, and cinctures. She returned to the hallway and went the six paces to the door she had opened at the beginning. She opened it again, quietly. The sleeping nun stirred in her narrow bed. Janus ignored her. She stooped and found the shoes exactly where they had been in the other room. She reached behind the door: the habit was there, covered with . . . not plastic but very stiff paper. Shit! It would be noisy. She lifted it carefully: it was. The paper crackled as Janus took the habit; it crackled loudly.

The nun rolled over. Janus knew what she would do: if the nun woke up, she would kill her.

The nun did not wake up.

But there it was again! Janus's stomach curdled. She would *never* kill what could not kill her. Such foolish impulse! What was happening to her nerves? She would *never* kill a toothless old nun! She redoubled her concentration, but she could not dispel the disturbing uneasiness. If her first instinct was no longer trustworthy, what was?

Janus returned to the empty room, removed the paper wrap from the brown habit, and quietly put it in the corner with the plastic wrap from the other one.

She bundled the habits and accessories together, hugged them to her breast and slipped into the hall. She went directly to the staircase door, opened it, and went down.

MacNeil was kneeling in front of Saint Mary, clutching three nickels, one quarter and four pennies. When the door leading from the cloister opened silently, she stood ready with the coins.

Janus came through the door. The coins fell and made their noise. Janus closed the door. The coins stopped.

Silence.

Janus gestured to MacNeil with her head, pointing the way for her. MacNeil walked down the length of the side aisle toward the rear of the chapel, not quickly. At the pew they had used, MacNeil stopped and retrieved Janus's shoes, and then Janus followed her out into the incredibly bright afternoon.

The sun had already turned its corner in the sky, however, and, in the first slight chill of the day's end, Janus noticed that she was soaked through with perspiration.

Roberta Winston was interviewing an attractive woman who appeared to be in her early thirties. They were walking along the sidewalk outside the cathedral, together with about forty other women, in the long, slow oval of the picket march. Some of the others carried signs lettered with slogans like END MALE SUPREMACY! and GOD IS LOVE, YES SHE IS! The *Post* reporter had interviewed seven of the women already.

Sister Sheehan was nowhere to be seen.

Now Winston was taking notes, even while they walked, as Margaret Baxter was speaking. Ms. Baxter was chairperson of the Washington chapter of the National Organization of

Women. She was tall, dressed in slacks and tan raincoat. Her hair fell to her shoulders, a careless blond downpour.

"This is just the latest in a long series of affronts to women. Clearly one of the major obstacles to the achievement of equality for women in this country is the Roman Catholic Church."

"Why do you say that, Ms. Baxter?" The reporter was detached, professional, as she asked her questions.

Margaret Baxter spoke rapidly. She was sure of what she was saying.

"Because the Church, for one thing, as in this case, refuses to recognize the validity of the mass when it's performed by a woman."

"But the Church would refuse to recognize a mass said by any person who was not ordained." The reporter winced to hear herself stating so easily the cardinal's position.

"Well, it's time they ordained women like the Episcopalians have."

"Of course, the Episcopal Church, Ms. Baxter" — Winston was wondering if she was overdoing the devil's advocate bit — "doesn't officially recognize those ordinations yet."

"Well," Margaret Baxter said impatiently, looking at the reporter: who the hell's side was she on, anyway? "Ordination is not the only injustice we're protesting here."

"What else brings you here?"

"We demand that the Catholic Church recognize the right of a woman to manage the fate of her own body."

"So the Church's teaching on abortion is one of the issues this picket line protests?"

"Certainly. The cardinal should call off the massive and elaborate lobbying effort he sponsors on Capitol Hill. He should abide by the Supreme Court decision of January 22, 1973. He should let women decide for themselves."

"Does Sister Sheehan agree that part of the reason for this demonstration is to promote free and legal abortions?"

"Why don't you ask her?"

"Thank you, I will."

As Roberta Winston stepped out of the picket line and took up a place on the curb from which she could observe it, she was aware of the fact that Margaret Baxter had little idea of Sister Sheehan's position. She had her own agenda, and was simply using the occasion of the conflict the nun's action engendered as one on which to press it. Even though Winston agreed with Baxter she knew that, politically, it would be foolish to confuse things by dragging in the abortion issue. If these women handled it right, they could bring immense pressure to bear from within the Catholic Church, as the Episcopal women were doing. But the focus on ordination had to be maintained.

The reporter considered whether to pursue the abortion angle in further interviews. She could get a good quote one way or the other from Dolores Sheehan. She was certain she could get some rabid and angry quotes from the college kids. It would spice up the story, but it could ruin the momentum of the support movement for the sister by scaring off her fellow nuns and the otherwise traditional Catholic women who felt she was being treated unfairly.

Roberta Winston decided to leave abortion out of it.

As Margaret Baxter passed her on her next circuit of picket-walking, the reporter joined her to ask one more question. It had occurred to her as an afterthought.

"Ms. Baxter, what is your religious affiliation?"

"I'm a humanist."

"Have you ever been a churchgoer?"

"Yes. I was a Catholic once."

"May I ask why you stopped being a member of the Church?"

"I married a Jew. Our families used their religions as clubs to beat each other with, so we got married by a J.P. and went our own way. A matter of growing up."

"Would you say, then . . ." Winston wondered what was kicking up the Mike Wallace in her. "Would you say, then, Ms. Baxter, that you gave up your religion because of your husband?"

Margaret Baxter stopped in her tracks and turned on the

reporter. "What kind of a question is that? Are you trying to make me look like a fool, or what?"

"No, Ms. Baxter, I'm just interested in you."

"I'm not stupid. I got the drift of your question. We're out here marching for you too, you know. Who the hell's side are you on?"

Roberta Winston was surprised at herself and at what she had just done. This entire business was confusing her. Why would she needle Margaret Baxter, with whom she sympathized? And why would she reply, to her question, "I'm a reporter. I'm on the story's side."

Cardinal O'Brien had been watching them.

He turned away from the bay window again and walked to his desk. He did not sit but stood still, the fingers of his left hand touching the top edge of his leather swivel chair.

Something was happening. He had a feeling in his breast, an ominous hollow feeling that frightened him. He wondered if that was the sort of feeling a man had before a heart attack.

He imagined himself standing on a low hill with all the world sloping away from him. He felt utterly alone.

"The world has nothing for you!" Was that Jesus speaking? It was the voice of the old man who had been his spiritual director when he was a young priest. "The world will kill you!"

Justin Cardinal O'Brien thought about that.

He had always assumed that he knew what the world was and that it was a different reality from the Church. That was the problem now: the Church and the world had become intermingled, confused with each other. It was the Church that marched outside his window now, the Church that had him worried, that frightened him, that left him feeling hollow. He expected that from the world, not from the Church.

He thought of himself standing on the low hill, watching them pass in their caravans, the wealth of nations, the armies of the world, the refugees from the chaos in Asia, those women in the street. And all passed by with one ear raised toward him, waiting for the word that would set things back in line, that would reveal to them all once more the real meaning of their lives. They wanted the word that would put an end to nonsense. They wanted it from him.

The word was *God*, wasn't it?

He saw himself standing on the low hill with all the world sloping away from him. He was standing on the Godspot, the place where the finitude of all that is becomes clear. And not only finitude, but corruption, the primordial infection of human life that turns members of the one family against each other. Belief in God begins in the experience of sin, he said to himself. We know our Redeemer lives because we know we need to be redeemed: he repeated it to himself.

Even to the cardinal it sounded tinny, weak, as if *God* had tipped his hat and walked out on the old pieties.

Cardinal O'Brien imagined himself standing on the low hill and raising his arms and giving a great sermon. And this is what he imagined himself saying: "Listen, world, if you would just take the time to hear God's promises. Behold the flowers of the field! If you would consider and consider and consider all would be well. The flowers are as good as any of us. They don't sow or reap, but they point their white fingers to their Father in heaven, giving him glory. They do not beat upon God's servants. They do not go on and on with questions. They receive and give. They obey the weather. They grow. They do what flowers are supposed to do. If all the world did likewise, then wars would end and no one would die alone, and you would all know why you had been created and where your heart belonged. Listen to me!"

He turned, let his eyes drift back to the window where he'd been standing. Even if he did say it, they wouldn't listen. There was no word he could say that would settle this. It was what he did now that counted.

It was the same in dealing with the terrorist. At a certain point you stopped talking and did something. You protected yourself and your house, or else you died and so did your children.

The cardinal decided to do something. He decided to go into the cathedral and pray.

He did not expect to see the men, four of them. No, five. They were walking slowly back and forth between each of the eight hundred and seventy pews. All of the cathedral lights were on, and it was very bright. They were from the embassy, he knew immediately. They were searching the church. Back and forth. Back and forth. It reminded him of the women who were going back and forth in the circuit of their picket line outside.

Cardinal O'Brien knelt in his customary pew toward the rear of the cathedral. One of the men, the one nearest him, nodded. The cardinal returned his nod gravely. He watched them. They moved like robots, back and forth, their eyes dashing about; now and then they stooped, checking the undershelves where the hymnals were stored.

The cardinal covered his face with his hands, but he couldn't shut the light out. He couldn't get the image of these foreigners searching his cathedral out of his mind.

Something was happening. The feeling in his breast intensified, the ominous hollow feeling that frightened him. He uncovered his eyes and watched the men searching, searching, searching, and knew it was not a heart attack of which he was afraid. And it was not the bomb they expected either.

Mrs. Tierney was leaving her apartment. She had not been able to sleep and had given up on her nap. She had been thinking about Bea and how lovely she would look with her hair done. Like a model, a Breck lady. Bea had forgotten how beautiful she was. Mrs. Tierney considered that when the girl had her hair done that womanly allure would return to her, that shine in her eyes. Mrs. Tierney knew she loved Bea like a daughter. She knew it from the ache in her breast, the ache she had never had for anyone but John. It was the ache of joy and pain, of wanting happiness for the child more than she wanted life for herself. She had that ache for her sister's girl now as if Bea were her very own, as if Bea had been the girl-infant she had longed for and never had.

It wasn't fair. Bea had come all this way. She would be so lovely. Mrs. Tierney appreciated her son's desire to spare her and her niece the aggravation of the troubles they were having with those nuns. But what could happen? It wasn't as if there were real danger involved. Bea should have the privilege of receiving communion from the cardinal. She should be able to go to the ceremony with the ambassador.

Mrs. Tierney had given careful consideration to what she was going to do. She would meet Bea at Annette's and the two of them would go over to the cathedral together in time for the ceremony at five-thirty. There was no reason to bother Johnny. They would sit in the back. Bea would be so beautiful. She would be so proud. They wouldn't be any trouble to anyone. Then she and Bea would be there when her son presented His Honor to His Eminence.

"Well, Parsley, shall we review things then, before the briefing of our staffs?"

"By all means, Brigadier."

They were in Cameron's office. Parsley approached the officer's desk. A large makeshift but apparently accurate diagram of the floor plan of the cathedral was spread across it. Cameron stood with his legs wide and hands at his hips. He was obviously ready to explain the diagram to Parsley, who was thinking as he saw it that it all seemed self-evident enough.

"Your men are circles," Cameron said, pointing. "Mine are crosses."

"I'd have thought squares," Parsley said, deadpan.

Cameron ignored him. "You will deploy here, here, here. This indicates the first balcony, and this, the ledges adjacent to the rose window. My people will cover there, there, and there. Clear?"

"Indeed so."

"As to the entrance security procedures." Cameron was pointing to the rectangle on the sketch that represented the main door in the rear of the cathedral.

"That's my department, Brigadier. You needn't worry over that."

Cameron went on as if Parsley hadn't spoken. "Each entrant shall be greeted, identified —"

"Cameron!" Parsley flashed with anger. "Don't instruct me! I am here to synchronize with you. I am not here to learn my trade."

"One moment, Parsley." Cameron was suddenly patient and therefore superior. "Consider: this is a potentially complex military operation. The command line must be exact and understood by all."

"My men take orders from me. Yours from you. That is clear enough."

"I'm afraid, my good man, it isn't. A force, however ragged, does not engage the enemy under the direction of two commanding officers."

"This isn't the battlefield at Waterloo, Cameron."

"Mr. Parsley, I am not interested in infringing upon your regular authority. Your section is your section. Mine is mine. Ordinarily the independence we both desire is quite suitable. Today, however, extraordinary circumstances require an extraordinary arrangement. One of us must be clearly in authority. All participants in the operation must understand that. It is crucial."

"I propose, in that case, Brigadier" — Parsley was going to tough it out with him — "that the line of command originate in my office."

"Impossible. This is a thoroughly military operation."

"It is a matter of security. I am chief of security."

"We are talking" — Cameron snapped "about a fucking goddamned war. A war about which you know nothing. A war about which I know everything."

"If you know everything about this war, Brigadier, why isn't it over?"

"Because bloody arseholes like you, Parsley, refuse to let soldiers be soldiers. Because soft-headed civilians buckle at the knees every time the issue is joined. It was the same in Burma, in Malaysia, in Cyprus. And, as the disgraceful rout this week demonstrates, it happened to the Yanks in Vietnam. It has happened repeatedly in Ulster. It will *not* happen here, today! A war is a goddamn war! It is not a political exercise. It is not an election. It is not a committee meeting. It is not a picnic for bureaucrats. Now, I'm telling you, Parsley, and only once, that this is *my* operation! You take your orders from me! Is that clear?"

"No. It is not. I suggest it is pointless for us to continue this discussion. Obviously, the ambassador must establish the order of authority."

"That's exactly what I mean. When the issue is joined you buckle. Rather than work this through with me, you run to the nearest handy snot-wiping daddy-figure."

"That strikes me as a peculiar sort of reference to the official representative of the very Crown you are presumably sworn to protect with your various and sundry wars. Or do you pursue them for their own sakes?"

"Ah, yes, the old bloodthirsty military routine. How patient you civilians are with us. We so love to kill and maim and sink our nightly fangs into the soft underflesh of our victims' throats. For Christ's sake, be original, at least, in your contempt. As for my attitude toward Ferris-Cogan, have you forgotten that he is *exactly* the one I am trying to safeguard? It is for the sake of that man's life and limb, not for some petty ego-need of mine, that I insist on proven military procedure."

"What exactly do you mean?"

"I mean we proceed as planned, as you and I have agreed, but under my ultimate authority."

"But with our separate areas of responsibility, correct?"

"Yes. As the diagram indicates."

"So, in effect, all we are arguing about is what is said at the final briefing."

"We are arguing, Parsley, about authority. The final briefing will establish it."

"I don't want you telling my people how to do their job."

"That is not my intention. Your shop is your shop. I expect its job, simply, to be done. In particular, I expect that no unauthorized person will gain entrance to the cathedral through either of the street portals."

"Rest assured."

"And I expect that Lady Ferris-Cogan and the girl will be surrounded at all times by security personnel."

"Neither the ambassador's wife, nor his daughter, will be in attendance. They will remain here."

"Excellent. Then we needn't worry about them. I shall personally accompany Sir Alisdair throughout the ceremony, appearing to be, in effect, his loyal aide-de-camp."

"I had expected to be with him myself."

"You would only draw attention, Parsley. You are a civilian. This is a highly ritualized occasion with certain military aspects to its ceremony. I will, of course, be uniformed in formal military dress. It will be the most natural thing in the world, even to my sidearm in its white patent holster. I will be at his shoulder every moment, and no one will think it the least bit unusual."

Parsley said nothing. He knew Cameron was right. The bastard had just argued him, not only out of his authority, but out of his own favored responsibility as the ambassador's personal bodyguard.

"Agreed," he said finally.

"Good," Cameron said. "Now that we understand each other, I am certain the operation will go off smoothly."

"Yes."

"We have scheduled the final briefing of our joint staff for fifteen-forty-five hours?"

"Correct."

"And positions for sixteen-fifteen."

"Correct."

"The investiture commences at seventeen-thirty."

"Check."

"Fine. If you will excuse me then, I will proceed to the ambassador's office for his briefing."

"Shall I accompany you?"

"I think not."

Ferris-Cogan had just finished his briefing of Lord Rees in London via the secure Scrambler-telephone. Rees had conveyed the prime minister's satisfaction with the procedures as outlined. There was agreement among Lord Rees, assistant secretary for Northern Ireland; Douglas-Home, the foreign minister; Lord Diplock, defense undersecretary; and Wilson himself that the terrorist had to be met head-on. Assured that maximum security would be in force in the cathedral, and that the odds were far better than even that the perpetrator would be seized if he tried anything, Wilson approved the plan as laid out by Ferris-Cogan. No one in London saw any need to involve American police forces before the fact. Lord Rees further indicated that, provided Janus, once arrested, was promptly gotten out of the country without publicity, American officials would be very unlikely to raise post-facto questions about minor irregularities. It was, after all, a matter of war. The United States understood what that was like.

Sir Alisdair had promised to contact Rees again by 2000 hours. Even though that was the middle of the night in London, Wilson and the others would be standing by.

"Best of luck," Lord Rees had said, signing off.

"Yes. Thanks," Ferris-Cogan had replied, dryly.

He knew that, with the attention of his government focused on how the affair was handled, the remainder of his career could depend on what happened in the next three hours. Indeed, his family's ancient longing to be reestablished among the hereditary peers of the lords temporal could depend on the next three hours. He realized, and laughed perversely as he did so, his life itself could depend on the next three hours. All of it — career, lordship, life — depended on how one mad

Irishman was inclined to spend the rest of that Wednesday in April 1975.

"The world is too much with me," Ferris-Cogan muttered to himself. He turned his attention to the framed parchment manuscript that sat on the margin of his desk. He had begun translating it earlier, and, with the same pleasure he took in unraveling a good *Times* crossword puzzle, he resumed his translation now. He had occasional reference to the battered Cassell's *Latin–English, English–Latin Dictionary* that he had fetched from his boxes, but, by and large, his Oxford Latin came back with a certain ease. He wrote out the translated fragment of Paul III's letter to More in longhand on a yellow legal pad.

Recognizing at the very beginning of our pontificate, which the divine providence of Almighty God, not for any merit of our own but by reason of its own great goodness, has committed to us, to what troubled times and to how many distresses in almost all affairs our pastoral solicitude and vigilance were called, we desired indeed to remedy the evils that have long afflicted and well nigh overwhelmed the Christian commonwealth, but we also, as men compassed with infirmity, felt our strength unequal to take upon ourselves such a burden. For while we realized that peace was necessary to free and preserve the commonwealth from the many dangers that threatened it, we found all filled with hatreds and dissensions, and particularly those princes to whom God has entrusted almost the entire direction of affairs at enmity with one another. Whilst we deemed it necessary for the integrity of the Christian religion and for the confirmation within us of the hope of heavenly things, that there be one fold and one shepherd for the Lord's flock, the unity of the Christian name was well nigh rent and torn asunder by schisms, dissensions and heresies. Wherefore, having been called, as we have said, in so great a tempest of discords and wars and in such restlessness of the waves to rule and pilot the bark of Peter, and not trusting sufficiently our own strength, we first of all cast our cares upon the Lord, that He might sustain us and provide our soul with firmness and strength, our understanding with prudence and wisdom. Then, considering these alliances and holy friendships which succor the tottering state of Christendom and preserve our own mission of unity, we give thanks that it has pleased the Lord our God to look favorably on us and grant us the gift of sons who with all zeal and love direct the energy of their souls to the defense of our poor name among the princes of infamy. Therefore we turn our heart to you, esteemed Son, and offer . . .

Here the page ended.

Ferris-Cogan was profoundly moved. He read the words again. He read them as if they were addressed to him. And then he remembered that, of course, they were.

The intercom buzzed. Radford, his secretary, announced Brigadier Cameron.

"Send him in."

And then the officer was explaining all the reasons why Ferris-Cogan would live safely through the next three hours.

The ambassador listened carefully, as carefully as his thoughts of the beheaded More would let him.

"**B**ut why aren't we going?"

Nancy didn't know what to say. Melissa was standing in the doorway of the solarium. Miss Wells was behind her, hanging back uncertainly in the corridor.

"You can go, Miss Wells," Nancy said. The woman nodded and disappeared without a sound.

The ambassador's wife put her number 7 brush down, came around from behind the easel, and went to her daughter. She stooped and hugged her without speaking.

The mother could feel the first tremors of the girl's sobbing. But Melissa controlled herself long enough to ask the question again.

"Why aren't we going?"

Nancy still did not reply.

"Is it because of me? Because I made Daddy angry?"

And then the little girl exploded into tears. Nancy held her, began rocking her, saying at last, "No, dear, no, no. That isn't it. Honestly."

"Why then?" she asked through her sobbing.

"Because of me, not you."

"Why?"

"Because Daddy and I had a quarrel and he asked me not to go."

"And me too?"

"Well, you couldn't very well go by yourself, now could you?"

"What was the quarrel about?"

"That's between your father and me, Melissa. I don't ask you what your quarrels are about."

"Sometimes you do."

"Well, not when they're with Daddy."

"Was your quarrel about me?"

"No, dear, it wasn't."

"Was it about God?"

"Melissa, aren't you nosy?" Wasn't she incisive?

Nancy considered her daughter's face. Tearstained and miserable, the little girl was convinced that she was to blame for whatever had befallen the family.

Why? Why? Nancy too wanted to know. Was it simply pettiness? Her own? Her husband's? Whatever his peeve, it hadn't been worth all this. Not this disappointment to Melissa, who had, in the course of her sessions with Father Tierney, associated the investiture with her own First Communion, which would take place in a few weeks.

Alisdair was being cruel beyond words. And not only to the girl. He had, in effect, repudiated Nancy's own effort to share in what she knew to be a moment of great significance for him.

Earlier, she had felt nothing but rage — hatred even. When her anger subsided over the afternoon, she had begun to feel the grim and desolate loneliness that only Alisdair seemed able to force on her. She felt as though she was being stared down at last by the old terror — that finally the man wasn't interested in her, did not want her or need her, much less love her. What else was he saying with his callous, capricious cruelty?

What troubled her most was that such bitter isolation could follow so closely on such intimacy as they had shared the day before. Had she been fooled?

Had he been frightened? Perhaps it was exactly that, his fear of her power, her achievement. Just when she was experiencing the height of her energy as an artist, and just when, with her first real show in London, she was about to gain serious recognition, and just when she, through her art, articulated her love for him as never before, he showed signs of wanting to destroy their relationship. Had she exceeded the limits he had set? She could be an amateur painter whose work he could proudly display after coffee: but could she be a serious artist who displayed her own work? She could be an affectionate partner who basked in his expression of their love for each other: but could she be the one who expressed it?

"Well, why?" Melissa persisted.

"Because, your father said so." It was the only fully truthful answer Nancy could think of.

"Well, it's not fair!" Melissa's face was twisted into the early stages of its most childish pout. As Nancy watched the transformation of her daughter's guilt into outrage, she realized that the girl was right. It wasn't fair! Why should this child be made to pay for her father's pettiness? And why should Nancy herself be the one who was left to explain, to make excuses, to bear the brunt of the disappointment?

Alisdair wasn't the only one who had something at stake in the cathedral ceremony. Melissa did too: if not an honor from the pope, some kind of message from God about her own place in His scheme of things. And, in some vague way that was beyond her capacity to say it or think it clearly even, the ambassador's wife knew that she too had a stake in the investiture of her husband. Around the occasion of that ceremony, their love for each other and their alienation from each other had both been given extraordinarily powerful expression. That meant something for her as well as for him.

"No," Nancy said, "it *isn't* fair!"

Why should he make this decision for his daughter and his wife?

Why should the two of them do his bidding when it issued from his small-mindedness, his fear?

Why should they not attend the ceremony?

And, Nancy thought, why should we not even love him in spite of the perverse invitation not to, wherever it came from?

Why not, indeed?

"Well," Melissa said forcefully, decisively, as if she could read her mother's mind, "why don't we go then?" The pout was gone: in its place, determination.

"Why not?" Nancy said, delighted in her daughter. They hugged each other. And then, pushing out into the corridor and toward their apartments, Nancy said, "Let's hurry and dress. We'll be late as it is!"

All was chaos in the sacristy.

It always was before a big service. Altar boys scurried in and out of the vaulted room and hovered in its gothic corners, lighting charcoal for the incense, unknotting the brass chains of the thurible, lighting procession candles, balancing the cross on the pole with one hand.

The honor guard, twenty knights of Malta, stout, older, feeling silly in their purple capes, white gloves, plumed hats, tried to keep the swords that hung from their broad sashes from hitting people when they turned around. The altar boys — all sidelong glances and swift stares — ached with envy at the knights' uniforms, not thinking they looked silly at all.

At the vesting case, which ran the length of the east wall, priests were donning layers of crisp, fresh linen, cinctures, stoles, white robes on black, surplices, or the fine silk cones of the concelebration chasubles. The red skullcap of Archbishop Benelli flashed through the bustling crowd like a punctuation mark. He was vesting with the help of an assistant who hung on to him like a stubborn thread. The priests were taking turns preening at the full-length mirror that hung inside the door of the closet where the albs were stored. Even the dullest, most ordinary man, before such a mirror at such a moment, in the ancient colors of religion can look almost beautiful. Two Italian monsignors, who would process next to the apostolic delegate as his chaplains, moved off to a side, looking like foreigners. Half a dozen younger priests, cathedral staff, the vice-chancellor, and the cardinal's chaplains talked in good spirits while they vested.

Ferris-Cogan, wearing tails and white gloves, was standing away from the clergy with Cameron, who wore the full dress uniform of Her Majesty's Special Guard: epaulettes, gold braid *forager* looped over his left shoulder, stiff Prussian collar, blood-red tunic, white sash, sky-blue trousers, beaked cap under his right arm, white patent leather holster and belt at his waist. Cameron and Ferris-Cogan stood as if at attention, not talking, watching the scene before them, fascinated.

John Tierney approached them, moving easily from the bustle around the vesting case. He was wearing the alb already, and was knotting the cord of his cincture around his waist.

"Everything seems all right," he said to the Englishmen in a low voice.

"We hardly expected trouble here, Father," Ferris-Cogan said with a false lightheartedness. The dignity and pomp of his dress were dispelled by an evident nervousness.

"Sacristies can be pretty dangerous places," Tierney said, reaching for banter, "especially if you're an altar boy late for the early mass."

"Indeed." Ferris-Cogan tried to smile, then fell silent, showing a strain and fright that Tierney had never seen in him before.

"The cardinal's outside," the priest said then. "He will have been greeting people at the entrance. He'll be here momentarily." He looked at his watch. "We should be right on time."

"Yes," Cameron said, raising his right wrist briskly and looking at his own watch. He showed absolutely no sign of nervousness. He was ramrod straight. He looked to Tierney as though he were ready for anything, and Tierney realized that, for Cameron, the great defeat now would be for nothing to happen. "We should be on time."

But Tierney didn't know whether he was saying it as an estimate or as a command.

Tierney noticed the radio wire stringing down from the

brigadier's right ear and into the high, stiff collar of his tunic.

Cameron was staring at him, as if waiting for a statement. The priest remembered the bartender, his miserable guilt, his agonized claim to have been tortured by the English. Tierney tried to imagine Cameron applying the red end of a cigarette to the man's feet. Even then, Cameron, staring at him, applied the edge of his antipathy to Tierney's taut surface, and the priest felt it burn.

Tierney turned to Ferris-Cogan. "Lady Nancy and Melissa . . ."

"Not attending."

"Just as well," Tierney said, and the ambassador nodded. Tierney went on, "I disinvited my mother and cousin too."

"I do hope, Father, they'll be able to join us for the reception at least."

"Thank you, Sir Alisdair. I was hoping they might."

"By all means."

There was a faint electronic crackle from Cameron's ear, and then the barest of murmurs. Both Ferris-Cogan and Tierney fell silent, watching the brigadier's impassive face. Finally he said, "Parsley reports some delay in the arrivals because of the demonstration. The dean is just coming in."

"Dean of the Diplomatic Corps," the ambassador explained to Tierney. "Andres Aguilar of Venezuela."

"I apologize, Sir Alisdair, for the commotion out front."

"Nothing you could control, is it, Father?"

"No."

"I thought not. No apologies needed. We'll be lucky if they don't invade the cathedral and demand to know why Great Britain's military attaché isn't a woman, eh, Brigadier?"

Cameron forced a smile, and the three men were silent and awkward.

Tierney excused himself and returned to the vesting case. At the center beneath the proud black wood crucifix were laid out the vestments Cardinal O'Brien would wear. Tierney, who had spread them on the counter himself, began to examine them again, making certain once more that each of eight pieces of ritual garb, the red velvet gloves, the red shoes, the pointed miter, and the crooked staff were not only there, but exactly in the places prescribed for them in the sacramentary.

"Are you ready, then?"

"Yes."

"And you rechecked the Beretta?"

"Yes."

"Remember, especially since it has no silencer, you are not to fire unless directed to do so by me."

"Yes."

"And said direction will consist simply of a glance. I will absolutely not look you in the eye unless I want you to make use of the weapon."

"Understood."

"All right. Leave the keys in the ignition."

"That's chancy in this city."

"It's the least of the chances we're taking. Improvisation is always desperate. When we return to this car we'll not have time to be fumbling for keys."

"As you say."

"One moment: your cord there. It's wrong."

"What, the cincture?"

"Yes. You've only two knots. There should be three."

"You sure?"

"Yes. One each for poverty, chastity, and obedience."

"Ah, just like me to forget my chastity."

"Quite funny. Fix it. The cardinal will know what good nuns look like."

"Right."

"Any questions, then?"

"No."

"All right. We're off."

"God bless."

"You too."

*   *   *

Just then Roberta Winston laid eyes for the first time that day on Sister Dolores Sheehan.

"Well, it's about time," the reporter said to herself as she moved along the crowded sidewalk toward the nun, who was standing near the street just below the cathedral entrance. Winston was in a hurry to get a comment from her so that she could wrap up the story on the day's demonstration.

At four o'clock there was supposed to have been some kind of rally with speakers and a folk singer. But it had fizzled. Betty Friedan was supposed to have shown, but didn't. There was no loudspeaker system, just the electronic bullhorn that the undergraduates had been shrieking through off and on all afternoon. A short, acne-faced girl had sung half a shrill song before giving up: no one had listened to her. By now, after five, some of the pickets had drifted away. The police had arrived in force an hour before, momentarily jacking up the demonstrators' spirits, making them think they were about to be arrested or challenged or ordered off. But the cops had come, as they put it, for some big church service. They couldn't have cared less about the women marchers, who took the police indifference as a kind of personal affront. It was then the women began to leave.

By now it was nearly down to the students and the dressed-to-the-nines nuns. The wives, Roberta Winston noted wryly, were all going home to their husbands.

"Well, Sister Sheehan," the reporter said in greeting, "you missed the best part."

"Hi, Roberta. Did I?"

"Not really. It's been kind of dull, actually."

"I thought it wiser to stay away."

"Why?"

"To keep the focus on the issue as much as possible. It shouldn't become a conflict of just personalities."

The reporter noticed that, in spite of the disclaimer, the woman was shining with a perceptible and radiant energy. She seemed to have been rendered almost, as it were, tipsy by her experience as the stormy center of the controversy. If she was trying now to become the *quiet* center, as perhaps more suitable to the thoughtful iconoclast she claimed to be, well, who could blame her? But if she wanted to be convincing as the reluctant rebel, Roberta Winston thought, she'd have to scrub the very pores of her face to wipe away that look of exhilaration.

"What's the latest on your trial, Sister?"

"Nothing new, Roberta. First hearing next Wednesday."

"Have you met with Father Tierney?"

"No. We spoke by phone."

"What did he say?"

"Same as the cardinal. He wanted me to resign."

"That *would* save them some trouble, wouldn't it?"

"Yes. What's going on at the cathedral?"

Sister Sheehan's eyes were fixed on a large Chrysler limousine that had just pulled up to the curb. An elegant black couple was getting out of the car. The dark-suited chauffeur was holding the door.

"A diplomatic function. A papal honor for the British ambassador."

"Oh, really? The Church goes on, doesn't it?"

"Did you expect it wouldn't?"

"Yes," the nun replied, half mocking herself and half making explicit the barb in the reporter's question. "I expected everything to come to a standstill until I'd been elected pope."

"No chance: you're not Italian."

"Look at that!" Sheehan said suddenly, pointing with her head toward two other nuns across the street who were making their way through the thirty or so circling women who formed the remainder of the picket line.

"Wow!" Roberta Winston said. "They're the first of the old-fashioned ones to come out on your side!"

The nuns were dressed in the traditional Franciscan habit, brown robes to their shoes, long, heavy-beaded rosaries swinging, white cinctures, faces framed in plaited white linen.

"Isn't that marvelous?" Sister Dolores said, thinking that if the more conservative orders would publicly support her, she couldn't lose.

"Wait a minute . . ."

The two nuns had walked past the picketers, past the cardboard posters, past the aggressive students who tried to enlist them in their circuit, breasting all the protest with their brisk stride that was determined, authoritative. Even from across the street, one could see that these two women knew their place.

"Terrific!" Sister Sheehan said bitterly, watching the nuns ascend the stairs to the proud, columned entrance. "A pair of VIP Franciscans!"

"René Chalmers, chargé d'affaires, Barbados."

"Yes, sir. Quite so," Parsley said. "Madame Chalmers," bowing slightly in her direction.

Parsley took the leather-bound credential in his hand and quickly read it, ran his finger over the seal, and compared the photograph with the black man's face.

It was always a bit of a surprise to hear these colonial blacks speaking with their precise British clip.

"Mr. Chalmers," Parsley apologized, "procedure requires, sir, the presentation of the tickets that accompanied the invitation itself." He returned the man's credentials.

"Ah," the man said, turning to his wife. She was withdrawing a folded white envelope from her handbag. She gave it to her husband, who withdrew the two white tickets with raised silver letters and handed them to Parsley.

"Thank you, sir," he said, bowing again.

He was relieved. He wouldn't have to run the metal detector over their bodies, a procedure guaranteed to provoke embarrassment, if not resentment, from people who were accustomed to a very high level of deference. On the other hand, they were also people who were inclined to understand the requirements of security in a world gone slightly mad.

So far most of the guests had been able to present the engraved tickets. Of those who hadn't, only the envoy from

Haiti had balked at being electronically searched. Parsley surmised that his bodyguard was armed, but a potentially sticky situation was avoided when the Haitian ordered his man back to the car. Parsley could never have allowed him into the cathedral, though, black as coal, it had been clear he wasn't an Irish assassin.

Mr. Chalmers and his wife moved by Parsley, and were greeted by Cardinal O'Brien, who took each by the hand and welcomed them warmly. Parsley had been impressed by the cardinal's friendliness and easy charm. He had never been in such proximity to a bishop before, and certainly not a Roman. Anglicans, it seemed to the security man, were stuffy by comparison. Or perhaps simply more dignified. In any case, Parsley preferred a bit more aloofness in his prelates.

"Well, Mr. Parsley," the cardinal said, joining him, "things seem to be going smoothly." He stepped to the threshold of the heavy exterior doors.

"Indeed, Your Eminence."

"Well, I should be getting back to the sacristy now."

But the cardinal was taking in the scene outside the cathedral. He was looking down on the sidewalk one last time. They were still out there, marching with their signs: the radicals, the students, the lesbians, the pro-abortionists, the renegade nuns. There was that reporter woman, and, with her — by God, the first time that day! — Sister Dolores. The two of them were standing there like a pair of actresses watching from the wings, the stars waiting to go on. The familiar anger stirred in his breast, but he forced it off as he had been doing all afternoon. There were other things to worry about.

Just as he was about to turn away from the door and move toward the sacristy, Cardinal O'Brien glimpsed the brown veiled heads of the two Franciscans bobbing through the picket line. Not them, too, he thought at first, and fixed his stare on them.

But then he saw that they were not part of the demonstration. Indeed, as they moved by the young women who wore bandannas and sloppy overalls the two nuns seemed aloof, even antagonized. The lesbians were trying to get the Franciscans to join them, and the Franciscans, God bless them, were refusing. They kept perfect monastic custody of their eyes, looking neither right nor left, but only straight ahead, giving the pickets not a smile, not a glance, not a hint of favor. These were nuns, real nuns!

They were wearing the habits, the cardinal saw, of the Franciscan Sisters of Perpetual Adoration, cloistered sisters, contemplatives, women who have no truck with popular causes, the Marys who sit only and worship their Lord. Of all sisters, these were the sort of whom Cardinal O'Brien was fondest. He cherished the presence of contemplative sisters in his archdiocese. They were the engine that made the whole machine run.

They were coming up the stairs toward the cardinal, lifting their long habits carefully, gathering their rosary beads, looking for all the world like nuns, like the valiant women of whom the Scriptures speak. O'Brien looked quickly toward Sister Sheehan and the reporter. They were watching the Franciscans, as he hoped they would be. That was what decided him. It was his chance to make one simple statement about their demonstration and their arrogance and their clothing and their contempt.

Cardinal O'Brien swept out of the vestibule, through the proud doorway and down the stairs toward the nuns. He displayed an energy and agility that, for once, he felt. No pain shot up from his knee. He met them on the landing that was half a dozen steps from the top.

"Sisters! Welcome!"

His arms were out and ready to embrace them both, but before he could, the two women were genuflecting in front of him, reaching for his hand to kiss it. He gave it to them. He let his eyes float across the street to the other sidewalk: Sister Sheehan was watching.

"Sisters, how good of you to come!"

"Your Eminence," one of them said. "You honor us."

He looked at her, saw that her eyes were brimming with emotion, and felt a profound gratitude that moved him to lift her to her feet and hold her to his breast.

He said simply and with great feeling, "Sister, thank you." And then he realized that he knew her, had certainly seen her before, probably at her convent on a holy day.

After a moment, pulling back from his embrace, she said, "May we visit the Blessed Sacrament, Your Eminence?"

"Indeed, Sister, and not only that: I am about to celebrate the Holy Sacrifice of the mass myself. You would honor me by attending."

"Thank you, Your Eminence," the sister said, and then added quickly, "Your Eminence, would you grant us dispensation that we might receive Holy Communion at your hand, since we received already this day at morning mass."

"Of course, Sister. I dispense you both. Receive again, if you choose, on the condition that you pray for me."

"We already do, Eminence. Thank you."

The other nun had said nothing in the exchange.

"Come then," the cardinal said, stepping between them, putting an arm around each, letting one last glance shoot toward Sister Sheehan and the reporter. They had seen it all: excellent.

He ushered the two nuns up the remaining stairs, though, from a distance, it might have seemed that he was not so much ushering them as leaning on them.

Inside the vestibule of the cathedral, where the fading light of day intermingled with the shadowy artificial light that drifted out on motes from the body of the church, Reginald Parsley stopped the cardinal.

"Your Eminence." He had stepped in his path when he realized the cardinal was leading the two nuns past the security check.

Cardinal O'Brien looked blankly at Parsley. Only after a couple of seconds did he seem to understand what the Englishman's problem was.

"Oh, Mr. Parsley. It's quite all right. These sisters are my guests."

"Yes, sir," Parsley said, then corrected himself, "Yes, Your Eminence." But he was staring into the face of one of the nuns. The three other security people were moving from the shadows to Parsley's side. One of them carried the phone-sized metal detector. Parsley put his hand out for it. "Quite so, Cardinal. Welcome, Sisters. Forgive us for the inconvenience, but we must —"

"Nonsense," Cardinal O'Brien said. "These sisters are *my* guests. I know them."

Parsley did not move. He was holding the metal detector in front of him. He flicked the switch to activate it. But he understood from the cardinal's tone and the fierce look in his eye that he was not to subject the nuns to the search.

"I see, sir," Parsley said, still not yielding, still staring into the face of one of the nuns. "Perhaps there are the required tickets?"

"Mr. Parsley," Justin Cardinal O'Brien said with strained patience, "the sisters are here on *my* invitation." Such was the emphasis that Parsley understood the prelate to be saying, "This is *my* cathedral, *my* ceremony, *my* responsibility. So get out of *my* way!"

He did.

Having stared so into the nun's face, Parsley was satisfied anyway. He expected that there would be an instinctive, visceral reaction in his very bowels if he ever locked eyes with the terrorist. The nun had met his stare, had not been shaken by it but only appropriately embarrassed. She had blushed bashfully.

Stepping aside, Parsley did not so much as nod even slightly to the cardinal. Even if they were only nuns, only women and harmless, it was not appropriate to alter procedure. But at this point it was only the principle of the thing: the cardinal knew them after all. It was not worth challenging the strange and obvious ire of the old man who brushed by him with his nuns like an owner leading his best quarterhorses into the visitor's circle.

"Hello, Hello. May I speak to Father Tierney? This is his mother."

She was in a phone booth in the Walgreen's at Dupont Circle. Everything was going wrong. There were no taxicabs. It was impossible to get to Saint Matthew's by bus. Her leg was roaring with pain. She couldn't take another step. And she had missed Bridgit at Annette's.

It was not like Mrs. Tierney to lose her composure. But now she was able to keep the quaver from her voice and the tears from her eyes only with the greatest effort. And to top everything — even if John *could* send a car for her — she was going to be late and by the time she got there her own hair would be a mess. What else could go wrong?

"I'm sorry, Mrs. Tierney, but your son is already in the cathedral. It would be impossible for him to come to the phone now."

"How's everything out front?"

"Fine, John, fine," the cardinal replied.

Tierney was holding the prelate's cincture for him. The murmurous crowd in the sacristy had fallen into a respectful silence when Cardinal O'Brien first entered, but it was quickly resuming the excited, chattering air it had before. The cardinal efficiently donned each of the vestment items as Tierney handed it to him in order.

"Two Franciscans came, John. Real ones."

"You mean sisters?"

"Yes. I showed them in myself."

"They passed Mr. Parsley's test, eh?" Tierney was kidding when he said it, but the cardinal's eyes flashed at him.

"You don't search Sisters of the Perpetual Adoration, Father! I would expect that from a Protestant, not from you!"

Tierney decided not to explain he was joking. Suddenly his

heart was pounding in his ears, and he could feel perspiration trickling down his neck. "One can't be too careful, Your Eminence."

The cardinal did not reply.

Tierney tried to ignore the anxiety that clutched him.

He turned away from the vested cardinal and surveyed the scene in the sacristy.

The knights of Malta were in line and waiting, their swords at ready. They would process as far as the sanctuary, where they would stop, present their arms in the ancient fashion, forming a canopy of upraised swords under which the rest of the procession would pass.

The teenaged boys who carried the procession cross, the thurible and boat, and the six candles were clustered together. Tierney snapped his fingers in their direction and they fell into place immediately.

The deacon with the Book, two subdeacons who would take the bishops' miters and staffs, and the half-dozen concelebrating priests were forming themselves into pairs behind the boys. The apostolic delegate and his uneasy chaplains were standing with Cardinal O'Brien, his chaplains, the ambassador, and Brigadier Cameron.

Once people had realized that Tierney was ready and that his glance was looking for an orderly formation, they quickly became silent.

"We will begin in just a moment." he said loudly enough to be heard, but still in a low voice. "We will process as in rehearsal, down the side aisle as far as the intersecting cross-aisle in the middle of the church. We will turn there and proceed to the center aisle, turning again and proceeding to the sanctuary. Fathers, if you will reverence the altar in pairs. Your Excellency, if you and Brigadier Cameron would proceed to the two chairs and kneelers on the right side of the altar. Your Eminence, of course, to the *cathedra*. Archbishop Benelli and monsignori, the priedieus adjacent to Cardinal O'Brien's chair. Everyone else knows his place, correct? Good. Then we will begin as soon as I give the signal to the organist. When the processional anthem and flourish begin, gentlemen, so will we."

Then Tierney turned back to Cardinal O'Brien and said in a low voice, "I'm just going to check quickly with Parsley . . ."

"But . . ." O'Brien was growing impatient, gesturing to Cameron. "The ambassador's man has a radio."

"I know," Tierney said, ignoring the objection. There was a feeling in his gut that wouldn't be ignored. He had to look the church over once for himself. He was the master of ceremonies: it was *his* domain now. Even these men of power, churchly and worldly, waited on his word. And he wouldn't give it until his inner clock told him it was exactly time. "But I want to be certain everything is set. It'll be just a moment."

Tierney left the sacristy, heading for the apse. As he went by the organist, who was hidden at his console in an alcove behind a large pillar off the edge of the sanctuary, he held up his forefinger and mouthed the word "Wait!"

But the organist, seeing the upraised single finger and misreading the word, thought Tierney had commanded, "Begin in one minute!" The organist, a precise and reliable man, started counting the seconds.

"I'm sorry, ma'am. You can't park here."

"Officer, I'm late for the service. Where can I park?"

"Not here, ma'am. Sorry."

"This is the ambassador's daughter. I'm his wife. We are due at the service."

"Oh. Yes, ma'am. I see now. I didn't notice the plates before."

"That's quite all right."

"You still can't park here. It's rush hour."

"Well, where can I park?"

"There's a lot behind Saint Matthew's."

"How do I find it?"

"Turn right at the corner, right again halfway down the

block. You'll see the lot. All the cars are there with the drivers. You won't be late. There's a side entrance to the cathedral right there."

"Thank you."

"Not at all. You have a pretty daughter there."

"Thank you again."

It took Tierney nearly a full minute to get to the rear of the cathedral. He wanted to talk to Parsley. Something was bothering him.

It was the nuns. The two Franciscans that Cardinal O'Brien had mentioned to him.

They were nowhere to be seen.

Tierney had looked at practically every person in the cathedral. He walked slowly down the right aisle, which, in a few minutes, would be crowded with the procession, past the confessional with its bright red lights glowing, past the dignified but relatively modest side entrance, past the large crucifix and rows of candles at its foot in the recessed cupola at the cross-aisle.

All the while he was looking at the persons seated in the pews. Only the forward two-thirds of the church was full. Here and there he noticed a person — now a man, then a woman — with a thin wire trickling down from ear to collar. In the balcony, which was closed to the public, he saw two men at each end. They would have rifles, he assumed. He could not see the men posted on the ledges near the great window, but he sensed their and other presences in the arching Byzantine darkness overhead.

He saw Parsley.

Tierney couldn't really imagine that a pair of Franciscan nuns known to the cardinal could be worth concern, but for some reason they were the focus of his anxiety, his sense that things were not yet quite right.

Suddenly the bartender's wretched voice filled his head: *Who'd have thought a woman? Who'd have thought a woman?* Who'd have thought a nun? Where were the nuns? Every time he turned around lately there was a nun to worry about.

He approached Parsley, but before he could speak, the great explosion of horns and pipes happened.

Tierney turned on his heel: what the hell was going on? Couldn't he wait? He had told the organist to wait!

But the anthem was sending its unleashed waves back and forth across the vault of the cathedral. The congregation was getting to its feet. The flourish was nearly over and the grand processional antiphon, the ancient Gregorian *Ecce Sacerdos Magnus*, was about to begin.

"Anything wrong, Father?" Parsley was at his elbow.

Tierney saw the procession cross bobbing in the doorway at the far end of the aisle. They were starting: goddamnit, they were starting without him! He was the goddamn master of ceremonies! Couldn't anybody get anything right?

"Anything wrong?" Parsley repeated.

"No, no. Just a missed cue, is all," Tierney said, forcing himself to calm down. "I'm supposed to be up there."

"Oh. Awkward. I see."

"I was just coming back to make sure everything is set. Everything all right?"

"Yes. Frankly, I doubt if he's anywhere near here, Father."

"And the two nuns left?"

"Sorry?"

"The nuns that Cardinal O'Brien brought in. They left, right? They're not in the church."

"They should be. Are you certain?"

"I don't see them. I just looked."

Tierney turned and looked over the church again. He could feel the tension from Parsley. Both men were suddenly alert, blood pounding its urgent way through their brains as they strained to see, strained to think.

Tierney saw the procession cross, the plumed-hatted, white-gloved knights bobbing in pompous cadence toward him. They were just passing the confessional, the small red lights of which still glowed across the shadows like jewels in the forehead of a dark-skinned woman. And then he knew.

"Jesus Christ!"

Tierney, who had not in years carelessly or irreverently used the Lord's name, said it again: "Jesus Christ!" The lights were on! The red lights were on! They were in the confessional!

The honor guard was just passing the purple curtains of the booths. The altar boys were just drawing next to them. Then the ambassador would be there, adjacent to the confessional, inches away from the weight that was tripping the switches that lit the two lights like blood.

Tierney began to run, gathering his robes at his waist as he did so, girding his loins like a Jew fleeing Egypt. The noise of his feet slapping the marble floor was lost under the blast of the mammoth organ. He tried to find Ferris-Cogan with his eyes, but he couldn't see him through the maze of plumes and crosses and candles.

He rushed by the side entrance and past the cross-bearer into the thick of the processing knights of Malta. He came on them so quickly and pushed by them so quickly that they ignored him and continued their slow, studied walk. At the cross-aisle they began making their turn toward the center as if nothing was happening.

It took Reginald Parsley exactly three seconds after Tierney began his dash down the aisle to understand what he had to do. He calmly raised to his mouth the small radio transmitter wired at his wrist and said simply, "Alert." He said it carefully, with precise diction, five times. And then he drew his gun and followed Tierney.

Cameron needed to hear the word only once. He swiveled instantly, in a perfect about-face, threw his left arm across the front of Ferris-Cogan's chest and his left foot and ankle behind Ferris-Cogan's legs and was in the process of a perfectly executed judo toss, throwing the ambassador to the floor.

But it was too late.

The gun barrel with the fat snout of its silencer was already protruding through the opening between the confessional curtain and the wooden frame of the booth. The targeting sight of the gun was already locked on the bridge of the ambassador's nose. The gunman's finger was already squeezing the tension out of the trigger.

But it was too late.

Tierney had seen the pistol barrel and had hurled himself through the last pair of altar boys, knocking both candles from their hands, making one of them think an earthquake had hit Washington, making the other think of his epileptic mother. Tierney dove into the curtained booth and crushed whoever it was between a wall and the seven furies that had been hiding in his breast.

The shot went high.

"Oh, damn! The door's locked, Melissa. That policeman should have known."

"I can hear the organ, Mommy. We *are* late."

"It's all right, darling. They're just starting."

"Shall we go to the other door?"

"Let me try this one again. They're very heavy doors, aren't they? Perhaps I didn't pull hard enough."

"Let's hurry, Mommy."

Ferris-Cogan was on the marble floor, covering his face with his arms. It was too soon for him to think about what was happening. It was too soon for him to be sick. He was all instinct, all self-preservation. These were the split seconds when a threatened man gave everything to the effort to find a dark, warm place in which to curl up.

Brigadier Cameron was just coming up from the crouch into which he had gone in taking down the ambassador. He was turning toward Tierney and the sound of the silenced gunshot. His right hand was snapping open the white dress holster at his side. He was moving by the first confessional booth, by the middle one where the confessor would sit, to the third. He saw Tierney grappling with a person who was resisting from behind the purple curtain. Cameron's right hand was around the cold steel of his service revolver and rising. He was pointing his gun at the struggling form behind the curtain. He was squeezing the trigger.

The shot went harmlessly into the curtain, just missing Tierney's left temple. Tierney turned on Cameron screaming, "The other! The other!"

Cameron didn't understand, but Tierney's voice and eyes had the full authority of a fellow soldier, and the brigadier responded. He withdrew slightly, shifting his weight, turning to see what the priest could have meant.

But there was nothing behind him or to his side that caused the instinctive reflex that saved a soldier when he met an enemy face to face.

Because, to Brigadier Cameron, the Franciscan nun who was suddenly right next to him, having slipped out of the first confessional as he had gone by it an instant before, was, in the midst of all the strange Roman pomp and panoply, not unusual enough.

Until he saw her eyes and knew he'd seen their hatred before.

Until he saw the gun barrel in the cave that the loose brown sleeve of her habit made around her right hand.

But it was too late.

He did not have time enough to stop her from killing him. He did have time, however, to kill her in return. But he did not use it. At the very last instant of his life his reflex failed him. It was not a matter of thinking or a conscious choice. Simply a split second of paralysis resulting from confused signals and a whole set of false expectations. He never expected to die at the hands of a woman.

The instant of Cameron's reflexive hesitation was all Oona MacNeil needed to get all that she wanted: a clean, point-blank shot at the man who epitomized the murderers of her brother. She squeezed her hand into a fist around the trigger. The Beretta jumped. Cameron's chest jolted upward with the force of the shot; he fell at her feet.

MacNeil was surprised that her gunshot was not louder. Janus had been concerned that the Beretta had no silencer.

Only after using the gun on the Englishman did Oona realize that the great organ was still playing.

She took in the scene immediately around her. Several altar boys were gaping, stunned, ten yards or so down the aisle. Beyond them was a pandemonium of plumed hats and white gloves. Immediately to her left were worshipers in pews who, with their hymnals and prayer books, seemed oblivious to what was happening. She did not look behind her, but, if she had, she'd have seen the white-robed priests scrambling back, trying to get out of the open space of the aisle, and behind them, being bumped and pushed with no idea why, the two bishops in their pointed hats.

She would have seen on the floor immediately behind her the ambassador, who was pressing himself into the cold marble, trying to get under it. She could have killed him easily.

But Oona MacNeil had only two thoughts now: to rescue her sister and to get out of there.

John Tierney had subdued Janus and was holding her fast against the back wall of the confessional. She was wrapped in the purple curtain that had been ripped from its pole when the priest crashed through it. Now he was pressing all his weight against what seemed like a large, bundled plaything. He knew the person was pinned. He was just feeling the lessening of tension that signals the first instant of surrender.

He was also feeling a cold, hard pressure against his neck: the barrel of a gun. He knew better than to mess with that. He released his hold on Janus and raised his arms so that whoever had the gun against his neck could see them. He backed out of the confessional and turned around slowly to face MacNeil. Janus slipped out behind him, freeing herself of the curtain, still garbed in the Franciscan habit.

MacNeil gestured with her pistol, directing Tierney to step clear of them. He did so, and she was grateful. She didn't want to kill a priest.

Both women turned and bolted for the side doors.

The arched doors opened easily as Janus hit the ornate brass plate that was the disguised fire bar.

The light from outside splashed into the cathedral, and, for the instant it took the two women to go through the door, their silhouettes offered two perfect targets.

Reginald Parsley chose one, taking careful aim. He had been caught in the panic of the honor guard and had wasted nearly four seconds trying to free himself of their desperate clutching. Now he was thirty feet from the door, standing with his legs apart, drawing his pistol down from its arch, holding it with his right hand, bracing it with his left, pointing his right index finger along the barrel, squeezing off the shot with his middle finger — all in less than one second.

The bullet exploded Oona MacNeil's head, knocking her forward, making her fall in front of Janus, making Janus stumble at the top of the dozen stairs that led down to the street. Janus knew without looking that Oona was dead. She had been prepared for that: the keys were in the car. Janus was trying to keep from falling.

She was trying to keep from colliding with the woman and little girl who had been standing outside the door.

The little girl was screaming.

The woman was stooping toward her.

Janus looked again. The ambassador's wife and child. Luck of the Irish.

John Tierney was standing in the doorway of the cathedral by then. He saw the woman in the nun's habit raising her pistol and pointing it at another woman, pointing it, he saw then, at Nancy Ferris-Cogan. He saw Melissa clinging to her mother, her face grotesquely twisted in terror.

"No!" he said. He said it loudly and stretched out the vowel sound so that, as he hurled himself down the stairs at Janus, his scream seemed like that of a man falling from a high cliff in an old movie.

Janus started at the scream, throwing her aim off one centimeter. When she fired at Nancy the bullet did not go through her left eye, but clipped her left brow, grazing her temple and slicing through her ear.

The ambassador's wife crumpled.

Janus turned to face the priest. For the barest instant she hesitated, an instant that should not have made a difference.

But he was faster than she was.

He had her exactly by her second of hesitation.

As he came at her, his right hand was drawn back across his left shoulder, and its edge was stiff, rigid as bone from the tip of its small finger to the taut flesh of its heel. He began to throw it at her like a weapon. His eyes were fixed on the starched white linen bib beneath her chin, fixed on the spot where he knew he would find the promontory of her thorax.

Even as his hand swept across and out from his chest, it all came back to him.

A whole world.

He had taken the first from behind, smashing his hand down on the man's shoulder near the neck. The cracking of bone had alerted the second NVA sentry, who lunged at Tierney with the blade of his bayonet. Tierney stepped away from it, crouched, brought his fingertips together and rammed them swiftly up into the man's neck. The man's feet left the ground with the force of the blow that separated his skull from his spinal cord. They were the first and second human beings Tierney had killed. He had thrown up that time. But not again.

It came back to him. It went away from him. His stomach was turning. His right hand was flying.

His left hand was just hitting the Luger that the woman had been raising toward him.

It was not a nun. It only looked like a nun. It was a killer. His mind roared. It had killed Nancy Ferris-Cogan. It would kill Melissa. It would kill him. It was not a woman. It was not a human being. It was not one of us. Kill it. Kill it. Kill it. His mind roared.

Never look it in the eye. That was the rule. Keep your eye fixed on the throat. It was like chopping wood. Like ball. Pick your spot, lock your eye on it, and let go.

Tierney let go with everything. His hand whipped into the linen mass at the woman's throat, propelled not only by the momentum of his swinging arm, but by the entire weight of his body, which he was throwing now into the blow. His timing was superb. The full force of his one hundred and eighty-five pounds was concentrated in the muscles of his right shoulder and arm for the instant of their exploding into the woman's neck. He left his feet when he connected. He hit her so hard that he crushed her windpipe, and her left jugular vein collapsed on its own vacuum. But he didn't stop at that. The edge of his hand carried through her neck clear to the bone column that joined her head to the rest of her body. He hit the woman so hard that her head came off.

It seemed like her head, but it wasn't. It was the starched bonnet and angled veil of the Franciscan habit. The stiff linen and shaped brown wool flew off her head as it first jerked forward over his hand, then whiplashed back with the blow.

That is when he raised his eye to her face.

And that was his mistake.

He saw her brows for the first time and her short brown hair. And he looked into her eyes, which were white, the pupils having turned up into her head. Her mouth was open, with blood spurting from the wreckage of her throat. He dropped his eyes involuntarily from the face, as if it had caught him in the midst of something shameful. Grotesque as it was, the twisted visage was familiar. An awful recognition was swelling in his stomach. Even before the chop of his deadly hand had finished its work, Tierney knew that he had just killed his own cousin, Bridgit Connor.

All the while he had been screaming "No!" like a man falling from a cliff in an old movie.

"By this holy anointing and of His most tender mercy may the Lord forgive you . . ." Tierney was bent over her, touching her with oil, taking refuge in the ancient sacrament.

She was dead before she hit the sidewalk. And Tierney knew it. But he had yelled for the sacred oils anyway. He was leaning over her, having just completed the ritual absolution, conditional forgiveness. No one could say precisely when the soul left the body. No one could say that his cousin, Bridgit Connor, was not in her last moment repentant. And so he had said the holy words.

Someone had shoved the sacramental oils into his hands. He wanted to touch her desperately. He wanted to take her up into his arms and hold her and, on behalf of the world, ask *her* forgiveness. She was no terrorist now, no traitor, no liar, but a kinswoman whom he had loved and whom the world had done cruelly. But how could he hold her: he had been its final instrument of cruelty.

He administered Extreme Unction, touching her eyes, her ears, her nostrils, her lips, her hands, and her feet with holy oil. He signed her with the cross at each place, sealing the five senses away from the world and its agonies forever.

He was numb. He could not think. He knew that as long as he lived he would never understand what had just occurred. Had Bridgit done what he saw her do? Had he himself done this? He would never understand how what is evil and what is good, what is hated and what is held dear, could be so twisted together that just when you had one you lost it and had the other.

He touched the oil to his cousin's flesh more tenderly than he had ever touched anything. He took refuge from his own tearing heart in the ancient words, which, as it were, lifted him up in a caress of their own. He gave himself over to the ineffable power of the sacrament.

"May the Lord forgive you whatever sins you have committed through your sight . . . or . . . hearing . . . or . . . sense of smell . . . or . . . speech . . . or touch . . ."

The priest's voice faltered as his eye drifted to the ugly black Luger that lay by his cousin's hand. He stared at it, could not speak for a moment, then continued, "Go forth, O Soul, out of this world in the name of the Father Almighty who created you . . ."

He turned from the gun.

He thought of Bridgit's laughing eye when they had teased his mother the night before. He saw the dark silhouette of her long, elegant neck against the floodlights of the city's monuments. He felt her hand pressing his wrist that noontime when she had looked behind his own surfaces and seen more of him than he had dared show her and, apparently, had wept at what they held in common. Had she been lying? He saw her blushing, turning away his compliments, showing him her awkwardness. He saw her eyes overflowing. Had she even then been trying to warn him of this other side? He remembered a hundred silences in which they had both known the extraordinary affection that teaches the meaning of family. Was there a message in her silence that he had missed?

And he remembered her husband, Peter, and the mystery surrounding his violent death years before. She would never speak of it. That pain, alone of all that he knew of his cousin, was a single clue for what would be his lifelong effort to understand how Bridgit Connor and the one called Janus could be the same woman.

Melissa's hysterical weeping caught Tierney's attention. He raised his head and saw the girl in her father's arms. Ferris-Cogan, while holding his daughter, was bending to touch Nancy, who was just then being lifted onto a stretcher. Her face was a mask of blood. The ambassador and the child went with her as attendants carried the wrecked woman off.

Tierney began to hear the other sounds as well: sirens, loud shouting, doors slamming, crowds of people murmuring, and, from inside the cathedral, silence.

He remembered the other woman-assailant, shot in the door, dead likely. He remembered the English officer whose name suddenly wouldn't come to him, shot in the cathedral, dead likely.

He looked down at his white alb; it was covered with blood. He fingered his stole; it was edged with gold. It meant he was a priest. He was in the act of praying for his cousin. He would be praying for them all, on behalf of them all. It was ordained that he do so. *He* was ordained that he do so. He would call down God on this. What else was there to do? He would hand it over to God, who had learned what there was to know about human blood from His Son. God would not forsake them. Not any of them. Not even now.

Indeed, Tierney forced himself to say, these are the moments when God and His people are most at one. These are the moments, according to the Scriptures, when God and His people are most at one.

Why then art thou sorrowful? he asked his soul.

And why should I not be? his soul replied, claiming its right to mourn.

Once more Tierney blessed the dead woman over whom he knelt. He said, "We commend to Thee, O Lord, the soul of Thy servant Bridgit. Dead to this world, may she live to Thee, and the sins she has committed in this life, through human frailty, do Thou in mercy . . . forgive."

EPILOGUE
THURSDAY, APRIL 24, 1975

PRESIDENT FORD SAYS AS FAR AS AMERICA IS CONCERNED THE WAR IN VIETNAM IS OVER.

John Tierney stared down at the *Washington Post*, focusing on its headline. He stooped and picked the paper up and started to read the story. "Saigon Panic Grows as Thousands Flee." But his eyes wouldn't hold the focus. He stopped reading. In the photograph above the fold dozens of Vietnamese were crowding onto a C-5A. He slowly bent the paper around his forefinger, slid it under his arm, and stepped back into his mother's apartment, closing the door softly on the vacant hallway.

He sat down again on the edge of the rollaway bed. He had not gotten to sleep at all. It was the bed's fault, he had said over and over to the night, knowing it wasn't.

But it was. It was the bed on which Bridgit had slept the night before. He would have preferred his own bed, of course, his own room. But this had been a night during which his mother could not be alone.

She had taken it all very badly. Of course. How could she have taken it otherwise? When her call to her sister in Derry was finally put through, she had collapsed. He had had to tell his aunt himself. When he finally succeeded in making her understand what had happened, his mother's sister had called hysterical curses down on him and hung up.

He was thinking now about Nancy Ferris-Cogan, wondering if she'd gained consciousness yet. If she hadn't it could mean the onset of a lengthy coma and certain brain damage.

He looked at his watch. Six-twelve. He could stop at the hospital on his way to the cathedral. He had time if he left now . . .

Absently he opened the newspaper again. It fell across his lap. The end of the war, Ford said. It occurred to Tierney that, where there should have been a reaction to those words — joy, elation, relief, or cynicism at least — there was a hole. *Panic Grows. Thousands Flee.* He felt nothing.

He got up, dressed quietly, looked in on his mother. She was still sleeping the heavy, drugged sleep of whatever the doctor had shot into her arm.

He hesitated. He didn't want her waking up alone. Not today. An old feeling stirred in his stomach. The feeling he had as a boy when he first left home. Walking out on his mother. Abandoning her. Letting her drown.

He went back into the living room and found the Pall Malls on the table by the rollaway. He lit one, hated it, and breathed the smoke in deeply. He stood at the window, smoking, watching the light spread on the city, wondering what it would do without a war.

"Johnny?"

He turned. She was standing in the doorway, robed, looking awful.

"Hi, Mom."

"How are you, son?"

"Okay. How are you?"

"Okay."

"Really?"

"Yes. You're dressed. You have to go?"

"I have the mass at eight."

"Couldn't someone else take it?"

"Sure, but I . . . want to say it, Mom."

"Of course, dear."

"I was thinking of stopping by the hospital."

"Of course."

"You don't mind?"

"No. I'm okay."

"Mom?" Tierney's eyes found his mother's. They looked at each other across the room, not speaking. Then she took a half-step toward him. Her arms floated up and away from her sides, beckoning. He went to her, went into her embrace, fell into an even older feeling: the warm, safe feeling of the cradle her arms made.

"Mom, I'm sorry," he kept saying, "I'm so sorry."

She said nothing, only pressed him to the ache and held him.

"Hello, I'm Father John Tierney."

The nurse looked up from her folder. She was sitting at her desk in the cubicle in the middle of the corridor outside the Intensive Care Unit.

"Good morning, Father." She smiled warmly. He could tell that she was Catholic.

"I'm here about Mrs. Ferris-Cogan. Is she still critical?"

"Yes, she is, Father. But there's some improvement."

"Did she regain consciousness?"

"Yes. About two hours ago."

"Oh, thank God."

"The doctors are quite encouraged."

"Is she sleeping?"

"No. The effort now is to keep her awake, for several hours more if possible. Her husband is with her."

"Do you think I . . ."

"Yes, Father. Come with me."

The nurse led him down the corridor to the private room where she'd been moved after gaining consciousness. The effort to keep her conscious would have disturbed the other critical patients in intensive care.

"Hello, Sir Alisdair," Tierney whispered.

"Father!" Ferris-Cogan stood, turning away from the high bed, and took the priest's hand in both of his own. "Father," he repeated.

The ambassador was wearing a gray cardigan over his formal white shirt, which was collarless and open at the neck. Tierney noticed its three pearl studs. Ferris-Cogan was alert, not showing any signs of weariness.

"Father, I'm so glad you came," he said, pulling the priest toward the bed, and turning, whispering, "Nancy, it's Father Tierney."

Nancy's face was covered with white bandages. On her right side was a large bulge. There was an opening for her nose and mouth.

She stirred; her head moved slightly. Tierney stepped to the bedside, where Ferris-Cogan joined the priest's hand to his wife's.

"Hello, Nancy."

She pressed his hand. That sign of life from her filled him with relief and gratitude. He was startled when she spoke. Somehow he had never expected to hear her voice again, and certainly not sounding so vibrant and alive.

"Father, I'm glad" was all she said, but it nearly ruined him. Recovering, he said, almost chuckling, "I'm glad too."

"Alisdair told me."

"He did?"

"Yes."

"Well, it was . . . awful, Nancy."

"Father." Ferris-Cogan touched him on the sleeve. "Excuse me, please. Nancy, I'll be right back."

The ambassador left them, slipping out of the room noiselessly. Tierney didn't know why. Perhaps Ferris-Cogan had sensed what Tierney only then knew — that he wanted very much to speak to the woman alone.

"Alisdair has been with me all night."

"I know. He loves you very much."

"Yes."

"Nancy, I want to tell you something."

"Yes?"

"I realized when I thought you were going to be killed that . . ." A pause. "You are very important to me." As soon as he said it he regretted it. But she increased the pressure on his hand. He wanted to see her eyes, but they were covered with bandages. He stared at her mouth: it hesitated, started to form a word, hesitated again.

He was afraid she would misunderstand him, not know what he meant. But what did he mean? He was trying to put words on a feeling that he hadn't admitted to having. It was a feeling for a woman, for this woman.

"Father," she said, apparently with difficulty, with much emotion, "you are very important to us."

He squeezed her hand in return.

Yes. It was a feeling for this woman, but for more too. Tierney's fondness for her was exactly as she was in relationship with her husband and daughter. She was the first woman he had allowed himself in years to want, but he wanted her to be where she was, who she was. His wanting her alive and well had been the one clear, unambiguous desire that had stirred all night long in his breast.

He considered that he was probably in some fashion in love with Nancy Ferris-Cogan. He both wished that circumstances allowed him to say so and was profoundly grateful that they did not. It was disturbing enough to be discovering this aching yearning in a part of himself that he thought was under control: disturbing enough to sense that the balance of solitudes at the heart of his life as a priest was tilting toward a choking loneliness. To have the yearning focused on this woman who had trusted him as a priest kicked up all the uneasiness of guilt. And to realize, as he did then, that his passion for her, hidden though it was, had been the source of the passion in which he had killed his cousin, was very nearly unbearable.

"How is your cousin?"

"What? I'm sorry, Nancy, what?" The question stunned him.

"Your cousin and mother. How are they? They were there, weren't they?"

Before Tierney could answer, someone touched his elbow. It was Alisdair. Tierney looked at him. He was shaking his head. He hadn't told her that; he did not want him to tell her. The priest looked down at the bandaged woman.

How was his cousin?

"My mother is fine."

But how was his cousin? How was her mother? How were her brothers? How were the men who had murdered her husband and her innocence? How were the victims of her own ruined conscience? How were the man and woman who had explored Washington at night in an easy affection? How was the man who, having been used and deceived, killed her?

"And my cousin is dead, Nancy."

"What?"

"She tried to kill you. She was the terrorist, Janus."

"I don't understand."

"Neither do I."

"But you . . ."

"Yes, I didn't know it was she until after."

"Oh, my God."

She was pressing his hand harder still. He could feel her pity, but it was leaving him unmoved. He had done only what was necessary. Since it had been necessary, he had done it regardless. That is what human life required at its worst and at its best.

"I'd have done it even . . ." His voice drifted off. Then he said, "Some things are more important than loving someone."

Neither Nancy nor Alisdair spoke. Tierney squeezed her hand once more, released it, thought of offering to bless her, thought better of it, nodded farewell to the ambassador, and left.

Cardinal O'Brien was hoping to catch Father Tierney before the mass began. He was walking as quickly as his dignity and stiff left knee would allow. He went down the center aisle of the cathedral, deliberately not looking at the confessional as he passed it. He would not look at the floor to see if the stains had been cleaned satisfactorily. They had still been in evidence the night before when he and Benelli had conducted, with the clergy, the ritual for the reconsecration of a profaned church. Now it was over. The sacrilege removed. He would not think about it anymore.

The cardinal was dealing with the trauma he had undergone by busily going about the running of his archdiocese.

Already that morning he had signed the pile of letters that had been waiting for two days for his crossed signature and seal. He had drafted the letter to the lawyers about the new mortgages for the eight bankrupt parishes. He had prepared his sermon for the Confirmation class he had at Saint Ambrose's that night. And he had written a letter that would be reproduced and sent to all his fellow ordinaries, explaining what was being done about the nun who attempted to say mass.

That was what he wanted to see Tierney about.

He swept into the sacristy. The priest was just putting the amice around his neck. No one else was there.

"Father John. Good. I want to talk to you."

"Good morning, Your Eminence." The night was having its effect on the priest. His eyes were red, his voice increasingly ragged. The cardinal had interrupted his silent reading of the prayers to be said while vesting. They were posted on the center panel of the vesting case. He had been saying, as he touched the square linen to his head and wrapped it around his shoulders, "I will wear the helmet of integrity . . ."

"John, I have this letter to the bishops. I want to get it out right away. What are the canon references you'll be depending on?"

"I'm sorry, Cardinal, what?" Tierney had heard what he asked. He just couldn't believe it.

"The canon references for the hearing."

"I don't know them offhand. They're on my desk."

"Good. I'll go up."

As if someone had thrown on a light in a dark room, Tierney saw that they must not continue this. They must not proceed with the case against the nun.

"Cardinal, don't do it."

"I don't mind, John."

"I mean, we should forget the case entirely."

"What, the case against Sister Sheehan? You can't be serious."

"I am serious. Punishing her has nothing to do with what the Church is for."

"It's not for punishment's sake. We're trying to maintain order. You said it yourself."

"I was wrong. It may look like maintaining order, but it's not. To pursue this now, after everything that's happened, would be to pile more chaos on everybody."

"Everything that's happened has nothing to do with the case against Sister Sheehan."

"Frankly, Cardinal, at this point, it's all of a piece to me."

"Well, you're wrong, Father. What would you have us do?"

"Forget it."

"And keep her on?"

"Yes, if she chose to stay. All I know is that we are the ones who destroy the true order of the tradition if we pursue this."

"Father . . ." The cardinal started to leave the sacristy, holding up the letter at Tierney. "We have no choice but to pursue it. We *can't* have the Sacraments made mock of in this archdiocese."

"As you say, Cardinal. But I refuse to do it."

"What?" The cardinal's tone softened. He was amazed.

"I refuse to have anything further to do with it."

"You choose to disobey me?"

"Yes."

"When you were ordained, Father, you solemnly swore to give your ordinary all obedience and respect." There was grief in the old man's voice. This was the last nail, and he knew it.

"I know it, Cardinal. I don't refuse lightly."

Once more, in a last effort, the prelate commanded, ordered, said with all authority: "You will not refuse at all, young man. You remain assigned as *Officialis* in this case."

"I will not do it."

Cardinal O'Brien looked at the priest from the sacristy door. The old man couldn't think of anything else to say, to do. The priest's eyes never wavered, never dropped. They were red and weary, but more, they were stark, determined.

Justin Cardinal O'Brien turned on his heel and left the sacristy. He did not walk up the side aisle past the confessional but crossed in front of the sanctuary, genuflected lamely, and then walked quickly down the center aisle, limping slightly and thinking about his heart attack.

Tierney finished vesting, did not look at himself in the full-length mirror, picked up his covered chalice, and walked out into the sanctuary.

The few people stood noisily. Men coughed. Women tried to find the right page in the missal.

Tierney genuflected, went to the altar, kissed it, placed the chalice on the stone that held the relics of the martyrs, and turned to face the people. He began to say the mass, as he had a thousand times before. Only now, the people noticed, his voice faltered, and he seemed to have trouble remembering what to do.